Cally's shotgun, of course, was gone.

"That wasn't fair," she whispered.

"Hmm?" Andrew drew away slightly and lifted her chin with his finger. "Are you all right?"

She could almost believe it was a sincere question. She found herself nodding. The odd fevered light was back in his eyes, and she felt her own temperature rise.

"I'm all right. Just don't talk about...you know."

"Don't threaten to shoot me," he whispered, drawing closer as if he were afraid she couldn't hear.

She knew she should pull away, but she wasn't sure her legs were steady yet. She didn't want to faint right here in front of him. She would let him hold her up a while longer. Meanwhile, she stared at him. How close did he think his lips had to be for her to hear...?

Dear Reader,

Sheriff Andrew Haywood was determined to carry out his promise made to Cally's dying father that he would look out for her. But the Kansas lawman was in for a surprise when he discovered that Cally didn't want anything to do with him, despite her father's wishes. *Cally and the Sheriff* do eventually work things out in Cassandra Austin's delightful new Western. Don't miss the fireworks.

Judith Stacy is back this month with *The Marriage Mishap*, the story of virtual strangers who wake up in bed together and discover they have gotten married.

In *Lord Sin* by Catherine Archer, a rakish nobleman and a vicar's daughter, whose lack of fortune and social position make her completely unsuitable, agree to a marriage of convenience, and discover love. And in Elizabeth Mayne's *Lady of the Lake*, a pagan princess surrenders her heritage and her heart to the Christian warrior who has been sent to marry her and unite their kingdoms.

Whatever your tastes in reading, we hope you enjoy all of our books, available wherever Harlequin Historicals are sold.

Sincerely,

Tracy Farrell
Senior Editor

Please address questions and book requests to:
Harlequin Reader Service
U.S.: 3010 Walden Ave., P.O. Box 1325, Buffalo, NY 14269
Canadian: P.O. Box 609, Fort Erie, Ont. L2A 5X3

CASSANDRA AUSTIN

CALLY and the SHERIFF

Harlequin Books

TORONTO • NEW YORK • LONDON
AMSTERDAM • PARIS • SYDNEY • HAMBURG
STOCKHOLM • ATHENS • TOKYO • MILAN
MADRID • WARSAW • BUDAPEST • AUCKLAND

ISBN 0-373-28981-2

CALLY AND THE SHERIFF

This edition published by arrangement with Harlequin Books S.A.

® and TM are trademarks of the publisher. Trademarks indicated with ® are registered in the United States Patent and Trademark Office, the Canadian Trade Marks Office and in other countries.

Printed in U.S.A.

Books by Cassandra Austin

Harlequin Historicals

Wait for the Sunrise #190
Trusting Sarah #279
Cally and the Sheriff #381

CASSANDRA AUSTIN

has always lived in north central Kansas, and was raised on museums and arrowhead hunts; when she began writing, America's Old West seemed the natural setting. Now she writes between—and sometimes during—4H, school events and the various activities of her three children. Her husband farms, and they live in the house where he grew up.

For Dad,
for lots of reasons

Chapter One

Salina, Kansas
1877

Cally slid off the mule and brushed at the dust on her oversize pants. She didn't like to come to town and neither did Royal. The poor dog tried to look in every direction at once and wouldn't get farther from Cally's side than the long hairs on his back.

Cally tied her father's mule in front of Mr. Lafferty's feed store as she always did when she was forced to come to town. She trusted Mr. Lafferty. He didn't look at her funny the way other people did. Of course, Mr. Lafferty was nearly blind.

She noticed with a little disappointment that Mr. Lafferty had already closed up his store. She hadn't meant to stop and visit him, but it was always nice to see a friendly face. And he usually fed her mule a little grain while she was gone. "Sweepings," he would explain. "Spilled the stuff and can't sell it now."

She rubbed the old mule's nose. "Don't worry,

Jewel, I won't be long," she said softly. Squaring her shoulders and drawing herself up to her full five feet two inches, she headed purposefully toward the sheriff's office. Royal trotted at her side.

Her eyes narrowed when she thought of that low-down sheriff. He had found every weapon she had tried to sneak in to Pa, but he wouldn't find this one. She had wrapped the butcher knife in leather and tucked it in her pants. He wouldn't dare find it. Somehow, she would slip it to Pa, or she would use it on that sheriff herself!

She prayed that tonight's plan would work. The only weapons left at home were the shotgun and the ax. They would be hard to sneak in to Pa.

Outside the sheriff's office, she motioned Royal to stay. He whimpered but complied. She pulled her hat down securely and pushed the door open, letting it slam behind her as she entered. The room was lit only by fading sunlight through the windows and one lamp on the sheriff's desk. Cally stood for a moment while her eyes adjusted to the dim light.

Sheriff Andrew Haywood was sitting with his long slender legs propped lazily on his desk, his head bent over a book in his lap. His straight dark hair, she noticed not for the first time, was ridiculously neat. He raised his head reluctantly, and snapped the book closed, bringing his boots to the floor with a bang. The cool gaze he leveled on her revealed nothing.

But he didn't frighten her. "I came to see Pa," she announced in a firm voice, sending a quick glance toward the cell where her father slumped against the wall.

"What a pleasant surprise."

Cally sneered at his sarcasm. She watched him come to his feet and walk slowly toward her, his broad shoulders blocking out the rest of the room. She wouldn't be intimidated by his air of authority or his size. When he stopped two feet in front of her, she was forced to tip her head back in order to look him in the eye. She was proud of her own cool, steady stare.

His chest beneath the perfectly laundered shirt expanded as he took a deep breath. "Hand it over."

Her eyes narrowed. "I'm unarmed," she said, perturbed at the way his gaze probed hers. It was all she could do not to look away.

He shook his head slowly. "You're never unarmed, Miss DuBois." He pronounced her name the way Pa did, "du Bwah." Most people said "boys." He did it to flatter her, to put her off guard.

She gritted her teeth as he continued. "You can't break your father out of jail. You'll go to jail yourself. Just give me the gun or knife or whatever you've brought this time, and make it easy for both of us."

Right then she decided she hated his voice. It was smooth and self-assured, deep and soft at the same time. A tempting voice, her mind warned. She could almost believe he really cared.

She stood her ground and watched him look her over. His searching eyes made her want to laugh. He would learn nothing from looking at the baggy clothes.

Abruptly he moved forward. She drew back involuntarily, but only a step. His hands dug into the huge pockets of her overcoat, then searched the hidden ones inside. She almost relaxed. Did he think she was stupid enough to try the same thing twice?

She smirked until his hands settled on her waist. A jolt like lightning charged through her with his warm touch. She gasped, a combination of surprise and fear. He was so close she could smell the soap his laundress used on his shirt. She watched his eyes light with understanding and tried too late to pull away.

Strong fingers locked around her slender arm while he grabbed a handful of britches that included the knife. She had no choice but to give it up. He wasn't even gentleman enough to turn his back while she loosened the rope belt and retrieved the leather-wrapped weapon.

She felt her cheeks burn and knew they were fiery red as she readjusted her clothes. She looked up to find his attention elsewhere. He was carefully unrolling the leather. She was pleased, at least, to see his face register some shock at the huge knife.

"I liked it better during the trial when you brought your father pies and such," Haywood said, carrying the knife to the desk and jerking open a drawer. "What did you plan to do with this?"

Cally looked longingly at the drawer's contents— Pa's razor, three knives and a pistol. The butcher knife clanked on top of the others, and Haywood slammed the drawer shut.

He straightened to look her in the eye. She squared her shoulders. "I was going to bury it in your gut."

Pa spoke for the first time. "Cally girl, I thought I taught you better. That's no way to talk to an officer of the law."

Cally exploded. "An officer of the law! He's a no-good, bushwhacking, bloodthirsty snake!"

Royal's concerned whimper could be heard through the door.

"Now Cally," Pa admonished, resting an obviously aching head against the bars.

"Now Cally! Pa! He's going to hang you!" Saying it aloud brought a sudden lump to her throat. She barely heard Royal as he whined and scratched at the door. She all but forgot about the lean lawman propped against his desk, watching her. Her attention centered on poor Pa behind bars.

"What am I gonna do?" she whispered. She walked slowly toward him.

He took her hand and pulled her into his arms as much as the bars would allow. "Ah, Cally girl, I'm so sorry. But you can't keep trying to bust me out."

She wanted to tell him she had to, but she didn't want the sheriff to overhear. It would be better if he thought she had given up. She tried to fake a sob and it came out a hiccup.

Pa patted her shoulder. "Have you thought about it, Cally? We'd have to run, and what would you have then? You can't think you could just take me home."

Of course she had thought about it. It wouldn't be easy, but she couldn't just let her father hang. She tried for a more realistic sob.

Andrew leaned against his desk, watching the pair. His desire to give them a few moments in private warred with his conviction that he didn't dare take his eyes off the girl. From where he stood, he couldn't see Cally's face; it was hidden under the brim of her absurd hat. He heard her sniff as she drew herself out of her father's arms.

When she reached into her hip pocket, Andrew came automatically to his feet and started toward her. She withdrew a jackknife, snapping it open an instant before he could stop her. Menacing him with it, she demanded, "Get the keys."

"You're not serious?" Andrew was more disgusted than frightened.

"Get the keys," she screamed.

The dog's bark caught the girl's attention for an instant. Andrew took the last step that separated them, grabbing for her wrist. Her arm swung up to ward him off, and the blade sliced into his upper arm. Andrew gave a startled grunt as he drew back.

High on Andrew's right sleeve a red streak appeared and slowly spread downward. Andrew gave it barely a thought. Cally stared at it in horror. She started to sway and the knife clattered to the floor.

With a muttered curse, Andrew caught her shoulders. "You can't be a killer if you faint at the sight of blood," he said, leading her to his chair.

"Ah, Cally girl, you know how you are," moaned the prisoner. "She can't even kill a chicken, Sheriff. She couldn't have meant to hurt you."

"Pa!" Cally wailed, burying her face in her hands.

Andrew planted himself between the trembling girl and the drawer full of weapons, being careful his own holstered gun was beyond her reach. The girl's dog was putting up such a commotion he was a little concerned it would come through the door. He pulled his handkerchief out of his pocket and wrapped it around his arm. "Damn," he muttered. "I should have known she'd eventually think of hiding two knives."

At the sound of his voice, she raised her head, her green eyes bright with hatred. The freckles across her nose stood out in stark relief against the too-pale skin. "I have to help Pa," she whispered.

"I know." The acknowledgment surprised even him. He couldn't get soft with this little hellion. He tried to keep his voice stern, but the girl was already about to cry. It tempered his tone more than he expected. "Please try to understand. There's nothing you can do. I could arrest you, too, for attempted—"

The sound of sobbing cut him off, this time from the cell. Emerald eyes shot daggers at him as Cally came to her feet and hurried to the bars. "Don't cry, Pa," she soothed.

Andrew retrieved the knife from the floor and tossed it in the drawer with the others. "You better go home, Miss DuBois." His prisoner was huddled on his bunk, shaking and sobbing. The waif that came to see him every day clung to the bars.

"Miss DuBois." She ignored his gentle touch on her shoulder. "You better go home. It'll be dark soon." He tugged her lightly. Her grip on the bars tightened. "Do you really want a test of strength, Miss DuBois?" He had intended for it to sound threatening, but it came out more a plea.

Cally turned and spit, hitting him squarely in the face, then marched out of his office, holding her head high. Royal growled at Haywood as she gave the office door an extra tug to be sure it slammed. She heard an answering thud and knew one of Sheriff Haywood's precious pictures had hit the floor.

"Good," she muttered as she stomped down the street. What kind of bloodthirsty killer framed the pictures of men he had killed and hung them where he could look at them all day? At least that was what she guessed they were. She hadn't asked him about the four Wanted posters that decorated the office wall. She didn't talk to him any more than she had to!

Royal ran beside her, head turned to watch her face, as she stormed down the street. The poor dog nearly fell over himself trying to keep up and watch her at the same time.

"Maybe he likes looking at ugly pictures of ugly men," she suggested to Royal and Jewel as she untied the reins. Swinging onto her mule's back, she realized she had let her anger at the sheriff get the better of her. Desperation settled heavily on her, and she hung her head. How was she going to get Pa out of jail? Sheriff Haywood ruined every plan. She couldn't let her own father hang! She was running out of ideas, and Pa was running out of time.

Andrew wiped his face with the back of his hand as he watched the baggy clothes and hat flounce out of his office. He never saw that coming! Twice now, she had actually spit in his face! Why did his guard seem to slip a little when he was around Cally DuBois?

He cringed when the door slammed and the picture of Wade Terris hit the floor. He stood still for a moment, getting his temper under control before he retrieved the picture.

The joints of the frame had been loosened by the fall. He slipped the poster out, grateful at least that he hadn't put glass in front of the pictures. He would be cussing little Cally DuBois for sure if he was forced to clean splintered glass off his floor.

He set the frame and poster on his desk and studied his prisoner. The sobbing had stopped with the slamming of the door. DuBois huddled on the bunk, asleep perhaps, but still shaking slightly. Trying to fix the frame would disturb the old man. He would leave it until later.

The cut on his arm stung like the devil. He probed it to be sure it wasn't bleeding and sat down at his desk with a sigh. He would have liked a doctor to stitch it closed, but he couldn't leave his prisoner unattended, not with his crazy daughter on the loose.

One of his deputies had quit and the other's wife was down with the flu. That meant he was here for the night, and the little cut didn't qualify as an emergency. It could wait until one of the volunteers checked with him in the morning.

He settled back in the chair. It still seemed like a foolish arrangement. Why couldn't Bill have found volunteers to look after his wife while he did his job? Granted, the couple had only been married a few months, and if Bill had come to work, he would probably have spent all his time worrying about his wife. Andrew wasn't entirely sure Bill wouldn't have given in to the temptation to leave his post to check on her.

To Andrew, the situation reinforced a long-held belief that lawmen shouldn't be married. It ruined their edge. And furthermore, he believed that most people, especially voters, agreed with him. They liked to know that nothing was more important than the job.

However, that hadn't discouraged Bill. Andrew had

never seriously considered firing him for getting married either, though the thought was appealing at the moment.

Andrew smiled to himself. Bill's job was secure, at least for now. He was having enough trouble finding a replacement for one deputy. So far, no one he had interviewed had come close to being qualified. Bill had suggested he was too particular, but he hated to settle for mediocrity.

Andrew turned down the flame in the lamp and closed his eyes, determined to rest while he could. Settling back in his chair, he slept, but not for long. The vision of a butcher knife flying in his direction brought him instantly awake.

He shook the sleep from his head, got up and locked the door. The office was nearly dark now, and he lit the gaslight on the wall by the door, keeping the flame low.

DuBois sat up, rubbing his face as if he were trying to get feeling back into it. Andrew hadn't meant to disturb DuBois, but since the old man was awake anyway, he decided to take a look at the damaged picture frame. He kept a hammer and other basic tools in his office. Turning up the wick in the lamp on his desk, he studied the joints of the frame.

"Why do you keep that dodger on the wall, son?" DuBois asked.

"I drew the picture," Andrew answered, then laughed at the pride he heard in his own voice.

"Ugly cuss."

"But a fair likeness." Andrew made short work of the frame as he talked. "I was working for the federal marshal then. I was their unofficial artist, you might

say. The drawing helped catch the man, I believe."
He returned the picture to the nail.

"Drew them other fellas too, did ya?"

Andrew nodded as he studied his prisoner. The man didn't look well. His face was pale, and, though he tried to hide it, his hands shook.

"Sheriff?"

"Yes, Mr. DuBois?"

"Might I have...?" He ran his hand across his mouth and shook his head, withdrawing the request. "I ain't been sober this long since the missus died. You remember her?"

DuBois looked up then, and Andrew saw the tears in the old man's eyes. Not so old, he corrected himself. He had discovered during the trial that Francis DuBois was barely past forty. "I'm sorry. I don't remember her."

DuBois hung his head, his shaking hands dangling between his knees. "You wouldn't," he muttered. "Pretty Irish lass, she was. Deirdre Calloway. Still can't believe she'd love me."

Andrew returned to his chair behind his desk. He shouldn't feel sorry for the man. DuBois had spent most of his time drunk, pulling crazy stunts during the worst of it. It had only been a matter of time before someone got hurt. True, the dead man wasn't much better, but that wasn't the point. The jury had found Francis DuBois guilty of manslaughter, and he would hang on Saturday.

Still, Andrew couldn't help but wonder. If the incident had had the opposite outcome, if Louis DuBois had been the one to die, would the banker's drunken brother-in-law have received equal justice?

"I like you, Haywood," DuBois said abruptly. "Always have. Do you know my Cally?"

Andrew came to stand beside the cell, studying the broken man. "Cally comes to see you every day," he said, absently rubbing the wound on his arm.

DuBois stared at the floor. "I remember the day she was born. I looked down at that red hair and turned-up nose, and I said to Deirdre, 'She's a Calloway.' And that's what we named her." His haggard face rose slowly. "Will you look out for my Cally, Sheriff?"

Andrew stared a moment. That was most certainly not part of his job! "There's got to be some family," he suggested.

DuBois shook his head. "I got none. Deirdre's...well, ya see, they never took to me. I'm afraid I lost track of them long ago."

Andrew turned away. He paced across the office and back. DuBois wiped his mouth with a shaky hand, no longer looking at him. After considering a moment, Andrew went to the desk and pulled out a flask and shot glass. He filled the glass half full and handed it through the bars to DuBois.

DuBois looked at it, licked his lips and glanced at Andrew. "Obliged," he said, reaching for the glass. He drank it back in one swallow. "Ain't been worth much since—"

His watery eyes turned to Andrew again. "She's right pretty, really. Always been a hard worker and not one to complain. Cooks real good, too. If you don't want her for yourself, you could see she hooks up with someone decent. I'd a done it afore now, but she never showed no inclination to marry and, well, I wanted her around.''

Andrew turned away from the cell. He didn't see how he could refuse. The damnedest thing was he did feel responsible. He had arrested the old man. He was going to lead him to the gallows.

He shook his head abruptly. That little wildcat could take care of herself!

DuBois persisted. ''I'd rest easier, knowin'.''

Andrew cursed himself even as he answered, ''I'll look out for her.''

The ride back to the farm had seemed long and dismal. Cally couldn't enjoy the quiet that settled around her as she left the town behind. She couldn't take any pleasure in the lovely sunset or the light wind that rustled the dry leaves. She had left Pa behind. She had failed again.

He had been right, of course. She had known all along that she couldn't just bring him home if she broke him out of jail. They would both have to run. Jewel was a wonderful mule, but her running days were over. They would have to trade her for something better as soon as possible.

And Queen, Royal's old mother, wouldn't want to leave the farm. Every evening when Cally went to see Pa, she told the old dog goodbye and prayed someone would come by and find her and the cow and the chickens soon.

Tears were threatening again, and she bit her lip. She didn't want to give up! Pa hadn't meant to hurt anybody. She had promised the judge that she would watch him better if they would let her take him home.

Even as she had pleaded, she had known he wasn't listening. What was done, was done, and Pa wasn't going to get a second chance.

The road dropped down to ford a small creek and Jewel and Royal splashed across the little trickle of water. Once they were away from the trees Cally could see the apple tree on the hill silhouetted in the distance, then the dark shape of the barn. As she rode closer the farmstead seemed to welcome her.

The little sod house Pa had built so long ago when Ma was still alive was the only home Cally could remember. She knew it wasn't fancy or pretty, but it was the best soddy there ever was. People didn't expect a soddy to last nearly as long as this one had. Pa had talked of building a real cabin, but she had never counted on it. This had been enough for the two of them.

The old barn had a leaky roof and the tiny chicken coop was barely tight enough to keep critters out, but this was home. This was where she was safe and happy, tending her garden and her animals, which were her only friends. That was as much as she had ever expected to do. But she had always expected Pa to be here with her.

Cally slid off Jewel's back and led her into the barn. She had already done the chores, but she checked on Belle, the milk cow, and made sure the barn door was securely closed.

Royal was beside her as she walked to the house. Queen came to her feet at the threshold, and followed them inside. As soon as the door was closed, Queen spread herself out against the door, resuming her previous position, this time inside.

Cally moved a chair out of her way and sat down on her bunk. Its side and head were against the paper-covered dirt wall, and Pa's bunk was across from it. The two were so close, a tall man might sit on one and rest his feet on the other. The trunk under the window barely fit between the two bunks. Clothes hung from pegs above the beds and on either side of the window.

A woodstove, table, two chairs and some crate shelves filled the rest of the house. Once in a while Cally noticed how tiny and crowded it was. Not lately, though. Lately it seemed almost empty.

She shook herself and rose, quickly getting ready for bed. As soon as she blew out the lamp, Royal came to lie on the floor beside her bed. The two dogs made her feel safe, and she slept almost instantly.

Early in the morning, Cally opened the door, letting the dogs out and the fresh air in. She dressed in the same clothes she had worn the day before and started her morning chores. By the time the sun was completely over the horizon, she had milked Belle and staked her and Jewel in grass for the day. She had fed the chickens, letting them out of the little coop into the pen, and had checked the fence, as she did every morning, for any signs that a raccoon had tried to find a way in.

Her own breakfast came last. She fixed a small bowl of corn meal mush, adding fresh cream. She carried it outside and sat in the old rocker to eat it. She liked to think of the little area in front of the house as her front porch, though its floor was dirt like the rest of her yard—and house, for that matter. Pa had built a little sunshade above the door, and set out an old table. Since the house was so crowded, Cally worked outside as much as possible. She would be confined enough to the small space inside all winter.

She thought of Pa, confined to his tiny cell, and gritted her teeth. It had been weeks since his arrest, but she still expected to find him sleeping on his cot every time she stepped into the cabin.

With a sigh she looked out at her garden. That and the animals would be the hardest things to leave. She loved her garden, and it had been good to her this summer. Her vines were loaded with ripe tomatoes waiting to be picked, and she had several jars of cucumber pickles, corn and beans already stored for winter.

"Stored away for whoever finds them," she said aloud. "'Cause we ain't staying." Last night she had almost given up, but this morning she was as determined as ever to save Pa. There wasn't anything else a daughter could do. She would go into town again toward evening.

But what weapons did she have left? The ax? The shotgun? The one knife she used to cut her food?

Royal sprawled on the ground and yawned noisily. She turned to stare at him. He twitched his ears at her scrutiny. "You wanna take on that coldhearted sheriff, boy?" she asked. She tried to picture it but couldn't. Sure, the dog could be threatening enough if she was in danger, but she wasn't sure he would actually attack.

Royal yawned again, giving her a good look at his sharp white teeth. The thought of them sinking into somebody's—anybody's—flesh made her shiver.

Could Royal just *scare* the sheriff into letting Pa go? She remembered Haywood's cool gaze. He was so sure of himself, she couldn't imagine him scared. She was afraid she knew what he would do. He would shoot poor Royal, cold-blooded killer that he was.

She couldn't put Royal in danger. She would have to think of something else. Maybe she was going about this wrong. Maybe she should burn down the sheriff's house at the edge of town to create a distraction. She shook her head. She couldn't quite see herself being that destructive.

With a sigh, she got up to take her bowl inside. Queen raised her head, and Cally stopped to ruffle her soft brown fur. Queen let her tongue fall out of her mouth to show her pleasure.

She was about to step over Queen when Royal barked. The dog was watching a tiny figure leave the road at the creek.

"Early for company," Cally commented, stepping over Queen and entering the soddy. She didn't look toward the empty cot. In a moment, she stepped outside carrying Pa's double-barreled shotgun. Pa had taught her that she could never be too careful, and she had no reason to expect friendly callers.

Cally returned in the rocking chair and laid the gun across her lap. She watched the figure become a horse and rider and eventually Sheriff Haywood on his sorrel mare. The moment she recognized him, she stood, bringing the stock to her shoulder.

Andrew pulled the mare to a stop at a respectful distance. "Morning, Miss DuBois."

Cally didn't answer.

Andrew took in the shotgun and the steady hands that held it. "Mind if I light down?"

"No need. You ain't staying."

Andrew wasn't surprised at the unfriendly words. The gun he hadn't counted on, though he probably should have. He would have to get it out of her hands before he told her what he had come for. He caught himself rubbing the cut on his arm and slowly settled his hand on the pommel.

"Miss DuBois, I'll only keep you a moment. If you like, I'll stay in the saddle, but I'd appreciate it if you would put the shotgun down."

It seemed to take the girl forever to decide. Andrew was almost tempted to smile at the picture she made. The squat little soddy seemed a perfect backdrop for the ragamuffin and her long-haired dogs, which could nearly pass as coyotes. The girl's face was hidden by the brim of the floppy hat, but he would bet she had him sighted down the barrel of the gun.

He found himself wanting to sketch the scene and mentally shook himself. It had been too long since he had indulged in his favorite hobby. How could he possibly want a picture of this scruffy trio?

Finally Cally lowered the shotgun and leaned it against the wall behind her. He knew she didn't trust him and had a feeling she would stay within easy reach of the gun. "State your piece," she said.

Andrew took a deep breath. "It's your father, miss. I came to tell you he...died last night."

Chapter Two

Andrew watched Cally stare at him. She had gone as pale as she had in his office when she nearly fainted. "Miss?" he asked. He wanted to rush to her side, but he didn't want to be shot.

"It...it's not Saturday. Why? I...I don't understand."

The stammered words helped him make up his mind. Andrew swung off his horse and strode to her, ignoring the dog's low growl. "I'm sorry, miss. You better sit down."

"You better explain, mister." Cally straightened and looked him in the eye. Andrew blinked at the change. Her face was still pale, but the green eyes gazed steadily into his. He had been inches away from taking her in his arms, prepared to comfort a weeping child. He eased back a little instead.

"We're not sure what happened, miss. I got Dr. Briggs as soon as I knew something was wrong. Doc said he thought it might have been his heart." The doctor had also said the old drunk might have been so used to alcohol he couldn't live without it, but

Andrew didn't think that would be much comfort to the daughter.

Cally stared hard at him as if trying to determine if he told the truth. "I'll drop over to the doctor's when I'm in town. Hear what he has to say," she said.

Andrew watched her. She was trying to be brave, but he wasn't fooled. The poor girl shouldn't be alone at a time like this. "You could ride into town with me."

"I got work to do. I'll be along later." She was suddenly occupied with the larger of her two scruffy dogs. "Where is he?" she whispered.

"He's laid out it the back of the Furniture House." Andrew considered her a moment. "Miss, can I send for anyone? A friend?"

"Got none. You can leave, now. I won't shoot you as you go." Her voice was soft but it didn't crack.

With a nod, Andrew walked to his horse, but turned back. "Miss, your father asked me to look out for you. I hate to leave you alone."

"I was alone before you came. I've been alone for weeks."

She spoke without looking at him. The hat brim hid her entire face, and all Andrew could see of Cally besides the ill-fitting clothes was the small rough hands that rubbed the dog's neck.

"I'll be out tomorrow," he said. He wasn't sure she had heard. He mounted and turned the mare toward town. One of the dogs barked once to encourage him on his way.

Cally didn't look up until she knew he had left. She watched his horse become a blur as her eyes filled with tears. "We won't need a plan now, will we, Royal?"

Royal leaned against her leg to offer comfort. She rubbed the soft warm head. "It don't hardly seem possible, Pa'd just die."

Cally brushed at her tears with her shirtsleeve. Turning, she lifted the shotgun and carried it inside, hanging it in its place above the door. Back outside she slumped into the rocking chair.

She stared at the ford over the creek where Haywood had disappeared. This was somehow his fault. A sheriff was supposed to take care of his prisoners, not let them die in their cells.

The tears were forming again, and she squinted her eyes to try to stop them. The realization that she wouldn't have to leave her home came to her and she brushed it away guiltily.

Royal's whine drew her attention. The dog slunk to her side, cautiously placing his head on her lap. She ruffled his fur and looked into the big, sad eyes. "I gotta talk to the undertaker," she muttered. "And the doctor." Her tears dried quickly. "Yes, I want to talk to that doctor."

When Cally rode into Salina an hour later, she wondered if she shouldn't have waited until evening. There was much more activity than she was used to. The little two-wheeled cart Jewel pulled bounced noisily over the rutted streets, drawing even more stares in her direction.

When she slid off Jewel's back in front of Lafferty's, Royal crowded her against the mule, and Cally had to push the dog out of the way before she could reach the hitching post.

The door to the feed store stood open, and Cally stepped inside. "Mr. Lafferty?"

"Would that be Cally, come to visit an old man?" Mr. Lafferty walked slowly toward her from the darkness of the back of the store.

Royal barked a cheerful greeting.

"Heard about yer papa, lass," the old man said. "'Twas a sorry thing." He laid a bony hand on her shoulder and added softly, "Still, I'm glad he didna hang."

Cally felt the tears sting her eyes and pretended it was the oat dust that caused it. "I've come to town to see him. Sheriff Haywood says he's at the Furniture House."

She was grateful Mr. Lafferty knew her well enough to realize that was a question. "It's just three doors down from me, lass. It has the tall red sign. The carpenters are undertakers as well, y'see, and they'll fix yer papa up nice. Would ye want me to be goin' wi' ye, lass?"

"No, thanks," Cally said quickly. The fewer witnesses, the better.

Mr. Lafferty's weak eyes narrowed, and she wondered what he was thinking. After a moment he patted her shoulder. "Ye know ye can be countin' on me if'n ye need anythin'."

"I know," was all she could say before the lump in her throat choked off her voice. She touched the old hand briefly then hurried into the sunlight. The brightness brought more tears to her eyes, and she hid beside Jewel as she brushed them away.

Rubbing the mule's nose, Cally looked up and down the street, quickly locating the tall red sign. She studied it and felt a wave of dread. Once she saw Pa's body there could be no more hoping he wasn't dead.

It would make more sense to talk to the doctor first, she decided quickly. Cally had been to Dr. Briggs's home after a couple of Pa's fights and knew it was just a few blocks away. She started down the street with Royal trying valiantly to turn her back.

"It's all right, boy," she murmured, patting Royal's head. The dog relented but growled low in his throat whenever someone passed too close to his charge. Several ladies stepped clear off the boardwalk to let them pass.

Andrew saw the little scarecrow and her dog as soon as they came into town. He had been expecting her and had positioned himself casually across from Lafferty's feed store. Cally was at least predictable.

He wasn't sure why he felt the need to watch her. He told himself his job included protecting Miss Cally DuBois from the rougher element of town. *And protecting the gentler element from Miss Cally DuBois.* He felt guilty even as he thought it. She was harmless now, surely.

When she left the feed store, Andrew guessed she was headed for the doctor's. He let her get well ahead of him before he angled across the street, stepping around a corner in time to see her enter the small frame house that belonged to Dr. Briggs. A moment later, the door reopened, and the huge dog was virtually pushed out.

Andrew smiled as he remembered the first time

Cally had come to visit her father. His reaction to Royal inside his office had been immediate and severe. He could imagine the doctor's was at least as strong.

The huge dog whimpered and turned in circles on the porch. Finally he sat, his eyes fixing squarely on the sheriff. Andrew had never intended to interrupt the girl's conversation with the doctor. He had only wanted to see to her safety and offer to help her any way he could. For one brief moment as he looked at Royal, it seemed presumptuous to the point of stupidity to think she needed his protection.

He decided to wait for Cally across the street from the doctor's office. He took one step toward a shade tree, and the dog came to his feet. One more step and the hairs on the dog's back bristled as his shoulder muscles tensed.

Andrew stopped. Royal relaxed.

Andrew took another step, and the dog bared his teeth, a low growl rumbling in his throat.

Andrew felt a surge of anger. He wasn't even walking toward the dog! Cally was inside, certainly out of his reach. He wondered, irrationally, if the dog recognized him, if Cally had given Royal orders to attack him on sight.

"It would be just like that little hellion," he muttered under his breath. Well, he wasn't going to let a dog keep him from doing his job! If he wanted to march up to the doctor's door and wait for Cally DuBois on the front steps, her trained beast wasn't going to stop him.

He took three determined steps directly toward the dog before he stopped. There was nothing like a snarl-

ing dog, poised to spring, to cool a man's anger and
remind him of the advantages of patience.

Andrew took a step backward. He and the dog
stared at each other and waited for Cally to finish her
conversation with the doctor.

When Cally first heard Royal's reaction to danger
she worried that a patient was being kept from the
doctor's door. She hurried to a window in time to see
the sheriff stop in his tracks. It almost made her smile.

"And that's when Haywood came to get you?" she
prompted, turning back to the doctor.

"Yes. I did try to revive him, Miss DuBois. But
when the heart stops…" He shook his head.

Cally couldn't bear the pity on the man's face. She
turned and opened the door, mumbling, "Thank you,
Doctor," as she went. She had to nudge Royal out of
her way before she could step out of the house.

Without a word to Royal, she walked toward the
sheriff, knowing her dog would keep himself between
her and any stranger. She wanted to see the cool, self-
assured sheriff back away.

The closer they got to Haywood, the more Royal
bristled, barking a warning between deep menacing
growls. The poor dog was trembling when Cally finally stopped, laying a hand on the dog's back to
reassure him. She felt guilty for using Royal that way.
Especially when it hadn't worked.

Haywood removed his hat. "Miss DuBois," he
said softly.

"Sheriff," Cally said, trying hard to sound as calm
as he did.

"I wanted to offer my assistance."

Cally wanted to scream. She looked directly into the sheriff's eyes and decided they were the color of dirt. The thought gave her enough strength to accuse him. "You killed my father."

He had the grace to look surprised—for a second, anyway. Then he looked angry. She had to admit it was quite a thing to say, but, oh, how she wanted to hurt him! She was prepared for him to answer in kind, some cutting remark that she could use to feed her anger.

He disappointed her again.

"Is that what the doctor told you?"

"Yes," she lied, telling herself it was a small lie and didn't really count. "You gave him a drink. That's what killed him."

Haywood blinked. That was all. Blinked! She had watched his dirt-brown eyes as long as she could. The cool gaze was giving her the chills. She lifted her chin with the last of her courage and went around him, walking purposefully toward the Furniture House.

Royal gave the sheriff a parting glance before joining her.

Cally wanted to mutter her frustration aloud to the dog as she walked, but the streets were too crowded. She didn't need to attract any more stares than she was already getting. Men and women in all manner of fine clothes were walking on the boardwalks or crossing the street, and they all seemed to think she was the most interesting thing to look at. Hardly any of them spared a glance at the tall buildings, wagons and horses or each other.

Under the tall red sign, Cally stopped and braced herself. With squared shoulders, she stepped through the open door of the big furniture store. A man with a drooping mustache hurried to meet her. "Young man! Leave that dog outside!"

Cally glared at him for a moment. With a wave of her hand and a soft word, Royal returned to the threshold and sat, effectively blocking the doorway.

The mustachioed man scowled. "What can I do for you?"

His tone implied he hoped it wouldn't take long. So did Cally. "Sheriff Haywood said my pa's here."

The man's scowl deepened. "I'm Cally DuBois," she added.

His demeanor changed drastically. "Oh, Miss DuBois. I'm so sorry. Please, come this way. We've laid the poor soul out in the back."

The dog growled, and they both turned to see two ladies hurry away. The undertaker glared at the dog but smiled sympathetically when he turned back to Cally. "We have a nice selection of coffins, and you'll be wanting the services of our hearse."

Cally's irritation at the man's phony thoughtfulness made her bold enough to ask, "Will the county pay for it?"

The man's mustache drooped a little lower. "I wouldn't think so." He opened a door and led her into a storeroom. Lighting a lamp, he crossed to a long narrow table where the body lay covered with a sheet.

Cally barely glanced at it. She felt her stomach tremble and wanted to run away. But this was what she had come for, and there were things to be settled. "If he'd hanged, would the county have paid then?" she asked.

"Perhaps. Now, our services can include mourners if your father wasn't...ahem...well, if he didn't..."

Royal growled again, and the man leaned to the side, trying to see the front room.

Cally knew he imagined more potential customers scurrying down the street. She was as eager as he was to have this done. "He died in jail," she persisted. "Why won't the county pay for his funeral?"

"Look, Miss, if the man was a derelict, the county will bury him in potter's field. But I can't imagine a good daughter letting such a thing happen. I am more than willing to discuss some financial arrangement so your father can be buried properly."

Cally's eyes narrowed at the man's harsh tones. "Maybe the sheriff killed him so the county wouldn't have to pay for his funeral."

The mustache twitched. "That's an outrageous accusation! The sheriff wouldn't be paying, in any case."

Cally shrugged, as if dismissing a small matter. "I'll take Pa home," she said. "My cart's outside."

The mustache seemed to take on a life of its own. "Why, you can't. That is—you'll still need a coffin."

Cally had already turned to go. "I'll make him one...from his cot. He won't be needing it anymore."

Cally marched out of the Furniture House, hoping her courage would last until she left town. She untied Jewel from the post in front of Lafferty's, barely noticing the trace of oats on the mule's nose, and led her forward until the cart was directly in front of the furniture store.

The undertaker watched her from his threshold, sputtering. Finally convinced of her determination, he drafted a passerby to help and went back inside. Cally rubbed Jewel's nose while she waited, trying not to think.

In a few minutes they returned and loaded the body into the cart. If the stranger spoke to Cally or even tipped his hat, she didn't notice. The sheet had slipped to reveal one worn boot hanging over the end of the cart. Cally stared at it, swallowing hard.

The undertaker delivered a parting shot. "I daresay you'll regret this, Miss DuBois."

It brought Cally back to her senses. Without responding, she swung onto Jewel's back, turned the mule in a wide circle and headed out of town.

Andrew watched her go, fighting the urge to follow. The girl intended to take her father's body home for burial. She intended to dig the grave herself, wrap the body, toss dirt on her own father's chest. He couldn't picture it. In fact, he couldn't allow it.

He had other responsibilities, however, and couldn't simply leave town. First, he would have to let his deputy know where he was going. Sick wife or not, the man could relay a message if someone needed to find him. And he would leave a note on his office door as well.

In less than half an hour, Andrew was on his way to the DuBois farm. He wanted to kick his horse into a run. It was a ridiculous notion, he knew. He needed to arrive in time to help her, but there was no need to beat her home. As slow as that mule was, he could almost do that anyway.

But he hated to think of Cally making the trip alone, even though it was scarcely two miles. His concern for the girl perplexed him. She had been riding into town every day for weeks, and he had never once worried about her safety. What had caused the change?

Will you look out for my Cally, Sheriff?

He heard the words as if they were spoken by a ghost. Was that really all it took to make him feel so protective, or had something about the girl touched him? He felt a twinge in his upper arm and muttered to himself, ''Yeah, the tip of her knife is what touched me.''

In a manner of speaking, as sheriff he looked out for everyone in the county, but he had never been anyone's guardian. He didn't know where to begin. Exactly what were his responsibilities to Miss Cally DuBois? It would surely take some time to decide, but for now he knew he couldn't let her bury her father by herself.

Cally rode the mule to a little rise near her house. A weathered wooden cross barely marked her mother's grave. All the way home, she had tried to remember what had happened when her mother died. Had neighbors come? Had Pa sent for a preacher? Had he bought a coffin? Or had he made one? It was all a little hazy.

She decided it didn't matter. She had no choice but to do this herself. When she had unhitched the cart in the shade of the apple tree and led Jewel to grass nearby, she decided it didn't seem right to leave Pa alone while she went for the spade. ''Royal, stay with Pa,'' she said.

As she walked the short distance to the barn, she decided nothing seemed right. Her whole world was upside-down, and she was supposed to make decisions she had never before thought about.

Was it wrong to bury Pa wrapped only in a sheet? Should she try to make a coffin from his cot? She had said it only to shut up the undertaker, but now she wished she could really do it.

She was at the barn door when Royal's warning bark brought her quickly around. Anger helped her forget all her questions. Sheriff Andrew Haywood was riding toward her.

He drew up a short distance away and dismounted. Why hadn't Royal warned her? As she turned toward her dog, her eyes widened in horror. As this most hated of men walked slowly toward her, Royal, her trusted friend and protector, left his post on the hill and went wagging to meet him.

She stared as Haywood and the dog greeted each other like long-lost friends. How had this happened? Then she remembered leading the snarling Royal toward the sheriff and laying her hand on the dog's head for reassurance as they stopped in front of Haywood. She groaned, closing her eyes in disbelief. Royal had misunderstood.

Well, there was little chance of explaining to the dog now. She decided her best reaction was to ignore him—them! She wouldn't so much as nod to the sheriff. She certainly wasn't going to call her dog! She spun around and went into the barn, grabbed her garden spade and walked back to the little cemetery without another glance in Haywood's direction.

Haywood had the nerve to mutter something to Royal as they followed her up the hill. She picked the spot and pushed the spade into the dry earth. Her tiny feet inside her father's old work shoes could barely press the spade into the ground. This would be harder than she'd thought, especially with Haywood watching.

"Do you have another shovel?"

She turned to discover that Haywood had removed his coat and was rolling up the sleeves of his starched white shirt. She lifted another puny spadeful of dirt. "It won't work any better than this."

"Go get it." His voice was soft, but she heard it as a command. She thought she would enjoy telling him where *he* could go when his hand came down on hers, warm and gentle. It reminded her of her father's loving touch and tears blurred her vision. She let go of the spade and escaped to the barn.

When she had herself under control again, she took the shovel to the rise, surprised at how much sod Haywood had broken in her absence. The shovel, though not as sharp as the spade, was wider, and she tried to use it to scoop up the dirt as Haywood loosened it. She only succeeded in bumping her shovel against the spade.

"I'll take care of this," he said gently.

Cally glared at him a moment. She hated to have any decision taken out of her hands, especially by Haywood, but it would be stupid to turn down his offer. She shrugged as if it made no difference.

After a moment of glaring at his back, she stalked to the barn, glancing over her shoulder once to see Royal lie down in the shade of the cart. Her dog's defection rankled as much as the sheriff's interference. Muttering to herself, she found a hammer and knocked two short boards off a stall divider that she never used. With the old nails, she fashioned the boards into a cross. It wasn't much, but it went with the cross at her mother's grave.

By the time she returned, Haywood had made considerable progress. It would have taken her forever to dig the grave. She would bite her tongue off before she admitted it to Haywood, though. She leaned the cross against the cart and sat down under the apple tree near Royal. Haywood didn't seem to notice that she had returned.

It was impossible to watch him work and not see the play of muscles across his back and shoulders as he broke dirt loose with the spade and tossed it aside with the shovel. A strong back like that could have the barn roof mended in no time, she thought. If the man felt guilty about Pa, maybe she shouldn't discourage him. All manner of odd jobs came to mind, and she bit her lip to keep from grinning.

With Pa gone, the farm was all she had. Somehow, she would keep what was left of it and survive with it alone. The weather was warm for September, but she knew there wouldn't be many more days before frost. She couldn't help feeling regret and resentment for the days she had wasted while she dreamed of rescuing Pa.

She tried to shake such thoughts away by concentrating on her future. She had yet to dig the potatoes, and, after the first frost, she would have to carry all the pumpkins and squash into her cellar. The hayloft would be a better place to store some of these things but the roof leaked. She watched Haywood's muscles flex as he shoved the spade into the dark earth, and imagined the roof repaired.

Besides harvesting her garden produce, she would have to chop enough wood to last through the winter.

She watched Haywood send another shovelful of dirt onto the pile. It was easy to picture him replenishing her woodpile.

Somehow, watching him too closely made her stomach nervous and her cheeks warm. Deliberately, she pulled her thoughts back to her plans.

She needed to put up as many jars of tomatoes from her neglected patch as she could. The money she made selling her pies and bread paid for flour, sugar and a few other supplies, but mostly she had to live through the winter on what she saved from the garden.

Cally was used to hard work and deciding upon a plan felt better than the persistent hopelessness of the weeks since Pa's arrest. In a way, she knew life would be easier. Pa, bless him, wasn't really much help. Cally scolded herself for the disloyal thought. Poor Pa was right beside her!

Haywood's shirt had become soaked with sweat, defining those useful muscles even more. Yes, her best bet was to humor the sheriff and play on his guilt as long as it lasted. With that in mind, she scrambled to her feet. She walked to the well and brought back a tin cup full of water. She didn't speak but stood in front of Haywood until he looked up.

He eyed her speculatively.

"It ain't poisoned," she said, thrusting the cup toward him.

"Thanks," he murmured. He tried to hide a grin as he brought the cup to his lips.

That grin made Cally furious. Her one act of kindness was suspect! Well, sure, it was more an act of encouragement than kindness, but he wasn't supposed to see it that way. Shoot! It was hard to be nice to this man! Maybe the barn roof wasn't worth it.

He handed the empty cup to her, and she snatched it out of his hand. She couldn't stay here and watch him anymore. Waiting for him to dig the grave was worse than digging it herself. She stomped back to the well and hung up the cup. At the house she took her bucket from its hook on the side of the house and went to the garden.

With a sigh she surveyed the tomatoes. Lately she had been picking only what she wanted to eat. "There are more rotten ones than good ones," she said to Royal before she remembered that Royal hadn't followed her. She looked toward the little hill where Royal lay in the shade of the cart, guarding Haywood while he worked. There was another mark against that interfering sheriff.

She picked overripe tomatoes and dropped them into her bucket, muttering to herself. She almost called Queen over so she would have an excuse to grumble aloud. She had tossed the second bucketful of spoiled tomatoes to the chickens when she saw Haywood approaching.

He had unbuttoned the damp shirt halfway to his waist revealing glimpses of his hairy, muscular chest. Dirt smudged his face and once-white shirt. His hair was in complete disarray. This, Cally decided, was the way she would remember Sheriff Andrew Haywood next time the always-perfect sheriff tried to tell her what to do!

Chapter Three

"The grave's dug, Miss Dubois."

It took Cally a moment to realize that Haywood had spoken.

He eyed her curiously as he went on in that soft voice, "I thought you'd want to say a few words over the body." He paused, waiting, but she didn't know what to do. "Do you have a Bible?"

Cally fought down a moment of panic. Nodding, she hurried to the well to wash. Inside the soddy, she found her mother's Bible and, hugging it to her breast, walked to the grave. Haywood had rebuttoned his shirt and was shrugging into his coat. He looked oddly formal for as dirty as he was.

He had laid Pa's body out on the ground and wrapped him more neatly in the sheet. She couldn't help staring at it.

"Do you want one last look?" he offered.

Cally shook her head. Haywood jumped easily into the hole, lifted the body gently, and laid it in the grave. He pulled himself back out and stood beside

Cally, his hands clasped in front of him. And waited. "Go ahead," he urged gently, indicating the Bible.

Cally swallowed. "I...can't." She sniffed. "Would you?"

Haywood nodded and took the Bible. Cally watched his hands as he turned the Bible over then leafed through it. In a moment, he found what he was looking for. His soft, warm voice read some verses that sounded faintly familiar to Cally. When he was done, he closed the Bible gently. "Did you want to say anything else?"

Cally shook her head, unwilling to look at him.

After what seemed like a long pause, he said, "It's sometimes customary for a family member to—"

Cally looked up as his voice trailed off. He held the small shovel toward her. The look on his face was more upsetting than the thought of throwing dirt on Pa's body. Compassion. Sympathy. She straightened her shoulders. If that was the custom, she didn't want to disappoint him. And she didn't want him thinking she was about to fall apart!

As calmly as she could, she took the shovel and slid it into the pile of dirt—dirt the color of his eyes, she reminded herself. Using all her irritation at Sheriff Haywood to give her strength, she lifted as large a load as she could handle.

As she let it fall into the grave, Haywood spoke gently, "Dust to dust. Ashes to ashes. We commit this body back to the earth from whence it sprang. Amen."

Cally watched him for a long moment before his eyes met hers again. "Are you a preacher?" she asked.

"No," was all he said. He took the shovel from her hands, handing her the Bible, and nodded toward the cart. "Why don't you hitch the mule to the cart and take it back to the barn? I'll finish up here." He was already removing the coat.

There he was, telling her what to do again! He turned his back on her as if he expected her to do just what she was told. Well, maybe *she* wanted to finish up here.

She watched those fascinating muscles flex as scoop after scoop of dirt fell on the corpse. Maybe she was being ridiculous. She hurried to Jewel, brought her to the cart and hitched her up. She called to Royal, and this time the dog followed her to the barn.

When the cart was put away and Jewel was staked once again, this time on grass as far from the grave as was practical, Cally walked slowly toward the house. She knew she should return to her garden. The tomatoes needed to be picked before they all rotted. Instead, she sat down on her rocker.

"He's truly gone," she whispered to herself. Royal whimpered in response to her sorrow and settled down beside her, his head resting on his paws, watching her with sad eyes. "I should have saved him."

Her eyes turned to the hill where Haywood worked steadily. Soon he would be done, and she would be alone again. He was the reason Pa was dead! When he left, things would be closer to normal. She would be glad when he was off her farm and out of her sight!

That didn't explain the stab of panic when she watched him drive her crude little cross into the fresh earth and, retrieving his hat and coat as well as the shovels, start toward the house. She didn't think he so much as glanced in her direction but left the tools beside the barn and walked slowly to the well. He splashed water over his face and neck, revealing his fatigue as he leaned against the low rock wall.

Cally's own stomach rumbled, and she glanced at the sun, now directly overhead. He could ride that horse into town and have a fancy meal at a restaurant, she told herself. *And I can eat alone.*

"I'll be on my way, Miss DuBois."

She had watched him walk toward her so wrapped up in her thoughts that she hadn't realized he watched her, too. She simply nodded, letting the chair rock gently.

He took a deep breath. "Miss, I hate to leave you out here alone. Won't you come into town with me? I could help you find someplace...."

"No!" She cut him off. "I have a place. Right here."

"Yes, ma'am." He stood quietly for a long moment as they watched each other.

He started to turn away.

"Do you—?" Cally stopped herself too late. She had caught his attention. She swallowed. "Do you want something to eat?" There. She had said it. Now what was she going to do?

"I need to get back into town. But thanks just the same."

He strode toward his horse, placing his hat on his head as he went. He tied the coat behind the saddle and sprang aboard. In a moment he was out of the yard.

How could he dare turn down her offer of a meal!

Who did he think he was? Too good to eat with her? She was the best cook in the county. Everybody said so. Didn't folks always snap up her pies and breads when she brought them to town?

"He better not ever show his face around here again," she told Royal. Feeling indignant was much more comfortable than feeling grateful. With renewed energy, she got up to fix herself some lunch.

Andrew rode into the barnyard of his rented house feeling nearly overwhelmed with pity for little Calloway DuBois. He had tortured himself all the way home wondering if perhaps he should have accepted her invitation to dinner. God knew he was hungry enough, but at the time he had thought he was saving the poor girl the trouble of cooking for someone after the ordeal of the funeral.

For nearly anyone else, the neighbors would have come with food enough to fill her larder for days. But few neighbors knew Cally or her father, and most that did weren't fond of them, especially since the trial. And, of course, this wasn't a publicized funeral.

So he had turned her down. Now he wondered if eating with her wouldn't have given him an opportunity to convince her to come with him to town. Clearly she couldn't stay on the farm by herself.

He led his horse to the barn and rubbed her down before turning her into the corral. He flexed his sore shoulders as he walked to the house. After some food and a hot bath, he would make inquiries about a position for Miss Cally DuBois. There must be employment for her somewhere, but if not, he would see to her needs while he continued looking for a job.

Or a husband. That, he admitted, would be the most thorough solution. By the time he had cleaned up and dressed in a fresh white shirt and twill trousers, he had virtually dismissed the idea. Considering the girl's disposition, finding a husband might prove impossible, even though men far outnumbered women in the community. For a moment he considered the man who would welcome the little hellion as a bride, and shuddered. She would need considerable training if she were to snare a man this side of a barbarian.

And training, of course, was another matter. How far, exactly, did his guardianship responsibilities go? Should he use some of his inheritance to send her to a school somewhere? The idea of Cally DuBois in a finishing school stretched the imagination.

By the time he left the house, he had a mental list of people to visit, but his first stop was Bill's house. The deputy answered his knock, looking somewhat haggard. "I wanted to let you know I was back in town," Andrew said, eyeing his deputy critically. "You aren't coming down with something now, are you?"

Bill sighed, running his hand through his already rumpled blond hair. "No, and I think she's a little better than she was this morning."

Andrew couldn't suppress a grin. "You look awful, friend."

Bill stepped out onto the porch, letting the door close behind him. "Just between you and me, looking after a sick wife is hell. I could chase a bandit clean to Mexico and not be so worn out. She keeps thinking of housework that needs to be done or she says it'll keep her awake."

"You made your..."

"Don't say it! Look, Andrew, three more days, tops. If she isn't better I'll see if some of her women friends can't take turns sitting with her. I've got to get out of this house."

Andrew gave his deputy a reassuring thump on the shoulder before he stepped off the porch. It was hard to build up much sympathy for the man. But then, he reminded himself, he wasn't really in a position to understand.

He tore his note from the nail beside his office door and started toward Dr. Briggs's house. A few steps down the boardwalk, he heard someone hail him and turned to see an elderly gent hurrying toward him.

"Mr. Sweeney," Andrew said as the man huffed up to him. "Is something wrong?"

"No, no," Sweeney said, reaching out to Andrew to steady himself while he struggled for breath. "I just...wanted to...catch you."

Andrew supported the old man as best he could and looked around for a place for him to sit. "Are you all right?"

With one last deep breath, Sweeney straightened. "Fine, fine. Can we go inside?"

"Of course." Andrew unlocked the door and motioned Sweeney in ahead of him. When the door was closed and the lamp on his desk lit, Andrew moved his chair near the one the old man had taken and sat. When he was sure Sweeney was recovered he asked, "What can I do for you?"

Sweeney smiled. "Why, I'm here about the deputy's job, of course."

Andrew hoped his jaw hadn't actually hit his chest.

"Mr. Sweeney," he began, searching for the most diplomatic words, "I was thinking of someone more...vigorous."

"Vigorous?"

"Well, sir, a deputy's job could get somewhat... strenuous."

Sweeney scowled at Andrew. "You saying I'm old?"

"Ah, no, sir, but—"

"Well, see here, young man, don't dismiss me because I've lived a few years. I could teach you a thing or two."

"I'm sure you could, sir, but—"

"Well, that's better. I was thinking I could start tomorrow. No sense wasting any time."

Andrew cleared his throat. "Mr. Sweeney..." He hesitated. How should he put this? He tried to be gentle. "I don't believe I can hire you as deputy."

Mr. Sweeney seemed completely surprised. "Why ever not? You just admitted I know more than you do."

"Yes, sir, but...you're not...I mean...you're—" Mr. Sweeney wasn't taking the hint. "Old," he finished.

Mr. Sweeney came to his feet. "I don't think I'd care to work for someone who has no respect for his elders."

Andrew rose and followed the old man out the door. "Sir, I don't want you to take this personally."

"No other way to take it, boy," Sweeney said, stalking away.

Andrew pulled the office door closed. He stood for a moment looking after the would-be deputy. The old man barely made it off the boardwalk without stumbling. Unfortunately, he had been one of the better applicants.

Andrew shook his head and turned in the other direction, toward Dr. Briggs's house. His run for the doctor the night before was fresh in his mind. He had been hesitant for a second about leaving DuBois alone but knew he could do nothing for him. By the time he and the doctor had returned, the old man was nearly gone.

Dr. Briggs answered the knock. "Good afternoon, Sheriff. What can I do for you?"

Andrew stepped inside and considered for a moment how best to approach the subject. He couldn't very well demand that Briggs tell him exactly what he had said to Cally. "I have a few questions about Mr. DuBois' death," he said.

The doctor offered him a chair and once they were seated, Andrew continued. "You suggested last night that it was his heart. Is that still your assumption?"

The doctor nodded. "Maybe." Dr. Briggs was a tall, thin, middle-aged man, friendly and usually straightforward.

"Maybe?" Andrew prompted.

"Well—" the doctor shifted in his seat "—the man was a drunkard. All that time since his arrest without a drink was giving him the shakes. The one drink he had that night might have been what stopped his heart."

Andrew grew very still. "You mean the drink I gave him killed him?"

"It's possible."

Dr. Briggs did not seem to realize how horrifying

this news was to Andrew. "You didn't mention this last night," he said.

"Things got a little hectic last night." The doctor seemed to finally notice Andrew's expression. "Look, Sheriff, it's just a theory. Even if it's true, no one could think it was anything but an accident. Besides, the man was going to hang in a few days."

Andrew nodded and rose to go. Sure, it was a minor detail. It wouldn't matter to anyone—but him and Cally.

He thanked the doctor and headed back downtown, hoping his visit with the attorney would be more rewarding. He climbed the stairs to Mr. Cobb's office and, after waiting a few minutes, was ushered into the inner office.

Cobb stood and shook his hand motioning him to a seat. "What can I do for you, Sheriff?"

"I need some advice," Andrew said as he was seated.

Cobb smiled. "That's what I'm here for."

"A dying man asked me to look after his daughter," Andrew said. "What are my legal obligations?"

Cobb stared at him a moment, and Andrew wondered if this sounded foolish to the attorney. Finally Cob asked, "Were there witnesses?"

"No." Andrew shifted forward in the seat. "I'm not trying to get out of this. I want to do right by her."

A feral smile slowly formed on Cobb's lips. "The DuBois girl, right?" He didn't wait for an answer. "There's a little land involved, if my memory serves. As her legal guardian you would control that."

Andrew was too surprised to object.

Cobb pulled a sheet of paper from a drawer and began making notes. "Is there family likely to come forward and challenge your right of guardianship?"

"No. You don't—"

"How old is the girl?" Cobb didn't look up from his notes. When Andrew didn't answer, he prompted, "Marriageable age?"

"Perhaps. Mr. Cobb, I'm not trying to steal the girl's land. I—"

"Of course you're not." Cobb finally looked up and winked. Andrew wanted to close the eye with his fist. "My suggestion is to see the girl married and demand a percentage for looking after her affairs. Forty is reasonable."

Andrew made one last effort to explain. "I simply want to know what my responsibilities are to the girl."

Mr. Cobb shook his head. "Not many, really. You'll want to do a few conspicuous acts of guardianship for this to hold up in court should someone challenge it. But DuBois was poor white trash. It doesn't take much to convince that kind you're on their side."

Andrew gritted his teeth. It was on the tip of his tongue to tell the attorney what he thought of his advice. Swearing at attorneys—or anyone else—wasn't his normal behavior. He took a deep breath. Perhaps the man could still be of help. "I thought, perhaps, I'd help the girl find a job."

"Oh, that's a good start."

Andrew tried to ignore the interruption. "Have you heard of any openings?"

Cobb was making notes again. "You might try the saloons. Is the girl at all pretty?"

Andrew had to get out of there before he did hit the man.

"Thank you, Mr. Cobb. You've been very informative."

As he rose to go, Cobb said, "I can have the papers drawn up for you and signed by a judge in just a few days."

"Don't bother."

"But—"

Andrew closed the door, cutting off the attorney. He started through the outer office then turned back to the clerk, who eyed him curiously. "Are you aware of anyone looking to employ a young woman?" he asked. "Domestic help, perhaps?"

The young clerk considered a moment. "Seems like there hasn't been much in the paper lately, except your search for a deputy." He grinned and Andrew pictured Cally applying along with every other misfit in town.

Andrew had turned to go when the clerk spoke again. "Wait. The Gwynns. I heard them talking to Mr. Cobb some time ago. They didn't want to advertise it, but they need a housekeeper. They're getting on in years and the house and meals and all are too much to handle. I'm surprised Mr. Cobb didn't mention them."

"I'm not," Andrew mumbled. "Thanks." He returned the clerk's smile and left, walking thoughtfully down the stairs. So much for learning his legal obligations. He would have to follow his own instincts. And his instincts told him a young woman, marriageable age or not, could not take care of herself on a farm two miles from town. He headed straight for the Gwynn sisters' home.

"Why, Sheriff Haywood. What brings you here?" The short stocky Easter Gwynn had opened the door. Noella appeared behind her, looking over her sister's shoulder.

"I understand that you ladies are interested in hiring a housekeeper."

Easter opened the door a little wider. "Why, yes, we are. Come in. Can we fix you some tea?"

"No, ma'am." Andrew followed the sisters into the parlor and sat on the edge of an uncomfortable but elegant chair. "I know of a girl who's been recently orphaned. She needs to find a position."

Easter smiled. Noella frowned. "Who is this person?" the latter asked.

Andrew almost cringed. "Cally DuBois."

The women looked at each other. No shock or horror was visible on their faces. Andrew wondered if they might not know who Cally was. That would make it easier, he thought, then felt guilty. He shouldn't be deceiving little old ladies.

"Isn't that the waif that sells the pies?" Easter asked.

"I believe so," said her sister.

"Imagine," breathed Easter.

"How soon can she start?" Noella asked, folding her hands primly on her narrow lap.

Andrew was surprised enough to ask, "You know her?"

"We know of her," Noella corrected.

"She's the best cook in the county," Easter said. Andrew was sure she started to lick her lips.

Noella spoke again. "I believe my sister asked when she could start."

"I don't know." Andrew felt a need to caution the ladies. "Cally—" What did he plan to say? Cally's a hellion? He grimaced. "Cally...hasn't agreed to it yet."

"Well." Noella came to her feet. "I will show you around, and you can convince the girl for us."

He followed the woman into a large modern kitchen, with Easter right behind him. "We will expect her to cook and clean," Noella said. "It won't be hard work. We're both healthy and don't need to be waited on hand and foot."

"Her room will be back here," said Easter, opening a door off the kitchen.

"It's very nice," he said. He had to tell them. He took a deep breath. "In fact, it's much nicer than what she's used to. Ladies, Miss DuBois has grown up in a soddy. I'm afraid she's...got a few rough edges." Did that really say what he meant?

Noella and Easter exchanged a look again. "Don't worry, Sheriff. We'll civilize her," Noella asserted.

Early in the evening, Andrew decided to lock up his office. He was still on duty, but almost anyone looking for him would know to come to the house on the edge of town. With no prisoner in the cell, he could spend the night in his bed, a luxury he hadn't experienced since his deputy's wife had taken sick three days before. In all that time, he hadn't been home except to feed his horses and to wash and change clothes. While he regretted the circumstances that made it possible tonight, he was more than ready for a quiet evening alone with his books or his sketchbook.

As he locked up the office and started down the darkening street, he realized he had waited longer than necessary, half-expecting to see Cally. Her visits had become a habit—like a toothache.

At home, he settled into a comfortable chair, gathering his sketchbook and pencils from the nearby table. In spite of the shock of his visit with Dr. Briggs and his frustration with Mr. Cobb, he wasn't totally unhappy with his afternoon's accomplishments. He had found a home for Cally.

He began sketching the women's faces as he remembered their conversation. Easter and Noella Gwynn seemed willing to overlook her lack of social graces. It was more than he had hoped for.

"We'll civilize her," Noella had said. He wondered if she realized the magnitude of that particular task.

Though it wouldn't necessarily impress Cally, the cozy room off the kitchen would be far more comfortable than her old sod house. Between the Gwynn's modern kitchen and large but tightly built house, the work would probably be easier than what the girl experienced now. Certainly, the gentlewomen would be far better influences on her developing mind than her drunken father!

Her father. As he continued to sketch, Andrew recalled Dr. Briggs's revelation. The fact that he had had no way of knowing the danger when he gave DuBois a drink was little comfort. He reminded himself that it was merely a possibility but still had trouble shaking off the guilt. He felt even more responsible for the girl than he had after DuBois' request.

He looked down at the picture he had drawn. The women that looked back at him seemed uncommonly stern. Had he seen them that way this afternoon? He tried to soften their features with a few light strokes, but they changed very little. The sisters' haughty noses and pursed lips defied his gentle efforts.

Poor Cally.

Andrew shook himself and tossed the sketchbook aside. She had spit in his face twice. His arm still smarted where she had cut him. She had threatened to stab him with a butcher knife. Which reminded him of a drawer full of weapons he had forgotten to return to her. Forgotten! He was almost afraid to return them to her.

He should be feeling sorry for the ladies. Stern was the least of what Cally DuBois needed.

Wasn't it?

The sun was streaming into the soddy when Cally fixed her breakfast. She had rescued her tomato patch the day before, washing and canning the ripe fruit and throwing the rotten ones to her chickens. She had been certain that she would sleep soundly after working so hard, but her night had been filled with strange dreams.

Of course, she had buried her father yesterday; she might have expected some unsettling dreams. But not like these. These had nothing to do with her father. The first dream, at least the first one she remembered, was the worst. Haywood had driven her away from her farm.

"It was a bad dream," she told Royal, feeling a need to hear a human voice. "He took the farm same as he took Pa." What she couldn't say aloud, not to her trusting friend, was that in the dream Royal had stood beside the sheriff. She was just feeling abandoned, she decided.

When she had fallen asleep again, she had watched Haywood walk toward her, tired and dirty as he had been after burying her father. Instead of inviting him to dinner, she had pulled a knife from her back pocket and slashed him with it. In the dream, it hadn't cut just his arm as it had in his office, but clear across his chest.

There was no need to let that dream make her feel bad, she told herself. However, her knees trembled and her head spun when she thought of the bright blood pouring down his white shirt. She had to banish the picture from her mind before she fainted. Her breakfast was ready, and she carried it to her rocking chair, turning her mind to the third dream.

In some ways, it was the strangest. She tried to remember it exactly. She was in her little cart under the apple tree. Strong arms had lifted her. She remembered a starched white shirt that smelled of laundry soap. She felt like a little girl being carried, but she knew she wasn't a child in the dream. Then he laid her…where? In the grave? She didn't think so.

She had jerked awake, to find her heart racing. Whatever it was, it still frightened her. Yet, unlike the first two dreams, it intrigued her. She wanted to remember it, relive every detail even as they seemed to fade away.

She finished her breakfast quickly, disgusted with herself for wasting time worrying about dreams that had already made her late since she had overslept because of them. She was taking the empty bowl into the house when Royal barked. A glance out the door told her she was about to have a visitor. She grabbed the shotgun and carried it outside.

Chapter Four

Sheriff Haywood cantered into her yard, and Royal went to meet him. For one brief moment, Cally considered the leaky barn roof and the dwindling woodpile. Then she remembered his efforts to get her to leave her farm. She weighed the shotgun in her hand as she considered. Its purpose was to discourage strangers, which Haywood wasn't—exactly. She had a feeling he wasn't frightened by it anyway. Still it let him know he wasn't welcome. She kept it in her hands as she watched him dismount.

"Surprised to see you back so soon," she said.

Haywood lifted a bag that had been tied to his saddle horn and started toward her. If he thought she was inhospitable after his help the day before, he didn't mention it.

"I didn't invite you in," she said, pleased with the chill in her voice.

He stopped. "These are yours," he said.

"Leave 'em where you stand."

He took his time, as if trying to decide if he should defy her. She wondered if he was gauging his own speed against her ability to swing the shotgun to her shoulder. No, that was foolish. He wasn't here to hurt her, just annoy the hell out of her. She gripped the shotgun tighter, wishing she knew what to say to make him leave her alone.

Haywood let the bag drop from his fingers. It hit the ground with a clatter. "Miss DuBois," he called louder than he needed to. She was supposed to feel guilty for making him stay so far from the house. "I'd like to talk to you."

"So talk. I can hear you."

She watched the sheriff clench his jaw. She had made him mad. She was elated. She bit her lip to keep him from seeing her grin.

Royal sniffed the discarded bag and turned in a circle to sit at the sheriff's feet. Cally wondered what would happen if she commanded her dog to kill. Sometime she was going to try it.

Haywood removed his hat, an odd gesture, it seemed to Cally. "I found a job for you in town," he said.

"I don't need a job."

"Miss DuBois, you can't stay out here by yourself all winter. There are two ladies who are willing to give you a home in exchange for housework. They're nice ladies, and I'm sure you'd—"

"I got my own housework."

"But surely you can't mean to stay."

Cally lost her patience. "Get on your horse and head on back to town now, Sheriff."

He didn't budge. "Your father asked me to look out for you."

Cally considered that for the briefest of moments.

"You sure that wasn't a warning?" She couldn't stop herself from grinning but was surprised to see Haywood do the same. She didn't think she had ever seen him smile. It made him look...different. She realized she had let her arms relax and brought the shotgun to chest level again. Just because he looked...different, didn't mean he was. She concentrated on glaring at him.

His smile faded, but he didn't look particularly worried. "Miss DuBois, what are you going to do when winter comes?"

A touch of arrogance in his tone made her certain he had seen her drop her guard. She glared all the harder. "I'll get by, I reckon."

He looked toward her woodpile. "How are you going to chop enough wood to keep from freezing? Do you plan to wade through the snow to do your chores morning and night?"

Cally was a little concerned about the wood, but she had him on this last argument. "Do you really think Pa ever did the chores?"

Unfortunately, he didn't seem to realize she had him. "If you don't freeze, you'll starve. Even a grown woman wouldn't try to make it by herself out here, and you're a child."

"I'm what?" Cally really considered swinging the shotgun to her shoulder. A child?

Haywood took his own sweet time deciding what to do. Was he wondering if she would really shoot him? She hoped he didn't push her that far; Pa's old shotgun hadn't been reliable in years. When she saw his stance relax, she hoped she had won—at least for now.

"You know where to find me if you need me," he said.

"I won't need you." Her voice, she noted with satisfaction, was as cold as ever.

Haywood rubbed Royal's ears, and the traitor leaned into his leg. "I'll check on you from time to time," he said, donning his hat before swinging into the saddle.

He turned the sorrel toward town, and Cally hollered after him, "I'll keep the shotgun handy!"

Andrew had the nerve to turn and wave at her to let her know he had heard—and didn't care.

She glared at the horse and rider until they disappeared, then at the sack in her yard. She knew it contained all the weapons he had taken away from her. She was glad to have them back. She really was. She just didn't want to look at them right now.

She took a deep breath and stomped across the yard, grabbed up the sack and stomped back to her house. She deposited the sack on the table, then turned and put the shotgun in its place.

She would dig her potatoes today. She would dig them all and take them to her root cellar. She marched to the barn to get the spade. "I'll boil a potato for dinner," she told the dog. "There's nothing better than fresh dug potatoes. I might even boil two. Too bad you don't like potatoes. Seems like you should since you like apples."

She knew she was babbling and to a dog even, but it was either that or think about that insufferable sheriff. "I'll check on you from time to time," she mocked.

Royal twitched his ears at the change in her tone.

"Meddling sheriff," she muttered, shoving the barn door open with more force than necessary. "Found me a job, did he? Like I have time for a job!"

She grabbed up the spade and left the barn. "Why, I've got so much to do here, I hardly know where to start."

She had stomped half the way back to her garden when she glanced down at the spade and stopped in her tracks. She stared at a small clump of dried mud that clung to the blade. Haywood had cleaned the spade and shovel before he brought them back to the barn, but a tiny bit of earth had remained to remind her of how the spade had been used. Yesterday.

Cally found herself sitting on the ground, her knees drawn up to cradle her face. In spite of how upset she had been, she hadn't cried the night Pa had been arrested. She couldn't remember even wanting to cry before that, though tears had threatened a few times since. But now the floodgates had opened, and she was powerless to stop the tears. Sorrow, loneliness and fear washed over her in turns.

Once she raised her head to let the breeze cool her damp face, hoping that would help her regain control. Royal, responding to what he saw in her face, whimpered, nuzzled her shoulder and licked at her ear, causing her to burst into fresh tears.

She didn't know how long she sat like that, in the middle of her yard with the offending spade discarded half a pace away, but in the end exhaustion won where willpower had failed.

She awoke later from a light doze and raised her head. "Potatoes," she reminded herself, stretching her stiff shoulders. "Lord, Royal, what if Haywood had ridden in and seen that? He'd be hauling me off to town hog-tied to the saddle, I reckon.''

She came unsteadily to her feet and took a deep breath. "If that wasn't the silliest thing." She rubbed her cheeks to make sure there were no more tears and brushed at her damp knees. She felt foolish, but in a strange way it had been good to cry. She felt released from a kind of tension that she had felt since Pa had been arrested.

The spot of dirt from her father's grave didn't bother her when she caught up the spade and headed for the garden. Digging the potatoes felt good, too. She inhaled the scent of the rich soil as she brushed it away from each one. Big ones and little ones went into the bucket, and she carried them to her cellar where she spread them on a piece of woven wire. Then it was back to her garden for another bucketful.

The soil in her garden was much more mellow than where Haywood had dug the grave. Of course the garden was fertilized and cultivated every year, and there was no apple tree sapping the moisture like on the hill. For some reason, it didn't hurt to make comparisons now. The cry and her garden had healed her, she decided.

She dipped the spade into the edge of the hole left by the last plant she had dug and lifted another clump of potatoes, watching them separate from the rich, dark brown dirt. *Dirt the color of Haywood's eyes.*

The thought startled her. This garden that she loved so much shouldn't remind her of *him!* He should have been the furthest thing from her mind.

She sat down beside her half-filled bucket to rest. She looked toward the hill where the two crosses stood. "Did you really ask him to look out for me, Pa?" she whispered. "*Him?* Pa, I can't believe you'd do that to me."

But in her heart she knew he had. Haywood wouldn't lie about that.

Andrew settled into his comfortable chair. He eyed his sketchbook but it didn't even tempt him this evening. It had been three days since he had visited the DuBois farm. The Gwynn sisters had come by again today asking when he would bring Cally in to meet them. He had hedged a little, not wanting to admit how obstinate the girl was. He had been certain she would come in herself by now.

He kicked a footstool into position and propped up his heels. Why did he keep thinking Cally would behave the way a normal young lady would? If he expected her to cooperate, he should have asked about a job at the livery.

He sat up suddenly. *Or Lafferty's feed store!* Why hadn't he thought of that sooner? He would ask tomorrow and, with any luck, could ride out to the farm with a new, perhaps more tempting, offer.

Smiling, he grabbed the sketchbook, turning the picture of the Gwynn sisters to the back, and started a quick sketch of Cally with baggy clothes and floppy hat. The outline complete, he concentrated on her face.

His mind had been occupied too much lately with Miss Cally DuBois. He hadn't even had more applicants for deputy to fill up his time. What he needed was a good long ride through some of the little communities in the county. While his deputy was home with his sick wife, it wasn't wise to leave the office for any length of time unless something specific called him away. He found himself wishing for a little trouble to have something new to think about.

Finally, this evening, Bill had come in saying his wife seemed to be through the worst of it. Andrew had wondered if the threat of having her women friends staying with her instead of her solicitous husband might have had some healing effect. At any rate, tonight Andrew had come home much relieved. Tomorrow he would make a wide swing though the county.

After he had talked to Lafferty. And after he had talked to Cally.

He looked down at his half-finished sketch. Were her lips really shaped like that? He had drawn them soft and full, extremely kissable. Her pert little nose, sprinkled with freckles, looked right, perhaps. But surely these weren't Cally's eyes? They were open wide with innocence and framed with beautiful dark lashes.

He had flattered her, he decided. He added a few more freckles, but it didn't change the overall effect. He should have drawn her angry, spitting in his face, her eyes narrowed and glaring. That he would have recognized!

He didn't know whom he had drawn, but it wasn't Cally. He set the sketch aside unfinished. He should check on the weather before he turned in. There had been some dangerous-looking clouds gathering in the west when he came home.

Outside, he was hit by a chilly wind that carried

the smell of rain. Lightning crackled constantly in the clouds in the west. They were in for a storm.

He pictured Cally alone in the leaky little soddy, hearing the thunder as the rain pounded relentlessly on her roof. A heavy enough rain would dissolve her house into a pile of mud!

Andrew had grabbed his coat and slicker from the hooks by the back door and started toward the corral before he was conscious of what he planned to do. He had known all along that she couldn't stay on the farm alone. Tonight was his chance to prove it to her.

The mare pranced around the corral, avoiding Andrew's loop. Her skittishness increased Andrew's concern, making him more impatient to rescue Cally. Keeping his own feelings under control, he calmed the horse with his voice and soon led her into the barn. Once inside she settled down while he saddled her. Andrew heard the first drops of rain on the barn roof and slipped into his slicker before leaving the barn.

The wind was increasing at an alarming rate. Lightning flashed like Chinese firecrackers. Thunder had become a constant rumble over the sound of the wind. He made it halfway to the farm before the sky opened and drenched him, turning the road to a river of mud in a matter of minutes. The thought of poor Cally, terror-stricken, possibly drowning, kept him struggling onward.

By the time he rode into the farmyard, the mare was fighting not only the mud but panic as well. Relief at seeing the house still standing was followed by the conviction that his horse would bolt as soon as he was off her back. He rode her toward the barn and, keeping a tight hold on the rein, dismounted and opened the rickety door.

The interior of the barn was dark but relatively dry. Flashes of lightning could be seen through a hole in the roof where rain poured in, sending a little river of water across the floor and out under the door. Good heavens, the girl had dug a trench to channel the water out of the barn!

In the uncertain light he made out two large forms in the barn. One would be the mule, the other the cow he had seen. He had determined a dry place to leave his horse when something cool and damp brushed his hand. He jumped before he recognized the friendly whimper of a dog.

"Why aren't you in with Cally?" he asked, scratching the dog's head. Almost immediately, the dog moved slowly away. So, this wasn't the friendly Royal. This was the old dog he had seen lying by the door. Cally must have left it in the barn to keep the animals calm. It seemed to be working. Even his horse was less skittish now.

Andrew tied the mare, hoping she wouldn't panic and pull the barn down around her. He removed her saddle and rubbed her down quickly, anxious now to see about Cally.

Cally lay awake, listening to the thunder. She had done all she could to prepare for the storm. Now she had to wait it out. By morning, her root cellar would be wet. Her barn would be wet. Her house would be wet, no doubt leaking mud for days to come. By morning, more than likely, everything she owned would be wet. There was nothing she could do about it now. She rolled over, trying to ignore the howl of the wind.

Royal came to his feet and whimpered.

"It's all right, boy," she murmured, hoping to reassure herself as well.

Royal wasn't to be calmed. He let out a sharp bark. Cally sat up in bed. "What is it, boy?"

Royal took up a position facing the door, barking insistently.

Cally swung out of the bed, making her way around Royal to grab the shotgun off the wall. She fumbled on the shelf for a tallow candle and her jar of matches, setting the shotgun on the table for a moment as she lit the candle. The soft glow filled the room when she heard a pounding on the door. She snatched up the shotgun. "The latch string's out," she called.

The door swung open, and a man filled her doorway. He stepped inside quickly, closing the door behind him. Royal, curse him, didn't growl. It was Sheriff Haywood. He didn't need to take off his hat and slicker and step into the candlelight for her to recognize him. He did it anyway.

And froze.

She had never seen anyone look so stunned. His eyes, staring first at her face, slowly trailed down her white nightgown to her bare feet and up again. He was obviously ignoring the shotgun. She considered lowering the gun now that she knew who the intruder was, but the look on his face was so strange she kept it where it was. "What are you doing here?" she asked, hoping to snap him out of his trance.

He didn't answer. He was breathing hard, and she

wondered if he had run some distance to seek shelter at her door. "Did you lose your horse?" she asked.

He blinked as if he had just awakened. "I put her in your barn."

Cally scowled. He shouldn't be out of breath from that short a run. Well, maybe if her yard was full of mud. She found herself disappointed in him, anyway. "Why are you out on a night like this?"

"I came to see you." He spoke in a strange whisper. She wondered if he had caught cold.

"You've seen me. You can go."

He was staring at her again. She decided he might be feverish. After a moment he spoke in that same strange whisper. "I'm not going back out in that storm."

She nodded. Now she understood. He was afraid of storms. The shotgun was getting heavy, but she didn't dare lower it. The look in his eyes made her stomach tremble. If he was afraid of storms why hadn't he stayed home? "You expect to stay here?" That thought made more than her stomach tremble.

He took a step toward her. Her house was so small that he would be able to snatch her shotgun out of her hands if he moved any closer. "I'll shoot!" she warned. She backed away as far as she could.

His expression changed from the strange fevered gaze to a flash of anger. "If you shoot me," he said, his voice back to the one she recognized, "I'll bleed. At this range, that shotgun will tear me in two and splatter blood and bone—"

He stopped abruptly, or she thought he did. The buzzing in her ears grew steadily louder as a black haze closed off her vision. Everything cleared just as quickly when she found herself leaning against Sheriff Haywood's body, his arms wrapped around her. Her shotgun, of course, was gone. "That wasn't fair," she whispered.

"Hmm?" He drew away slightly and lifted her chin with his finger. "Are you all right?"

She could almost believe it was a sincere question. She found herself nodding. The odd fevered light was back in his eyes. It must be a catching kind of fever; she felt her own temperature rise.

"I'm all right. Just don't talk about...you know."

"Don't threaten to shoot me," he whispered, drawing closer as if he were afraid she couldn't hear.

She knew she should pull away, but she wasn't sure her legs were steady yet. She didn't want to faint right here in front of him. She would let him hold her up a while longer. Meanwhile, she stared at him. How close did he think his lips had to be for her to hear?

Then his lips actually touched hers! It hadn't occurred to her that he would want to kiss her! It was a strange sensation, his lips right against hers like that. They felt cool in spite of his fever and he smelled like the rain. She felt her stomach quiver while little shivers went down her legs and up her body.

He must have felt her legs shudder because now he held her much tighter. She clutched his coat, trying to still the trembling in her hands. Very slowly, he raised his head. She followed it up as far as her toes would stretch but eventually her lips were free.

He cleared his throat as he loosened his arms. "I can't stay here."

He released her rather suddenly, and she grabbed a chair to steady herself. Without looking at her again, he threw on his slicker and hat and vanished into the storm.

She stared at the door for a full minute, wondering if she had just had another strange dream. She touched her lips. No. He had been here all right. And suffering from a fever. She decided to brew some herb tea to see if she could keep herself from catching it.

Andrew slogged through the mud to the barn. He raised his face to the rain and let it trickle down the back of his neck. He had to cool off. He was a fool. He had no business worrying about Cally in the first place. And he certainly had no business kissing her! He opened the barn door and stepped inside. "Too big a fool to even stay home out of the rain."

He shed the slicker and hat, tossing them over a stall divider. In all his life, as far back as he could remember, he had never been such a fool. In fact, he prided himself on his good sense.

Good sense? What was he doing here?

He settled down in a corner, thoroughly miserable. Cally didn't need to be rescued. She didn't want him checking on her. Why did he fool himself into thinking otherwise? Why hadn't he learned from his previous encounters with her?

Of course, none of those encounters had prepared him for tonight.

If he wasn't such a fool, he would be warm and dry right now. He would be at home. He would be sleeping. In his own bed! He would still believe that the sketch he had drawn was somebody else, not Cally.

But he *had* been a fool. He had come and seen her, seen the startling red-blond hair tumbling around her shoulders, her slender body barely hidden beneath a simple white gown, her emerald eyes, wide with innocence. Lord, he was sure she had never even been kissed before!

Andrew groaned. If he thought the mare would cooperate, he would ride for home right now. Pneumonia couldn't possibly be any worse than this.

The old dog joined him in the corner, evidently wanting to quiet his fears. "How could I have known?" he asked. The dog lay down with her head across Andrew's leg. "There's no way I could have guessed she looked like that. She surprised me into kissing her." Andrew took a deep breath, resting his hand on the dog's back. "She'll never trust me now."

The tea Cally drank before returning to bed hadn't helped. If anything, it had made it worse. Cally felt the fever burn her body all night. Smaller versions of the strange trembling she had felt in her stomach when he kissed her, came back again and again. She wondered how serious the fever might be. If the sheriff died, she would have to try to explain her symptoms to the doctor.

She wished she still had Pa to talk to, although somehow she doubted he would have been much help with this. It might have been nice to at least share her worry with someone. She wasn't lonely for company, of course. Haywood was the one who thought she couldn't be alone.

And Haywood was the reason Pa was dead, she reminded herself. She shouldn't feel guilty about sending him out into the storm, sick as he was. She tried to work up her fury at the sheriff, but this strange fever that possessed her simply let it wash away. For some reason, she felt too good to be angry. With that rather confusing thought she drifted off to sleep.

And dreamed. Her cheek rested against a starched white shirt. Strong arms held her. Warm masculine lips hovered above hers—and never quite touched her. When she woke up, the fever was worse.

She expected to be dizzy or sick to her stomach when she got up, and was relieved to find she merely felt hungry. And perhaps a little giddy. She let Royal out, surveyed the muddy yard and went about her morning chores.

Andrew spent a restless night. The storm seemed to rage for hours. The barn was damp and drafty. The corner where he huddled was hard and bug-infested. Whenever he drifted off to sleep, one of the animals chose that moment to snort or stomp. When he slept at all, he dreamed of Cally. Those dreams caused as much discomfort as all the other conditions put together. And when he happened to moan in his sleep, the old dog whimpered and nuzzled to comfort him.

He couldn't believe he had given up a chance to sleep in his own bed because of a misguided concern for Cally DuBois. He fell into an exhausted sleep about an hour before dawn.

The sound of the rickety door opening startled him awake. He sat up suddenly, bumping his head on the wall behind him. He groaned and the dog whimpered. At the same moment he registered a gasp from the figure in the doorway. He had clearly startled Cally as much as she had him. Last night he had forgotten to mention that he would be staying in her barn.

She watched him suspiciously as he came to his feet. He tried to straighten his coat and adjust his shirtsleeves. He ran a hand over his stubbled chin, imagining he looked a sight. But even that didn't quite explain the curious way she peered at him, leaning forward and moving so the light fell on him as if she were looking for something specific.

He wanted to think she was worried about his well-being, but knew better. Lord, but it disconcerted him to look at her now, decked out in those baggy clothes, knowing how she looked without...

He swallowed hard. "Morning, Miss DuBois," he managed.

The dog at her feet and the dog at his looked them both over, then trotted off toward the house. Cally spared a glance toward them and Andrew smiled. She still smarted at Royal's defection. Her watchdog had turned into a friendly pup where he was concerned. Now if she could just follow the dog's example.

"I have to milk the cow," she said abruptly. She still stood in the doorway, perhaps afraid to come inside. Poor girl. He had truly frightened her last night.

"I'll be on my way, then." Somehow, it was harder to pull his gaze from her than it should have been. He couldn't really see her anyway, silhouetted as she was in the doorway, but he could imagine the red hair and the emerald eyes and the soft curves. He cleared his throat, taking a tentative step toward the mare.

"You feeling all right this morning? Any fever...?'' Her voice trailed off as if she wasn't sure what she was asking.

"I'm fine," he answered. "You?"

"Fine," she said quickly. "I have to milk the cow."

He nodded and turned away, only to turn back once again. "Cally," he started before he caught himself. "Miss DuBois, I don't think you should stay here alone." He raised his hand as she stiffened. "Please hear me out. I only have your best interests in mind. I think you should come into town."

Noting the stubborn lift of her chin, he added quickly, "At least meet the Gwynn sisters. Would you do that for me? If you don't like them, I can ask around some more. Mr. Lafferty, perhaps?"

He took a step toward her, and she backed away. It hurt him to know she was scared of him. It ought to please him. Surely it would be easier to get her to do as he suggested if she was frightened of him. Wouldn't it?

"Sure," she said.

That was just the answer he wanted. Why didn't it please him? What difference did it make *why* she agreed as long as she agreed? Right? "Next time you're in town then? You can come by my office, and I'll take you to meet them."

"Fine." She edged toward the milk cow, her back practically pressed against the barn wall, trying to stay as far away from him as possible. "I have to—"

"Milk the cow." He nodded. "I know." The nicest thing he could do for her now would be to get out of her way. She was evidently safe enough out here for now. He had to think of the long run and that meant giving her time to make up her own mind. A few more days of trying to do everything for herself were bound to have the desired effect.

He saddled the mare as quickly as he could, trying not to listen to her coaxing voice as she talked to the cow. He tried not to believe that he was abandoning a child to look after herself. After all, he was beginning to respect her self-sufficiency and courage.

But mostly he tried not to think about the surprising young woman he had discovered last night. That young woman didn't belong out here. She didn't belong in those baggy clothes. She belonged—good heavens, he couldn't believe what he was thinking!

Chapter Five

Cally heard Andrew leave. She was relieved that he hadn't said goodbye. It was better for him to just go. That way she didn't have to speak to him again, and she wasn't sure of her voice.

This crazy fever she suffered from was definitely tied up with that man. The sight of him, rumpled and sleepy, brought it on. His voice, as smooth as warm honey, made it worse. By staying as far away from him as she could, she had kept it under control.

As she milked Belle, she tried to put all the pieces together, the light in his eyes when he saw her last night, the touch, the heat, the quivers. It was kind of like when a bitch or a cow was in season, she decided. Haywood had just shown up at the wrong time. It had never happened to her before, because nobody but Pa had ever been around. All she had to do was stay away from Haywood until it passed.

And make certain he never touched her.

Andrew was doubting the wisdom of the idea before he stepped across Mr. Lafferty's threshold. Yesterday, it had seemed like a perfect place for the little tomboy to work. His whole picture of the girl had changed since then, or was at least confused. The idea was still worth a try, he decided.

The store was dimly lit and apparently empty. Andrew was about to turn to go when a figure left the dim shadows at the back of the building and came toward him slowly.

"Who's there?" Mr. Lafferty called.

"Sheriff Haywood."

"Well, 'tis nice to hear yer voice, lad. You be needin' more oats for that fine mare of yers?"

Andrew went to meet him and clasped his hand. "I came about something else altogether. I believe you know Cally DuBois."

"Bonnie wee lass, that one. Sweet thing." Lafferty nodded thoughtfully. That didn't exactly fit Andrew's assessment of the girl, but he let it pass. "Fine cook, too. Brings me muffins and the like, says they broke comin' from the pan, but she doesn't fool this old man."

Andrew smiled. A generous Cally? "She's all alone now, you know. I've been trying to find her a job in town. I worry about her on that farm alone."

"Do ye, now?" The old man's weak eyes narrowed.

Andrew shifted uncomfortably. "Mr. Lafferty, I'm here to see if you would consider hiring the girl to help out here."

Lafferty shook his head. "A feed store's no place for a gentle lass like that one, Sheriff. Around all the dust and dirt, rough men comin' in and the like. It wouldn't do, sir. Not for one like Cally."

"She's a little rough herself, sometimes," Andrew argued. "I think she'd like it better than the other prospect I've gotten."

"No, Sheriff. The girl deserves somethin' grand. I'd think on it, I suppose, if I be needin' the help. Good luck with her, though. I'm sure you'll find just the thing for Cally."

Andrew wanted to argue further, but Lafferty had already turned and started toward the back of the shadowy store. With a sigh, he stepped into the sunlight. The Gwynns were still his best hope.

"When was the last time you talked to her, Sheriff?"

Both Gwynn sisters had come to his office this time. Noella looked coldly down her long, thin nose as she spoke, never mind that Andrew was a good eight inches taller than she. Easter wrung her chubby hands in front of her wide frame, and looked distraught.

"Two or three days," Andrew said, blinking away the sudden picture of Cally in the white gown. The vision came to him often enough, especially this time of the evening when the girl used to visit her father. He didn't need anyone to remind him of his last visit to the farm. "She promised to meet you next time she was in town."

"When will that be?" asked Noella.

"We can't hold this position forever, you know," Easter added.

"I'm afraid I can't make any promises. She's been...well, she's still grieving. We have to give her time to realize what's best."

"She's being stubborn," stated Noella, nodding down at her sister.

"As stubborn as that mule she rides," agreed Easter.

Andrew hadn't noticed that Cally's mule was particularly stubborn, but otherwise he had to agree. "She is somewhat—independent."

"Don't worry. We'll snap that out of her soon enough," declared Easter.

Andrew cringed. The more he listened to the sisters, the less he liked them. He wished he had some other choice. No one else needed a scruffy girl with a stubborn streak, even if she could cook and clean and care for animals—even if she had adorably childish freckles, startling red-blond hair, expressive emerald eyes and full, soft lips. He shook his head to clear it.

Noella was talking again. "We've almost decided to go out to that farm and bring the girl in ourselves."

Andrew pictured the shotgun leveled on the two ladies. "I'm not sure that would be wise."

The outer door opened, and Andrew excused himself, moving to greet a young boy as he entered. With his back to the ladies, he allowed a grin to surface. It certainly wouldn't be wise, but it might be fun.

"Telegram for you, sir," the boy said, handing a folded sheet to the sheriff and waiting for the coin he knew he could expect.

"Thanks, Taylor," Andrew said, resisting the urge to ruffle the boy's hair. At the advanced age of eleven, that would be insulting.

"You want I should wait for an answer or anything?" Taylor asked hopefully.

"Shouldn't you be home for supper?" Andrew grinned as the boy scuffed one toe on the floor before turning to leave.

When Taylor had left the office, Andrew unfolded the sheet and scanned it quickly. Instantly forgetting his guests, he read it through more carefully. It was from his old boss, Federal Marshal Kenneth Yates. Wade Terris and Parker Stedwell had escaped from the penitentiary in Leavenworth. He gazed at the pictures on the wall. Terris, with his wide scarred face and squinting eyes, and Stedwell, almost dapper in his derby hat, stared back at him. The safecracker and the forger. Were they partners now?

Andrew had taken part in the apprehension of both, and remembered their vows of revenge. Terris always struck him as the more dangerous of the two, but Stedwell was smarter. An extremely clever and cool-nerved thief.

"Ahem!"

Andrew swung around to face the ladies. "Sorry. Bad news." They didn't seem impressed. He tossed the telegram on his desk and reached for his coat. "Look. I'm going to be gone for a few days. I'll bring Miss DuBois in tonight."

The Gwynn sisters nodded to each other, evidently certain that their persistence had won the day. They didn't seem to take Andrew's hint to hurry as he held the door open but took their time departing his office.

Andrew's long strides took him home quickly. He would ride east, stopping in sheriffs' offices along the way for any news. With some luck, he could join up with the posse somewhere between Salina and Leavenworth.

Of course there was no guarantee the convicts had headed this way. He could locate the posse from the marshal's office in Topeka if he hadn't met them sooner. He couldn't imagine that the convicts would travel far. More likely they would hole up someplace and make plans, if they hadn't already made them.

As Andrew hitched up his wagon, he considered where they might go. Abilene would be a good place to get lost. But so would a lot of other places. Maybe it was prideful of him to think that they would be after him. There were several other lawmen who played a part in their captures; somehow he had just gotten a little more credit. When the law caught up with them the second time, he wanted to be part of it again. He could already feel the thrill of the chase.

But first, he had to take care of Cally. He couldn't leave her out there alone when he left. She had to be in town where she was safe, in the Gwynns' care where he wouldn't worry about her. This time, he wouldn't take no for an answer.

Andrew stopped the wagon outside Cally's sod house just as she stepped through her door, shotgun first. He hopped off the seat and strolled toward her, doffing his hat. "Evening, Miss DuBois," he said, as if the gun were a friendly greeting. "You recovered from the storm?"

She narrowed her eyes at him but didn't speak.

He stopped several paces away from her. With Cally he was never sure what was the best tack. Probably because nothing he had tried so far had worked. He decided to try plain and simple. "I've come to take you to town."

"I don't wanna go." He thought her voice sounded a little shaky and wondered if her resistance might be weakening after all. At least she had set the shotgun aside.

He tried his gentlest voice, the one he used on skittish horses. "I have to leave town for a few days. I can't leave you out here alone while I'm gone."

"I'm alone out here when you ain't gone." She had raised her head a little to talk to him. The wind tugged at her hat.

"True, but I've been within fairly easy reach if you needed me."

"How often have I needed you?"

Andrew opened his mouth to speak but couldn't think of a good response.

She went on, straightening to look him in the eye. "I got my shotgun. Royal here doesn't let anyone near me."

Andrew grinned. "Except me."

She faltered a little, but before Andrew could press his advantage she spoke again, her voice tinged with irritation. "You just don't have call to worry about me."

Andrew shook his head. "But I do. I can't ride away, knowing you're out here alone. I wouldn't be able to do my job. I need to know you're safe." In frustration he added, "I'll arrest you if I have to."

He saw her startled expression and hated to think he was convincing her by scaring her. It made him feel cruel.

He was considering how to soften his words when the wind finally tugged the floppy hat clear off her head. A cloud of bright hair tumbled over her shoulders. Caught by the sun, it was even more stunning than it had been the first time he saw it.

She faced the wind for a second to make her hair blow behind her head instead of across her face. It made a stunning picture. Her face in the sunlight, green eyes and freckles. She was simply adorable.

Suddenly she caught her breath. She stepped backward before Andrew realized he had approached her. She grabbed up the shotgun but instead of raising it to her shoulder, she held it toward him with both hands, offering it to him or warding him off, he couldn't tell.

"I...I'll come," she stammered. "I'll do whatever you say. Just promise not to kiss me again."

Andrew bit back a curse. His face had obviously given his thoughts away. It galled him to think she would rather be arrested than kissed by him. He took the shotgun, uncertain what he ought to say, deciding that he was better off saying nothing until his temper was under control. He set the shotgun aside.

"What should I take?" she asked softly.

Her resignation made him feel as if he had just been kicked in the stomach. "Whatever you need for a few days in town." She went inside the little house, and Andrew followed. "When I get back, I'll help you move anything else you want." She looked at him sharply, and he added, "If you decide to stay with the Gwynns."

She turned her back and stuffed a few things in a worn flour sack. In a moment she appeared ready to leave. Andrew backed out the door, certain she wouldn't walk around him. He reached out for the sack, and she gave it to him reluctantly. As he set it in the back of the wagon, she retrieved her hat and stuffed her hair under it again. He moved to help her into the wagon, but she climbed aboard herself.

"What about my animals?" she asked.

"We'll stop at Ned's on our way to town. One of his boys will be glad to come over and take care of them." He started the wagon moving as he spoke. He had a feeling she might still change her mind.

"Ned? Ned's been trying to buy this land out from under us for years. He's got all of it already but just what's around the house."

"He can't take the farm just by doing your chores," Andrew said. Even as he tried to reassure her he filed the information away for the future. He glanced at the young woman beside him to see if he had effectively hidden his thoughts.

She wasn't looking at him. Her lips were pursed in a pretty pout. He looked away quickly.

After a moment she spoke softly. "Nobody does someone else's chores for free. I can't pay Ned's boy nothing." The admission was forced between clenched teeth.

Andrew felt like the lowest form of life for making her suffer. "I'll take care of it, Cally." He meant to reassure her, not hurt her pride. He wanted to take her in his arms and comfort her. No, if he was honest, that wasn't exactly what he wanted.

"Royal's coming with me."

Andrew hauled on the reins. Sure enough, the big dog trotted along beside the wagon. "I'm sorry, Cally. The Gwynns won't allow pets."

Cally raised huge eyes to him. "Royal can't stay here by himself. He needs people."

"Cally."

"He needs someone to watch over."

Andrew turned the wagon back toward the farm. "He can watch over the farm and your other animals."

"That's Queen's job," she said matter-of-factly.

Andrew stopped the wagon again. He took a deep breath. "What do you suggest?" She started to rise, and he grabbed her arm. "Besides going back." Before he finished the brief sentence, she had shrunk as far from him as the wagon seat would allow. What did she imagine he would do to her? Probably just what he had been imagining.

Cally whispered, "You could take him with you."

That was quite an offer considering how devoted she and the dog were. Andrew knew it was a surprising admission of trust. He was flattered. And it wasn't totally unheard of, traveling with a dog. For Cally, he actually considered it for a moment. But he didn't want a dog along, especially one he didn't really know. What if something happened to Royal? Cally would never forgive him. He steeled himself for her reaction, and said, "We'll shut him in the barn."

The emerald eyes filled with anger, and Andrew turned away. What hobby should he take up next, he wondered, drowning kittens? He pulled the wagon up close to the barn, and had no trouble coaxing the dog inside and closing the door.

He was half-afraid Cally would have retrieved her shotgun and barricaded herself in the soddy while he was at it. But she sat, stiff and silent on the wagon seat. There was a certain determination in the set of her jaw that made him uneasy. They pulled out of the yard followed by Royal's persistent barks.

Cally still sat with her teeth clenched when he stopped at Ned's. Andrew thought she would have some special instructions for her animals' care, but she didn't say a word. By the time he pulled up in front of the Gwynns' big house, his frustration outweighed any guilt he had felt earlier. He was ready to dump her off and run.

The sisters opened the door and stood on their porch waiting for them. Andrew jumped down and hurried around the wagon, but Cally had scrambled down unassisted. He retrieved her flour sack and took her arm, escorting her up the steps.

"Miss Easter and Miss Noella Gwynn, this is Miss Cally DuBois." Cally tried to tug her arm out of his grip. "Cally, say hello to the Gwynn sisters."

"Hello," she spit.

Andrew pretended that was as cordial a greeting as he had expected. The sisters were looking the girl over with somewhat sour expressions.

"I believe the first step is a bath," said Noella, more to her sister than anyone else.

"Are you hungry, dear?" Easter asked.

Cally shook her head. She turned her huge eyes toward Andrew, then squinted them into a glare that made him want to groan.

"Of course you're hungry. Come on into the kitchen, dear. You can eat while the water heats for your bath." Easter reached out to take the girl's arm while Noella stepped back, obviously not wanting to get too close until the girl was properly scrubbed.

Andrew literally handed Cally over to the woman.

She was safe now, and he needed to prepare for his trip. "Goodbye, Cally," he said, giving her the flour sack. He hoped she would look at him again until he remembered her glower of a moment before. With a last tip of his hat to the ladies, he returned to the wagon and left.

Cally refused to turn and watch him go. The shorter and more rounded of the women coaxed her toward the kitchen. A bath and food didn't sound too bad, she decided. She had worked hard the past few days trying to rescue her garden after the heavy rain. Her house had required constant cleaning, too, as mud continued to drip from the ceiling at odd moments ever since the rain.

The Gwynn sisters' house was certainly grand. They entered a funny little room with no furniture except an undersized table and lots of doors. The short woman led her through one of these doors into a room bigger than her whole house. Cally stood in the middle of it and turned in a slow circle. There was a table with chairs that matched, a huge cookstove with fancy ironwork and a pump right inside the house. There was also a funny short cupboard with tightly latched doors that Cally promised herself she would investigate as soon as the women were gone.

"This is the kitchen," said the short one. She had stepped into another room and returned with two cloth-covered dishes. "Sit down, dear," she said as she placed the dishes on the table.

"I think we should call her Calloway," said the tall woman as she pumped the handle at the sink. "I am Miss Noella, and she is Miss Easter."

"Then I'm Miss Cally," she said, hoping to upset the ladies. It worked. Noella bristled and exchanged a look with her sister. Easter turned nervous eyes back to Cally.

It was Noella who attempted to instruct her. "If you work for us, it isn't proper for us to address you with a title. I suppose we could call you—" she paused as if the word tasted bad "—Cally, if you prefer it to Calloway." The woman's tone was cold, and Cally decided she didn't like *Miss* Noella.

Easter must have read rebellion in her face because she reached out and patted Cally's hand. "It's all right, dear. You—"

Noella cleared her throat, and Easter faltered.

"Cally. You wouldn't know something like that."

Of course not. I also wouldn't know any better than to sit here and let you two fill my bath. Cally watched Easter slice off thick chunks of bread and cheese and decided that one night here might not be so bad. Especially if she pretended not to know anything.

Cally would have been willing to let the old ladies drag the brass tub into the kitchen, but Noella told her sharply to help. She helped empty the buckets of hot water into the tub, too.

Easter left the kitchen for a moment and returned with loaded arms. "Here's soap, a towel," she said, putting each item on the table. "A gown to sleep in, some undergarments. The wardrobe in your room has your dresses, and your aprons are in the chest of drawers."

"Just leave those...clothes you're wearing in a pile by the door," added Noella. "You can burn them in the morning." She looked down her nose at Cally.

"We'll need to see about some more appropriate shoes, but that can wait. We expect breakfast by seven in the morning."

"We'll come in and help you find things tomorrow," Easter added. "Then we can discuss the rest of your duties."

"I suggest you go to bed as soon as you've cleaned up the kitchen after your bath." Noella turned to leave the room but stopped at the door, evidently waiting on her sister.

"Go to bed where?" asked Cally, longing already for her own little cot.

"Your room is through there," said Easter, pointing to the door past the sink. She followed her sister out, and the door was closed behind them.

Cally sighed. She should be grateful they didn't stay and "discuss her duties" during her bath. She was almost surprised the tall Noella didn't want to watch to make sure she got adequately clean.

After another glance at the door the women had left through, Cally crept to the odd cupboard. Cautiously, she lifted the latch that held the door and eased it open. Cold air rushed out to greet her, and she slammed the door closed. She stood and stared at it a moment then opened it again. Butter and milk sat on the shelves as if they were in no danger of turning sour. Was this a newfangled icebox Pa had talked about? He had seen one in the restaurant, he said. She hadn't imagined that regular folks could have them, too.

She closed the door again and turned her attention back to the tub. She had always known most folks lived better than she did. It had never bothered her before, and she wasn't going to let it now.

Cally picked up the soap and sniffed. It smelled heavenly! She quickly threw off her hat and clothes, stepping gingerly into the hot water. No sense passing up a hot bath with scented soap. As she sank into the tub, rubbing the soap to fill the air with its fragrance, she had to hold back a giggle. Did the old ladies think seven was early? She would be home milking Belle long before that. And Haywood wouldn't be around to drag her back.

Haywood. He must think he was quite a man, getting her to come here when he knew she didn't want to. She slid down the tub to wet her hair and resurfaced to lather it with the soap. She had gone along all right, but at least she had kept him from kissing her.

She hadn't been able to keep him from touching her, though. In the wagon and at the door, he had touched her arm, sending that strange tingling through her. She had hoped that the problem would have passed by now. That strange fire in his eyes had told her otherwise, and she had made him promise just in time.

He made her life so confusing. If he would just leave her alone, she would be fine, but he had to keep coming around, telling her this and that, claiming he was worried about her. And this story that Pa had asked him to look after her, she hated to believe that. Pa did some mighty strange things sometimes, so it was most likely true.

Everybody seemed to think that the sheriff was an honest man. But then she had also overheard women whispering that he was strong and brave and handsome and everything else. What did a bunch of gossips know? He was the low-down skunk who had killed Pa. Well, sort of. Maybe. Anyway, he *was* trying to ruin her life!

She sank into the tub and rinsed the soap out of her hair. This huge tub was such a relaxing way to bathe. It seemed odd to step out onto a wood floor. Her feet would still be clean when she went to bed! She rubbed herself dry with an unusually soft towel and pulled her nightgown out of her flour sack. She left the old ladies' things lying on the table.

She took a few minutes to try to dry her hair. She ran her fingers through the tangles and rubbed it with the towel, only to create more tangles. With a shrug, she tossed the damp towel on the floor.

Gathering her clothes, she walked cautiously toward the door Easter had indicated. She pushed it with her fingertips and peered inside. It wasn't yet dark outside and light filtered through filmy white curtains. This room was almost as big as the kitchen! It contained a bed twice as wide as her own, covered with a worn but colorful quilt. There was a wardrobe and a chest of drawers. She couldn't resist a peek.

The wardrobe contained three dresses, all gray, all of a coarse serviceable fabric. She wrinkled her nose. She wasn't fond of dresses; they got in the way. Anyway, she had outgrown her last one years ago. But if she decided suddenly to wear dresses again she would choose some a little more interesting than these.

In the drawers she found aprons and piles of odd garments, evidently intended to wear under the dresses. Some contained strips of something stiff, and

Cally imagined they would be quite uncomfortable. Others were creamy white and soft and inviting. She thought for a moment about taking a few of the things with her, but dismissed the idea, slamming the drawer.

She sat down on the bed, laughing at the way it gave under her weight. An honest-to-goodness feather mattress! No wonder the old ladies had warned her that breakfast was at seven. In a bed like this a person would want to sleep the day away.

She snuggled under the covers, thinking about the trick she was playing on the old ladies and Haywood. Her last thoughts before she fell asleep would be of scented soap and feather beds. Or so she thought until Haywood's face intruded. That soft voice when he said he was worried about her seemed to murmur in her ears.

She rolled over, sniffing the sweet scent in her damp hair. "Iceboxes and wood floors," she murmured.

Haywood's face wouldn't leave her alone. The tingling started in her stomach as it always did when she thought of him.

"Mr. Perfect Sheriff," she mumbled. She forced herself to picture him dirty and tired, his hair wind-blown and wet with sweat, clinging to his forehead.

The tingling turned to warm liquid and spread through her body. She found she had no choice but to give in to it. She let the warmth reach clear to her fingers and toes. She would be glad when this fever passed. She closed her eyes and fell asleep, remembering Haywood's kiss.

Chapter Six

Andrew intended to ride out before dawn. After delivering Cally to the Gwynns, he made all the other arrangements. His deputy knew he would be gone. The county commissioners considered his trip a vacation but agreed to let him go. He was heading home to pack his saddlebags when some extremely loud whispering caught his attention.

"But we gotta get help!"

"No! Shhh! Somebody's coming."

Andrew rounded a corner and stopped in front of Schoolmaster Jarrell's house. In the side yard stood a small boy looking up into a cottonwood tree. In the gathering darkness Haywood could make out a dark shape high in the tree. "What's the trouble?" he asked softly as he approached.

The boy turned quickly. "Howdy, Sheriff," he said with exaggerated carelessness. He grinned, revealing two oversize front teeth with empty spaces on either side.

"Aren't you the Russell boy?" Andrew asked.

"Yes, sir. Mikey." He stuck his thumbs in the

straps of his overalls and tried to cross his feet at the ankles. He barely caught himself before he fell.

"Well, Mikey," Andrew said, listening to strange little noises from the branches above him. "Shouldn't you be home?"

"No, sir," replied the boy, still smiling.

Andrew turned and looked into the tree. "Taylor, is that you?"

"Mikey, you are so stupid."

"I am not neither! You're the one what's stuck!"

Andrew put a hand on the little boy's shoulder, quieting him. "Just tell me what the trouble is, Taylor. We'll worry about exactly why you're in that tree once you're safely on the ground."

Andrew could hear Taylor squirming a little on the branch. "My britches is caught, and I can't reach it. I can't even get the darn thing to rip and let me go."

"Don't try too hard," Andrew cautioned. "You might fall."

Andrew stepped closer to the tree trunk as he tried to gauge the pattern of potential foot- and handholds. It was growing darker by the moment, and climbing the tree after the boy didn't look promising. He was a little out of practice. Besides, his weight could break a branch that had held the boy safely. "Maybe Mr. Jarrell has a ladder."

"We can't ask him," blurted Mikey. "'Cause then he'll know we're here."

Taylor whispered harshly above them, "He's gonna know we're here if I fall out and die on his yard."

"He won't know I was here." The boy took off at a run as if he could see in the dark.

"Darn little coward," Taylor muttered.

"Just sit still," Andrew said. "I'll get some help."

Andrew tried Mr. Jarrell first. He looked back at the boy in the tree as he waited for the schoolmaster to come to the door. "Yes?" asked the man suspiciously, raising a lantern high to shine on Andrew.

"Mr. Jarrell, do you have a ladder I could borrow?"

"Why?"

"There's a child caught in your tree."

Jarrell looked at him, at the tree and finally back at Andrew. "Not in my tree, sir."

"Uh, yes, there is," Andrew said.

"In my tree? The schoolmaster brushed past Andrew and peered into the tree before he would believe it contained a boy. "There's a boy up there."

"Yes, sir. He's stuck. Do you have a ladder I could borrow to help him down?"

"What's he doing up there?"

Andrew was growing short on patience. "Let's get him down and ask him. A ladder, sir?"

"No," Jarrell said, still staring into the tree. "I don't own one."

"All right," Andrew said. "Just sit still, Taylor. I'll be right back."

"I'll be here," called the boy.

Andrew left Jarrell at the base of the tree holding the lantern aloft. He was forced to ask one neighbor after another, all of whom reported to the schoolmaster's yard to discuss the boy in the tree. The yard was getting crowded before Andrew found anyone who admitted to owning a ladder.

Finally, with the ladder propped against a relatively

stable branch and two of the neighbors holding the bottom, Andrew went up the ladder and untangled the boy's britches from the limb. When Taylor was on the ground, the neighbors applauded and slowly drifted off toward their homes.

All except the schoolmaster. Before Taylor could make his escape, Mr. Jarrell caught his ear. "And what were you doing in my tree, young man?"

"I was sittin' there stuck. What did it look like?"

"Don't get smart with me." He tightened his grip on the ear, and Taylor opened his mouth in silent protest. "Sheriff, I want you to see this boy home and make sure he's properly punished."

"I can do that," Andrew said quickly, taking the boy's arm in hopes of freeing his ear.

"Be sure you explain all the trouble he's caused," the schoolmaster added before turning Taylor loose and taking his lantern back in the house.

"He's an old meany," Taylor grumbled, rubbing his ear.

"I'll walk you home," Andrew said. "And on the way you can explain what you were doing in Mr. Jarrell's tree."

"I already told you what I was doing."

Andrew scowled down at the boy. "*Why* were you in the tree?"

Taylor dragged his feet as they walked down the street toward his home. "Are you gonna tell my pa?"

"I haven't decided," Andrew said.

Finally the boy took a deep breath. "Mr. Jarrell is the meanest man in the world. He makes fun of Mikey all the time. Sometimes Mikey comes to school with a button missin' or a hole in his pants.

Mean ol' Mr. Jarrell always has to say something to make him feel ashamed. Mikey's mother's dead! My old man can't sew on a button. Can yours?''

Andrew didn't answer. Taylor's house was in sight and he slowed his own steps, hoping to get all of the story out of the boy before they reached the house.

"Anyways," Taylor continued, "Mikey don't always get his work done, since he has to help more at home. He ain't even got a sister, you know. I got both a sister and a ma. Course, if ya got a ma, a sister ain't much use."

"Taylor, that still doesn't tell me what you were planning to do."

Taylor stopped walking altogether. He looked toward his house, and Andrew turned too. There were no lights. The boy's family had gone to bed. Finally the boy spoke again. "Mean old Jarrell deserved it."

"Deserved what, Taylor?" Andrew didn't have to work at making his voice stern.

Taylor answered just above a whisper. "He said Mikey's ma was lucky she died and didn't have to see what a stupid boy he was."

Andrew shook his head. Maybe Jarrell deserved it. That didn't make what the boy was doing right, whatever that might have been. He prodded again, more gently. "Tell me what you were planning."

The boy shrugged. "I just climbed his tree."

"Come on, Taylor. You can't expect me to believe that." He grinned at the boy. "Tell me what you were going to do."

Coaxing didn't work either. All he got was a shrug. Andrew suspected Taylor had hopes of trying again. He held the boy's shoulders and crouched to look him in the eye. "Listen, Taylor, it's right to want to protect someone who is smaller and weaker. I admire your loyalty to your friend. But playing tricks on Mr. Jarrell is just going to make life harder for both you and Mikey."

Taylor didn't look as if he believed it entirely. Andrew imagined he thought if the trick had worked it would have been worth any punishment. And of course, there was always the hope of not getting caught. "If anything happens to Mr. Jarrell now, he's going to suspect you, you know."

Taylor wrinkled his nose. "I don't care if he's mean to me as long he leaves Mikey alone."

Andrew sighed. "You could have gotten hurt tonight, Taylor."

The boy nodded. "I was a little scared."

"That's good, Taylor. You should have been scared. Now, promise me you won't bother Mr. Jarrell again."

Taylor suddenly grinned, and Andrew knew he was thinking ahead to the possible outcome of such a promise. "Oh, yes sir, Sheriff. I promise."

"Good." Andrew let the boy go and watched him dart away and scramble up a tree. In a moment he climbed through an upstairs window and was safe inside.

As Andrew walked through the partially lighted streets toward his home he reflected on his decision to let the boy go. Had he been lenient because he identified with the boy's need to protect his friend? But wouldn't Taylor have learned respect for authority if he had roused his father? Did anybody ever know if they were doing the right thing when it came to children? Or when it came to anybody else?

He thought of Cally in the big, strange house with women she didn't know, then shook the thought away. Surely he had done the best thing for her. Cally was safer with the Gwynns than on the farm alone. She would be more comfortable, too, if she gave it a chance. She was probably sleeping soundly by now. He didn't need to worry about her. He had other things to worry about, like his trip tomorrow.

An hour later he was ready to turn in himself. His saddlebags were packed and waiting at his kitchen door. All he needed was a good night's sleep.

All he got were fitful dreams. The Gwynn sisters loomed large and cruel in his imagination, mixed up with the angry schoolteacher. Poor Cally shrank to a tiny child, younger even than the boys.

He repeated to himself all his reasons for moving her into town, but none of them altered the fact that it wasn't what she wanted. He had taken her away from her home and shut her dog in the barn. The way she shrank away from him on the wagon seat showed how much she hated him.

Just what were his goals here, anyway? he asked himself. DuBois had asked him to look after Cally. "See she hooks up with someone decent," were his words. Working for the Gwynn sisters certainly qualified, probably beyond the old man's expectations. Why should he care if she didn't *like* it?

Cally was a child. Well, not exactly, but she had grown up in such isolation, it was nearly the same. She didn't know what was best for her. Her safety and future mattered more than what she thought she wanted. Didn't it?

And it certainly shouldn't matter if she didn't like *him*. If she shrank from his touch and glared at him, he should be all the happier to be rid of her. The little spitfire should be *grateful*. If she wasn't, he should walk cheerfully away.

He should be worrying about the poor old ladies who had gotten themselves into more than they imagined. How many times had the girl tried to sneak weapons in to her father? How many times had she spit in his face while he tried his best to be decent and polite to her?

The cut on his arm had nearly healed. He rubbed it now, trying to refresh his memory of her uncivilized behavior. Instead, he remembered the freckles on her pale face when she nearly fainted. Which reminded him of her huge emerald eyes. Which in turn reminded him of her startling hair. And that, of course, led him to remember the tempting body barely hidden by the thin white gown.

Andrew groaned as his body responded to the image. She was not worth losing sleep over! He should be thinking of Stedwell and Terris. He should be using his head to guess their plans.

"I should be sleeping!" he muttered aloud. The ride tomorrow would lend itself to considering Stedwell and Terris. He needed to sleep, which he finally did just before dawn.

The nearly sleepless night took its toll. Andrew was still saddling his horse at seven o'clock the next morning when Noella and Easter Gwynn marched into his yard.

"Thank goodness, you haven't left," Noella called.

"You have to go after her," said Easter.

"Oh, Lord," mumbled Andrew.

"She ran off in the night."

"She didn't bother to make her bed."

"She didn't even bother to dump her bathwater!" This last outburst was from Noella. Andrew glanced at the long nose, wrinkled with distaste.

I would have run away, too. He shook off the foolish thought. "I'll go talk to her," he said, preparing to mount.

Easter wrung her hands. "Where could she have gone?"

"Home."

"She could never make it all the way home on foot!" declared Noella.

"Sure she could. It's less than two miles." Andrew swung into the saddle. "I'll try to bring her back, but I'm not making any promises." He tipped his hat before reining the mare around and cantering out of the yard. The Gwynn sisters had a lot to learn about Cally DuBois.

She would be home. She would be armed. And she would tell him to leave. He would—what? Throw her across his saddle, bound hand and foot? Threaten to kiss her to get her to behave? He was really looking forward to matching wits with someone reasonable like Terris or Stedwell.

He could see her in the chicken pen as he neared the farm. Royal barked an alarm, and she took off for the house. A moment later she stepped out carrying the blasted shotgun. He reined up and dismounted, struggling with his temper.

"I thought you'd be on your way by now," she called to him as she leaned the shotgun against the soddy.

"What are you doing here?" It was a stupid question, but it beat swearing at her.

"I had chores to do."

"Ned's boys would have done the chores."

"They ain't their chores, they're mine."

Andrew strode toward her. "Will you go back to the Gwynns when your chores are done?"

"To do their chores, too? Why should I?"

Andrew felt the anger drain away. Why indeed? To ease his mind. "Cally, they'll take care of you."

"Take care of me like I'm a child?"

Andrew didn't answer. He realized he should have denied it when he saw her eyes harden.

"They want me to wear ugly gray dresses," she added.

"They'd be beautiful on you." He hadn't meant to say it. His loose tongue was caused by his lack of sleep, surely.

Her reaction was instantaneous. "Oh no, you don't." She eased closer to the shotgun. "You don't come near me, and you don't go flashing those fevered eyes at me, neither."

Andrew considered her a moment. Fevered eyes, huh? Maybe she was right. It was foolish to want to protect someone who wanted to shoot him. She could protect herself the same way. "You win," he said.

"Good," she said.

"I'll be on my way." But he continued to stand and look at her.

"Just ride right on out." She didn't turn away.

"I promise not to worry about you ever again."

"Never did make sense."

He nodded and after another moment started to leave. Turning back, he tried one last time. "Cally, one night isn't really giving it a chance."

"Forget it, Haywood. I went into town last night to get rid of you. It's not my fault you didn't leave like you said. You'd be on the road to wherever, none the wiser, if the Gwynn sisters hadn't squealed. Or did you stop by their house to say goodbye?"

Andrew couldn't resist a grin. "They squealed. Was that the plan all along, to agree to go then run back as soon I left town?"

"Not all along. Only after you shut poor Royal in the barn."

Andrew took a deep breath. "Take care of yourself, then."

"Always have."

He tipped his hat and turned. This time he mounted and reined the mare around, leaving the farm. Cally watched him go and found herself smiling. Well, she had to kind of like him. Foolish as it was, he did worry about her. No one else ever had much.

"Wonder how long he'll be gone," she said to Royal as she put the shotgun away. "What you reckon he's doing, anyway? Maybe he's gonna add another ugly mug to that collection on his wall."

She laughed. "Reckon he would'a hung my picture up there if he had got me to stay at the old ladies'." She reached down and scratched the dog's ears. "Would'a been about as bad as being shot."

* * *

Andrew could see the town of Topeka in the distance. It had been a long, tiring and, so far, fruitless trip. The lawmen in Abilene and Chapman had no new information. They had all received telegrams from Marshal Yates at the time of the escape, but none of them had heard anything about the marshal's posse since.

Someone at Yates's office would have gotten word from the posse by now. He had to face the fact that it was probably beyond his reach. He slowed the horse to a walk as he entered the dimly lit street. Morning would be soon enough to get the answers; now he needed rest.

A sign across the boardwalk ahead advertised a livery stable. No one was around so he helped himself to some oats, planning to tally it in the morning. He unsaddled the mare and as he rubbed her down his mind was on Stedwell and Terris. He was convinced that they wouldn't travel far before going into hiding. They had surely known where they were headed before they broke out.

Somehow, he had expected to figure out more than that. All these days of solitude had provided him with ample time to think. Knowing their past history, he should have figured out where they would go, what they would hope to do. Hell, for all he knew they could have headed for the Black Hills gold mines, or silver towns in Arizona. He had no idea.

However, during those same days of solitude, he had become completely convinced that the rain had caused Cally's roof to cave in, wolves had attacked her livestock and a prairie fire had burned her barn to the ground.

As he turned the mare into the corral, he cursed himself for a fool. He had passed up a bed in Abilene the first night in an effort to get a few more miles down the road. He had pushed himself and his mare harder than necessary because of this feeling that he had been away too long.

As he walked the short distance to the hotel, he realized that between his deputy's sick wife and his misguided concern for Cally, he had missed an awful lot of sleep. Women caused lawmen at least as much trouble as the outlaws. He had always known it, but he had fallen into the trap anyway.

He shoved the hotel door open and practically stomped to the desk. "One room, one night," he said to the young clerk.

"Yes, sir." The clerk trembled as he turned the register toward him and handed him a pen. "Anything else, sir?"

"No." Andrew took the key that the clerk offered and headed for the steps. He heard the clerk call the directions to the room after him. Inside, he dropped his gear on a chair by the door and lit a gaslight. He had to get that little gal settled safely someplace before he drove himself crazy from worry and lack of sleep.

He caught a glimpse of himself in a small framed mirror and did a double take. He looked half-demented already. Five days' growth of beard hid half his face. His eyes were bloodshot and sunken. No wonder the clerk was nervous. He would probably scare little Cally to death.

He moaned and turned from the mirror. Why couldn't he get Cally off his mind? Hadn't he promised himself not to worry about her? How long had he kept that promise? A day? An hour?

He stripped off his dusty clothes and turned down the light. The bed was comfortable, a perfect opportunity to catch up on much-needed sleep. In fact, what would it hurt if he slept until noon? He didn't have to get up to milk a cow. He shook off the image of Cally waking him as she came to the barn to do just that.

"Sleep." He murmured the command as his exhaustion finally caught up with him.

That same night, in a little rented house in Abilene, Val Milton paced his upstairs bedroom while he waited for his woman to join him. Fancy was busy downstairs making sure their guests had everything they needed. He thanked God he had had a few days warning before her brother and his cell mate had shown up at his door, and the back door at that. Fancy had actually warned him that Parker would be breaking out of prison half a day before it happened.

He smiled to himself. He had a feeling her knowledge went beyond just an advance warning. Fancy's willingness to jump into unusual situations was one of the best things about her. He had always considered her jailbird brother one of the worst. He had even thought about leaving her when she first came back from Leavenworth with this latest bit of news. But Fancy Stedwell was a little hard to leave.

Fancy had always been honest with him, as far as he knew. She had told him about her brother when they first hooked up. She made irregular visits to Leavenworth, never suggesting he go along. He should have guessed it would come to this eventually.

Val walked to the window and leaned against the frame, gazing into the street. Lamplight filtered through dirty windows and smoky doorways onto the boardwalk and street. In another hour the games would be getting interesting, and he would join them. Abilene had been profitable, but it was probably time to move on.

He had discovered, to his surprise, that he kind of liked Fancy's brother, Parker. The man's suggestion that they rob a bank in Salina and frame Sheriff Haywood kept coming back to him. Stedwell had been half-joking, but Val smelled an opportunity. He hadn't worked it all out yet, but he would.

This cell mate, Wade Terris, was a different matter. He was equally determined to seek revenge on Sheriff Haywood. In fact, that seemed the one thing the two escapees had in common. Haywood had been key in both their arrests, and they blamed him rather than their own ineptness.

Val was certain that Terris didn't understand finesse. The fool would probably rather march into Salina and murder the lawman. Never mind that it would land him right back in prison, or worse.

He heard Fancy's light step on the stairs and turned to the door as it opened. Fancy was dressed in a high-necked gown of deep blue satin that hugged her shapely body clear to her thighs before flaring into a full skirt. Her bustle wagged at him as she turned to close the door. Fancy could make the most modest fashions look decadent.

"Are they settled in?" he asked as he watched her walk toward him.

"I think so. I'm sorry about this, Val," she said, her blue eyes smoldering seductively. "He is my brother. Can he stay with us for a few days, at least?"

"It's all right, Fancy," he said, opening his arms for her. Fancy never simply stepped into his arms, she slid up against him—just a little. He smiled down at her. "Will you come with me tonight?"

She ran her tongue across his jaw. "Do you want me to?" She pretended an interest in his cravat and diamond stickpin, her long fingernails scratching the cloth.

"You know I do." He lifted her face, and added before he captured her lips, "You're my luck."

She squirmed closer against him. When he released her mouth she asked breathlessly, "Are you in a hurry?"

"Never."

By the time Andrew walked into the marshal's office at eight the next morning, he had shaved and bathed and felt like himself again. The secretary looked up, and Andrew introduced himself, asking, "Has there been any word from Yates's posse?"

"Mr. Yates will be glad to see you, sir." The young man stood and tapped on the inner office door. He stuck his head inside and in a moment motioned Andrew forward.

"Andy," greeted the big man, coming to his feet behind his desk.

"I didn't expect to find you here, Ken." Andrew shook the offered hand.

Yates indicated a chair and returned to his own. "You thought we'd still be out after Terris and Stedwell. I hate to say it, Andy, but we gave it up. There was just no trail to follow. Is that what brought you here?"

Andrew nodded. "Stedwell led us on a merry chase last time. Not to mention the trouble Terris caused. I expected to get word of the posse before I got this far."

"Figured to join 'em, huh?" Yates's chair creaked as he leaned back. "Sorry to disappoint you, Andy. They holed up somewhere, I guess."

"Any idea where? Or with whom?"

Yates sighed. "The only lead we had was a visitor a couple days before the escape. An old woman who gave her name as Mrs. Luella Canary got permission to visit Stedwell. We've been trying to find out who she is and where she came from but so far it seems to be a dead end."

"Do you have a description?"

"Not much of one, I'm afraid."

Andrew was thoughtful for a moment. "I'd like to talk to the prison guards who saw this visitor." It would take two more days to ride to Leavenworth. Two more days before he could start home. He caught himself as his mind added, *Home to Cally.*

"Do you think Stedwell and Terris will stick together?" he asked.

Yates shook his head. "They don't make a likely pair, do they? It's hard to tell, though. They might admire each other's talents."

"And may plan to put them to use for their mutual benefit." Andrew was silent a moment. "I've come this far, I guess I'll head on to Leavenworth. If you hear anything, you'll let me know, won't you?''

"Of course, Andy. Are you thinking this could get personal?"

Andrew smiled at his old friend. "Crossed my mind."

Andrew started to rise, and Yates stood as well. "I still think you should have stayed with us instead of settling for one little county where every time you turn around you're running for reelection," he said, walking with Andrew toward the door.

"I wanted to settled down."

"Did you?"

The question took Andrew by surprise. "Sort of, I guess." They shook hands, and Andrew headed for the hotel to get his gear.

Val turned up two recent issues of a Salina paper. He sat in front of the dining room window, letting the afternoon sun warm his propped-up legs, while he browsed through them. Wade Terris sat sullenly in the shadows across the room. Val deliberately ignored him. It seemed the best way to treat the man. With half an ear, he listened to the brother and sister talk in the kitchen. Fancy's occasional giggle brought a smile to his lips.

There wasn't much of interest happening in Salina, he decided, and the editor of this particular paper was not very imaginative. A nice feud always made for better copy. He had no idea what he hoped to find, anyway. He was about to fold up the paper when a name caught his eye. Francis DuBois. Why did that name ring a bell?

Chapter Seven

The article read:

> Francis DuBois died last night in the county jail.
> He was there awaiting execution for manslaugh-
> ter in relation to the death of Harley Nichols. In
> the opinion of this editor, the men were two of
> a kind and the community will miss neither.
> DuBois leaves a grown daughter still at home
> and a small farmstead which will doubtless come
> up for sale in the near future.

"Francis DuBois," Val murmured. He rose and
crossed the room to the writing desk. From a drawer
he lifted a stack of papers, IOUs, most of which were
too small to bother collecting. He had looked through
them a day or so earlier, when he first thought of
leaving town. He shuffled through them quickly.
"Francis DuBois," he said, dropping all but one of
the papers back in the drawer.

"Who the hell is that?" Terris asked.

Val waved a hand at the man to stop him from

interrupting his train of thought. The IOU was only for twenty-five dollars, but Stedwell's talents could make it for far more, with the man's little homestead as collateral. That would provide them with a base of operations, give him a reason for being in Salina and get them started on their plans. By God, they would rob a bank and frame the sheriff. Only Val Milton would make a few plans of his own.

But first he and these two convicts had to come to an understanding. He had to convince them to trust him, and that wouldn't be easy. Val paced to the window and looked out. He could guess that Terris was watching him. If he became partners with these men, they would want to know what he stood to gain. Helping them out of the goodness of his heart wasn't going to be credible.

There was laughter from the kitchen. He turned toward it, thinking. Could he convince them that love was his motive? Without a word, he walked into the kitchen. Terris quickly followed. "Fancy, run down to the butcher and see if he has any pork chops."

Fancy's lips pouted. "I don't want to cook. Let's get dinner from the restaurant again."

"We don't want them wondering why we have guests again tonight, baby." He pulled his wallet from his pocket. "Stop at the bakery, too." At her pretty frown he added, "I'll do the cooking, if you'll do the shopping."

Fancy came to her feet, finally relenting. As he opened the wallet to count out some money she lifted it all from his fingers. "I'll see what else I can find," she whispered as she passed him.

Val smiled after her. She could easily spend every

dollar in that wallet, but it didn't really matter. "I hope she saves back enough for the chops," he said as he heard the front door close.

"Pretty free with your money," Stedwell commented.

Val shrugged. "Is this talk of getting even with Haywood for real?"

The men glanced at each other. It was Stedwell who spoke. "It's for real. Do you have an idea?"

"Your idea, actually. Let's take the bank in Salina and frame Haywood. Let him have a taste of what you two have experienced."

"Sounds good," said Stedwell. "You got a grudge against this sheriff, too?"

Val shook his head.

"Then why help us?"

His fledgling plan could depend on the next few moments. "All I want is your promise to leave Fancy alone. Don't contact her in any way." Stedwell looked startled, and Val continued. "She broke you out of prison. No, she didn't tell me, but I can guess. That's a federal offense, man! She could wind up in prison! Do you want that for your sister?"

"Hey, we never asked for her help," Terris argued.

"You didn't need to." Val leaned toward Stedwell. "She'd help her brother if he needed help. I don't want her to even know where you are. If I help you set up this sheriff, you disappear from her life and never contact her again."

Val could tell that Stedwell was shocked. He was faintly aware that he should feel guilty about doing this to Fancy, but he had never found his conscience strong enough to make him uncomfortable. He gave

Stedwell a moment to think it over. When he thought the man was about to resist Val added, "It's what you would do anyway if you cared about her."

Andrew passed the sketch across the table to the guard. He had found three guards who had seen Stedwell's last visitor. He had tried his best to draw the old women each of them described. The three sketches didn't look much alike. One odd thing they had in common, though, was a decidedly youthful jaw and neck. His fourth sketch, based on all three descriptions, was a young woman with stage makeup and a wig. The first two guards had agreed that it was the woman. Andrew watched the third guard now as he studied it.

"Well, maybe," he conceded. "But I really thought she was old." He passed the sketch back to Andrew, scowling. "She walked so bent over, you know, and her voice was kind of cracked like."

Andrew nodded, satisfied. He didn't see any need to push the guard into an admission that he had been fooled. He thanked him for his time and headed back to the hotel, eager to start home.

By the time he tied the saddlebag behind the saddle, the idea of riding back the way he had come seemed decidedly unappealing. After a moment's reflection, he mounted and headed toward the train station.

When the next westbound train pulled away from the siding Andrew's mare was in a stock car and Andrew was settled in a passenger coach. He pulled his hat over his eyes and shifted his shoulders against the hard seat back, trying to make himself comfortable.

Yes, this had been a wise decision. There was no need now to be ready to ride off in any direction. Both he and his mare deserved a rest. He hadn't chosen the train because it would make better time getting home. He wasn't worried that he had been away too long. He wasn't even going to check on Cally when he got back.

Unless she had left word for him. Or had decided to move in with the Gwynns while he was gone. Or there had been another storm. Or any reports of... well...anything.

He groaned aloud and crossed his arms. He would think about his work. He had had the newspaper repeat the notice that he wanted to hire a second deputy. This time he had listed some minimum qualifications. There ought to have been some response by now.

Maybe he should try advertising for a husband for Cally. He imagined the notice.

Wanted: One husband for independent, ill-tempered, uneducated, poorly dressed female. Must not be afraid of shotguns.

He chuckled aloud. In the same ad, he would list her good qualities.

Can cook and care for animals. Willing to guard homestead. Loyal.

Andrew sobered. Loyal. He had never seen anyone more loyal to kin than Cally. She had the same loyalty to her pets and even her old cow. A man could do worse than find a loyal wife. If she would transfer that loyalty to him—

Andrew gritted his teeth. His mind wandered in the most foolish directions. Of course he knew it was brought on by lack of sleep. He had pushed himself hard the past few days. If he could catch up on his sleep during this trip home, he could go back to being the competent sheriff the people of Saline County deserved.

Unfortunately, that was a big if.

Haywood sat in his office going through a stack of Wanted posters. None of them looked familiar. When he had gone all the way through them he stacked them up, tapped the edges until they were even and turned the pile over.

Reaching for a pencil, he reflected on the fact that he had been back in Salina for two days and hadn't been out to Cally's once. He was rather proud of that. He hadn't advertised for a husband for her either, though that was at least as tempting as riding to her farm. The pencil brushed over the paper, forming Cally's likeness. Andrew couldn't help but chuckle. He had a dozen sketches of her at home.

He was starting to wonder if he was falling in love with the girl. Ever since he had mentally listed her good qualities he had found his attitude toward her changed. Perhaps he should go out to the farm after all. Coming face-to-face with her shotgun again would probably be the best cure.

The door opened, and Andrew came to his feet, glad for any interruption. A smile spread across his face as Taylor and Mikey came inside.

"What can I do for you, boys?" Andrew asked.

The boys looked at each other then came forward, choosing seats across from the desk and scooting backward into them. Andrew sat as well, waiting.

Finally Taylor spoke. "We came to get hired as your deputy."

"My deputies?" Andrew looked from one little boy to the other.

"No, sir," said Mikey, grinning at his friend.

Taylor grinned too. "Not deputies. Deputy."

"That's right," said Mikey. "On account of us wantin' a job and you needin' a deputy."

"Boys," Andrew began. He didn't want to hurt their feelings by laughing. It was hard to take them seriously, though. He said gently, "The ad said over twenty years old."

Taylor grinned. "Together we're twenty-one. You wouldn't have to pay us both, see? We'd split it."

Mikey nodded, grinning hopefully.

Andrew watched them a moment then narrowed his eyes. "What do you fellas need money for, anyway?"

They looked at each other sharply. Taylor shook his head; Mikey shrugged. With a sigh, Taylor turned back to Andrew. "We gotta pay for a window."

"Mr. Jarrell's?"

"No," they answered quickly.

"This was an accident," Taylor explained.

"We was playin' baseball," Mikey said.

"Mikey's gettin' real good at whackin' them balls." Taylor smiled proudly at his friend.

"Whose window?" Andrew persisted.

"It was Pa's," said Mikey.

Andrew nodded his relief and studied the two

young faces. "We may be able to work something out. Not as deputies," he added quickly, seeing their eager responses. "I had something more like general errand boys in mind."

The boys were openly disappointed. "But we'd make a real good deputy," Mikey grumbled.

"You're too young, fellas. Adding your ages together won't work. You'll just have to grow up first." At their downcast looks he reluctantly added, "You could think of this as deputy training."

They brightened immediately. "Honest?" Taylor breathed.

Andrew nodded. "Starting Monday you can come here after school and work for me for about thirty minutes. Penny a piece. All right?"

"We gotta wait clear till Monday?" Mikey asked.

Andrew sighed. "Come by my house after supper tonight. I'll see if I have anything for you to do."

The boys nodded and scrambled off their chairs. They started for the door, but Taylor turned back. "Will we get to arrest anybody?"

Andrew kept his face admirably straight. "Not tonight."

When the boys had gone and the door was closed, Andrew let himself laugh. Too bad he couldn't average their ages with Mr. Sweeney's.

A moment later the door opened again. The man who entered was slender, medium height and well dressed. The swallow-tailed coat, while somewhat dusty, looked new and expensive. The corners of his stiff white collar folded down to form small triangles above a diamond nestled in a cravat. Andrew couldn't help but think, right age, wrong appearance.

"The name's Val Milton," the stranger said, extending a hand toward Andrew.

Andrew came around the desk to meet him. "Sheriff Andrew Haywood." The hand that he grasped was completely free of calluses.

"Then you're the man I need to see. I've come to town to collect a gambling debt, but I'm afraid I've run into some complications."

Andrew sat back against his desk, studying the man intently. "What sort of complications?"

"It seems the man's dead." He took a small sheet of paper from his pocket and handed it to Haywood. "Well, you can imagine how I feel about this tragedy, but I took the note in good faith."

Andrew accepted the paper reluctantly. He read it through twice and shook his head. Francis DuBois had gambled away his daughter's home.

"Even though the date for payment is past, I would be willing to work something out with the heirs. Do you think DuBois left eight hundred dollars?"

Andrew bit back a bitter laugh and shook his head. "I doubt if he left eight."

"The homestead was listed as collateral. Do you know what's become of it?"

Andrew gave himself a moment before he answered. "His daughter's living on it."

"Oh dear. I don't much care for the idea of running someone out of their home, but I don't feel I can just let it ride. Bad for business, you understand." He smiled.

Andrew frowned. Damn DuBois. This was just like him. Andrew took a moment to consider. If this note was legitimate, his duty called for him to confiscate the property for the gambler. Cally could identify her father's handwriting, but how honest would she be?

He could advise her to get a lawyer and fight Milton in court. But Cally couldn't afford a lawyer, and would that be the best thing for her anyway? Wasn't this the perfect opportunity to get Cally off the farm and into town where he could look after her?

He took a deep breath and leveled his eyes on the gambler. "I'll ride out there now and talk to her."

"Mind if I ride along?"

Andrew cringed. "I think I would rather try to explain this to Miss DuBois alone. Would you trust me with the note? I want her to see the handwriting." He didn't say that she wouldn't be likely to believe him if she didn't see the note for herself.

Milton hesitated only a moment. "Of course, Sheriff. I'm registered at the City Hotel, but I'll probably be in the Antlers." He gave Andrew a knowing grin.

Andrew nodded absently. "I'll find you as soon as I get back."

Andrew sat on the edge of his desk for a moment after Milton had left his office. He lifted the sketch and studied the innocent face. He had drawn her smiling, though he could only remember having seen her smile once. He knew he had drawn what he wanted to see, rather than what was. After a moment he returned it to the pile of Wanted posters and shuffled them, thinking to lose Cally's picture among the rest. The girl had him mooning around like a lovesick boy.

Cally stretched her arms over her head, then took off her hat, tossing her head to fill her hair with the breeze. It was really quite a lovely day. The sun seemed to make everything sparkle, even her nearly spent garden.

Because of the rain, she had cut some tall grass with her butcher knife and spread it under each of her squash and pumpkins so they wouldn't spoil in the mud. She was still getting a few tomatoes, though the vines were looking sadly bedraggled. She liked to go into her little root cellar just to look at all she had harvested.

"This is a wonderful way to live," she told Royal. She took the bucket of tomatoes to the house and greeted Queen with a pat on the head. "We don't need anyone else, do we?"

Both dogs watched her, obviously agreeing.

"We'll be fine here all winter, even if we have a blizzard like we did a couple years ago. We were fine then too, thanks to my garden."

Cally knew she didn't have enough wood cut for the winter, though it didn't take much to heat the house. It had seemed best to take care of the garden until frost, then work at gathering the wood. She didn't say any of this, however, not wanting to hear her own worries aloud.

She left the bucket by the door and sat down in her rocker. She deserved a little rest, she decided. Royal took up a position at her side. "In a way, I look forward to winter," she said. "I can catch up on the mending, and maybe stitch up some more of Pa's old clothes to fit me." She tried to pretend it sounded like fun.

She rested a hand on Royal's head. "It's nice, just us here, don't you think? We don't need a man around, telling us what to do. Even Haywood finally got that message." She laughed. "Though for a while there, I didn't think he ever would."

She rocked awhile in silence, listening to the birds chirp and the dogs pant. "How long's it been since he was here? A week or more, I reckon." The fever must have passed, she decided. She was certainly glad he wasn't still coming around looking at her funny and trying to kiss her and such. "I didn't need that," she said.

Cally closed her eyes and rested her head against the back of the rocker. After another quiet spell, she said drowsily, "The nicest thing about being way out here is I don't even have to think about the sheriff."

After a few minutes, Royal's sharp bark brought her out of her doze. "Company?" She got to her feet and entered the house, returning with the shotgun. She raised the gun to her shoulder and watched the horse and rider come closer. When she recognized Sheriff Haywood she lowered the gun, stomping her foot on the hard ground. "Oh, shoot! It's Haywood!"

Haywood dismounted and trailed the reins on the ground, approaching her slowly. Cally was tempted to raise the shotgun again, but it wasn't any use. Haywood knew by now she wouldn't shoot him. She leaned the shotgun against the wall behind her and stomped her foot one more time before she spoke. "I thought you'd forgotten about me. I'd forgotten about you."

The man had the nerve to grin. "Believe me, I tried. I'm here on official business."

"You gonna officially demand that I go live with the old ladies?"

Haywood seemed to hesitate. Something about his

manner made Cally wary. He reached in his pocket and withdrew a paper before he spoke. "Cally, did your father ever go to Abilene?"

Cally shrugged. "He'd go off for a few days once in a while. I don't know where he went."

Haywood took a step closer, and Cally stiffened. "Do you know if he gambled?" he asked.

Cally lifted her chin. "I suppose so," she said. She knew so. They fought about it from time to time. Pa would always swear he would never gamble again.

"Would you recognize your father's handwriting?" Haywood stepped close enough to hand her the piece of paper. Cally took it from him, unfolding it carefully. The small page was a mess of scrolls and curls in blue ink. She swallowed. She was supposed to identify this somehow?

Then she remembered Pa writing something in the Bible after Ma died. She remembered it clearly because it had seemed so odd. She hadn't understood why Ma's dying added anything to the Bible.

Without a word to Haywood she turned and carried the note into her soddy. Haywood was in a sudden rush to follow her in. She gave him a curious glance over her shoulder. When she reached for the Bible on the little shelf beside the stove, he seemed to relax. She gave him a questioning look, but he didn't offer an explanation.

Cally peered at him closely. It was dark in the soddy so she wasn't sure if he showed signs of the fever again. She decided it would be best to get outside, where she could see him better and he would have more trouble cornering her. She turned and left the cabin, giving him a wide berth and moving well away from the door as he followed.

Feeling safe once again, she handed him the Bible and the note. "Pa wrote in here somewhere," she said.

Haywood turned the Bible and opened it to the front. He found the page almost immediately and looked at it closely. He placed the note next to it and studied them both.

Cally wondered what they both said. Of course they wouldn't say the same thing so she didn't see how it would help him. She wondered fleetingly why she would want to help the sheriff with anything.

Finally he closed the Bible and handed it back. "It's the same, Cally. I'm sorry."

Cally shrugged. "Why are you sorry?"

Haywood watched her with an odd expression, but at least it didn't seem fevered. Cally tried to take comfort in that.

"Cally, didn't you read the note?"

Cally glared at Haywood. He wasn't leaving her any way to keep from telling him. She lifted her chin, ready to spit in his face if he laughed. "I can't read." Her voice would have curdled milk.

Haywood didn't flinch. He looked more sorry than surprised. She began to wonder if he would respond at all. When he did all he said was, "Oh."

Cally considered spitting at him anyway. When he spoke again, his voice took on that warm honey quality she had heard before. "You better sit down."

She blinked twice, responding to the voice rather than the words. Something was wrong.

Haywood took her arm, and warm tingles curled

through her body. She ought to pull away. He drew her the two steps to the rocker and eased her into it. Crouching in front of her, he said, "Cally, your father took a trip to Abilene last spring. He gambled with a man named Val Milton and lost. He wrote this note, saying he owes eight hundred dollars and putting up this homestead if he didn't pay it off."

Cally stared at him, unwilling to understand what he was saying. This was something Pa had done; it had nothing to do with her.

Haywood seemed to expect her to speak, but she couldn't. He looked so sad, Cally was tempted to touch his cheek. She didn't, of course, remembering the fever in time.

"Cally, I'm the sheriff. It's my duty to confiscate this property for Mr. Milton. You have to come to town."

It seemed completely incredible. "Mr. Milton wants my farm?"

"I think he'd rather have the eight hundred dollars. But the farm is what he gets."

Cally closed her eyes and let everything sink in. She had worried Pa would do something like this. Still it seemed so unfair. "How soon?"

Haywood came to his feet. He paced off a few steps and turned back. "Milton will have to have the deed registered. There'll be some formalities, but he'll get the farm in the end. It won't get any easier if you wait."

"Now?" she asked.

Haywood sighed, looking off in the distance. She wondered if he saw the same things she always saw, or if he was just thinking of his duty. He took Pa, now he was taking her home. Haywood had taken everything! Well, maybe she wasn't being exactly fair either, but it was such a blow.

His voice was almost too soft to hear when he spoke again. "How about tomorrow morning? I'll bring the wagon and help you move into town. I'll make sure, but I think the Gwynns will still take you in."

Cally came to her feet. "What about Royal and Queen? What about all my animals? They were never Pa's. He couldn't have gambled them away." She knew that wasn't quite true but it should have been.

He stepped toward her. "I'll find a place for them, Cally. It'll be all right." He put his hands on her shoulders, and she shook them off.

It wouldn't be all right! How could he say it would? She turned around and went into her house. She wanted to slam the door but knew that would send a shower of dirt down on her head. Besides, she couldn't do it without hurting Queen. Instead she pushed the door closed enough for Haywood to know he wasn't welcome.

She sat down on her cot and looked around at the cluttered room. It seemed incredible that she had been so happy a moment ago only to discover that she had lost everything. She took a deep breath, trying to get past the anger and think clearly. Somehow, she'd find a way to get it back.

Haywood stood staring at the half-closed door. He wanted to follow Cally in and take her in his arms. The two dogs looking at him so trustingly made him feel worse. He turned and walked slowly toward his horse.

The poor girl couldn't even read, and he had forced her to admit it. He felt guilty now for thinking she intended to toss the note in the stove. She had trusted him enough to take his word for what the note meant.

Her father had written her date of birth in the front of the little Bible. He wondered if she knew that in a little less than three weeks she would turn eighteen.

After a last look at the little soddy, Andrew mounted and turned toward town. Eighteen was hardly a child, but it was too young for a woman to be on her own. Especially a woman like Cally. He wasn't sure why he felt that way. Because she seemed so vulnerable, he supposed. He pictured her trying to sneak the butcher knife in to her father but dismissed it.

Nothing would convince him that she didn't need his help. Discovering that she was a little older than he had previously thought made no difference. She was alone. She was his responsibility. He would tell the Gwynns she was coming, then he would find a home for two dogs, a cow, a mule and a few chickens. How hard could that be?

By the time he got to town he decided he couldn't go around asking people to take in Cally's dogs. Selling her milk cow didn't seem right. Who would want a worn-out mule? He remembered her father saying she didn't have the heart to kill a chicken. How could he let them end up in someone else's pot? He went instead to his landlord.

* * *

Taylor and Mikey swaggered down the street toward Sheriff Haywood's house. "What you reckon he'll have for us to do?" Mikey asked.

"Spy on somebody, maybe" Taylor suggested. "Sneak through a window where he can't fit. Gather ev'dence."

"What's ev'dence?"

"Things left behind what makes a lawman know who done the deed."

"What deed?"

"Whatever." Taylor nodded knowingly, and Mikey did the same.

They stepped up to the front door where Taylor knocked loudly. They waited, listening for any sound from the house, then Taylor knocked again.

"You reckon we're early?" Mikey asked, cupping his hands to peer in a window.

"Let's go around back. Maybe he wants us to be more secret-like."

The boys jumped off the porch and ran around the house. The sheriff was back there all right, but he didn't look as if he had any law-enforcing in mind, secret or otherwise. He was carrying shovels from the barn.

"Hi, boys," he greeted them. "Ready to do some work?"

Chapter Eight

"This ain't deputy work," Mikey groused. He tossed another shovelful of debris from the floor of the chicken house into the cart Haywood had left outside the door. He felt as if they had been working for hours.

Taylor didn't answer.

"I can't even pretend this is deputy work."

Taylor stopped scooping and looked out the door. "Just be quiet," he said softly. "It might be a test. Sheriff Haywood might wanna see if we can follow orders without question." He narrowed his eyes. "He might be testing to see if we're tough. He wouldn't want to trust no deputy what was afraid of—"

"Chicken poop," Mikey provided, rubbing his nose.

"Yeah," Taylor said seriously.

"Afraid ain't exactly what I'm feelin'," Mikey said. Before going back to work, he cast his friend a look that said, you got me into this.

"Maybe he's gonna hold a prisoner in here," Taylor suggested.

Mikey glared at him.

"Maybe not." Taylor went back to work. "It could be worse," he offered after a few minutes. "It could be fresh."

The sun had just peeked over the horizon when Cally sat down in the rocking chair to wait. Her little trunk, with all she owned that was worth taking, was inside ready for Haywood to carry to his wagon. The cow and mule were staked near the house. Her chickens were in the crates that had recently been her kitchen shelves.

As she had pried the boards loose from the barn stall to use as lids for those crates, she remembered fashioning her father's cross. She was leaving her parents' graves, as well as her home. How could she be expected to do that?

She had spent most of the night trying to come up with a solution. She had considered holding Haywood off with her shotgun, but knew he was convinced she wouldn't shoot. If he didn't scare, she would have to actually shoot him. She couldn't quite bring herself to picture Haywood shot, not to mention the fact that Pa's shotgun might explode in her face.

Besides, the deputy and all manner of marshals would come after her if she shot him, and she couldn't shoot everybody that came. Eventually she would have to run, and then she would lose the farm anyway. Or they would hang her.

Even now, she tried to think of a less bloody plan that would save her home. What if she simply didn't go? Haywood could argue and coax, and she could dig in her heels and refuse to budge. He wouldn't shoot her. He would be patient and polite, but eventually he would become frustrated and angry. She would like to see him angry, she thought, grinning down at Royal beside her.

Her mind had been playing that scene last night as she drifted off to sleep. Even in her imagination Haywood wouldn't cooperate. The dream came back to her now in surprising detail. Haywood had lifted her in his arms and carried her to the wagon. Only he hadn't put her down. In the dream he held her in his strong arms, her cheek against the clean white shirt, his face hovering over hers as she waited to be kissed.

She remembered coming awake this morning with a sense of peace that was out of place considering her dilemma. "The fever," she had mumbled then, but now she wasn't so sure. These feelings seemed to return too often and too easily to be explained as an illness or even a natural cycle. For some reason that was beyond her understanding, she longed to be in Haywood's arms.

She tried to bring her thoughts back to her immediate problem. With a sigh, she voiced the conclusion she had reached earlier that morning. "I don't see any way out, Royal. I'll have to move to town. I don't know what'll become of you and Queen." Her voice caught, and she buried her face in Royal's soft fur. They had been together since Royal was a pup more than five years ago. He had always been there when she needed a friend, something she couldn't say for anyone else. And Queen—she could barely remember a time before she had guarded the door.

In a moment, she sat up. "I'll show Haywood that I'm not a child who needs to be looked after. I'll work for the old ladies, and I'll save my money. Then I'll buy back you and Queen and Belle and Jewel. Then I'll buy back this farm, and everything will be right again.''

She knew it was impossible. She knew she was dreaming. But she couldn't bear to believe anything else.

She sat and rocked for nearly half an hour before she saw Haywood and his wagon emerge from the creek. She didn't move until he had pulled to a stop at her door. She watched his eyes fall on her crated chickens and knew the moment he realized she was resigned to go.

''My trunk's in the house.'' She urged Queen out of the doorway and went inside. He followed her in, and, as before, his presence seemed to fill the tiny space.

''Is this all you're taking?'' he asked gently, lifting the trunk.

Cally looked around the little room again. She couldn't picture any of her pots and baking pans in the Gwynns' kitchen. Her dented tin plates and bowls wouldn't look right at their table. There wasn't even much sense in bringing many of her own clothes since she would be wearing gray dresses and white aprons from now on. ''That and my shotgun's all from in here. My root cellar's full of food, though.''

Haywood set the trunk back down on the packed dirt floor. ''Cally, leave the shotgun here.''

''It's my shotgun.''

''You won't need it in town.''

Cally narrowed her eyes. He was being patient and coaxing, just like she predicted. It made her furious.

She wanted him to understand how horrible this was for her. Short of that, she would settle for hurting his feelings. "Why? 'Cause you'll take care of me?"

He had the nerve to smile. "Exactly," he said, lifting the trunk again.

She followed him outside, the shotgun in her hands. As he slid the trunk into the wagon bed, she slid the shotgun in beside it. Haywood quietly lifted it and carried it back inside the soddy. Cally glared after him. At least he didn't know her father's old pistol along with his knives and razor were in the trunk.

"Fetch a candle," she called, "and I'll show you the cellar." She knew he would find the candle lying on her table. She could guess he carried matches in his pocket since he was always ready for anything. He had even thought to bring several empty crates. If she had known, she wouldn't have used her kitchen shelves for the chickens. She didn't try very hard to fight back her resentment.

Haywood managed to catch up with her in time to help with the cellar door. "You won't need the food, Cally," he started. "The Gwynns will..." He had reached the bottom of the rock steps and struck the light. He looked at the neat shelves lined with sealed jars. "You've worked hard, haven't you?"

"I could survive the winter here," she responded proudly. She didn't add that she didn't need him or the Gwynn sisters. She was sure he heard that in her voice.

She could see he debated with himself whether to take all her hard work to town or not. Well, she had already decided. She wasn't leaving this food for the no-account gambler who was taking her farm! "If the

Gwynns don't want it, I'll sell it from Mr. Lafferty's store.''

Haywood turned toward her, grinning again. "Lafferty's Feed and Canned Goods?''

"Sounds good to me.'' She decided she hated his grin.

Haywood handed her the candle. "I'll get the crates. Do you have some straw to pack between the jars?''

Cally shook her head. "Pa's old clothes, maybe?''

Andrew agreed and twenty minutes later the crates full of canned goods were all packed in the wagon. Somehow, out of the little cellar, there didn't seem to be nearly as much food as she thought. She had talked him into taking most of the potatoes, but he wouldn't promise that she could come back later for her pumpkins and squash. She made a secret vow to raid her own garden at night.

The chickens responded with squawks of outrage as Haywood lifted the two crates into the wagon. Her rocking chair followed. Cally called Queen and patted the wagon bed to coax her in. The old dog obeyed slowly, jumping in and circling three times before lying down. Belle and Jewel were tied behind the wagon and Cally climbed to the seat, narrowly avoiding Haywood's offered hand.

When Haywood was seated beside her, she asked the question she had been postponing. "Where are you going to take the animals?''

Haywood hesitated long enough to make Cally worry. If they were all destined to die, she was getting out right now! She was nearly trembling with anger by the time he finally answered. "Well, I asked around a little, but I didn't have much luck. For now, I guess they come home with me.''

Cally stared at him, sure she had misunderstood.

''The mayor owns the place where I live. I talked to him first to be sure, but he doesn't care. I've got plenty of room, and I'm not far from the Gwynns'.''

''So I can still take care of them?'' She was almost afraid to hope.

Haywood laughed. ''I'd like that. The chickens are the only thing that could cause a problem. There's a little chicken coop but no pen, and I'm not sure I like the idea of them having the run of the yard, not to mention the neighbors'. I'll get a pen up as soon as possible.''

Cally was so happy, she almost wanted to hug Haywood. All her animals would be safe. She could see them whenever she wanted. She wouldn't have to buy them back after all.

She knew Haywood watched her with a smile on his face, even though she refused to look at him directly. She didn't want him to think that he had made her happy. She watched Royal trot along beside the wagon as an excuse to turn her head away from Sheriff Haywood.

At the edge of town, Haywood turned the wagon in his drive, passed the house and stopped in his barnyard. Cally tried not to show her admiration for the big house and even bigger barn. She had known which house Haywood rented, but she hadn't allowed herself a close look at it before. It was nice. In fact, to Cally, it looked like a mansion. But then, the Gwynns lived in a mansion, too.

Haywood untied Jewel and Belle from the back of

the wagon and turned them into the corral while Cally slowly climbed from the wagon seat. She told herself that she was glad he didn't offer to help her down.

"Come, Queen," she said, as she walked around the wagon. "This is your new home." The dog came to her feet, and Cally ruffled the fur on her neck, adding more softly, "Just until I can get the farm back."

Queen jumped out of the wagon, shook herself and ambled toward the inviting shade under the back-door overhang. Cally couldn't help but grin as the dog sniffed at the walk and the door and finally spread herself across the doorsill just as she did at home.

She heard Haywood's footsteps crunch in the gravel behind her, then the startled squawk of the chickens. She turned to the wagon and grabbed the second crate, following Haywood to the chicken house.

Haywood set his crate down and opened the door, holding it wide for Cally to enter. "You can thank Taylor and Mikey for cleaning in here," he said.

Light through the south window shone on a patch of wood floor that showed definite signs of a recent sweeping. Fresh straw was in the nests that lined one wall, and a tub of water and a pan of oats stood under the window.

"Taylor and Mikey?"

"Deputies in training," he mumbled. "Never mind." Haywood closed the door behind them and pried the lid off one crate. "Do you think they'll be all right if I keep them shut in until I get the pen up?"

Cally shrugged. "I guess." The house was bigger

than their house and pen put together and tighter than her soddy. He didn't need to know that, though.

The chickens fluttered out of the crate, creating a storm of dust and feathers. In a moment the second crate was opened and all six hens were free to investigate their new home.

Cally couldn't help but think they wouldn't want to go back to their old coop. She caught herself before she said it aloud. She couldn't let Haywood know what she planned. *Because he'll tell you it's foolish, and he'll be right.* She brushed the thought aside and left the chicken house without another word to Haywood.

He followed her out quietly. Being patient and polite, she thought irritably. He could make a better home for her chickens, her mule and her cow than she could. Even Queen was settled happily at his door. But he would never make Royal feel at home. The dog waited for her and trotted beside her as she walked back to the wagon.

While Haywood carried her half-filled sack of feed and her milk bucket to the barn, Cally knelt and put her arms around Royal's neck. "You have to stay here, boy. Can you understand? I'll come back and see you twice every day." She buried her face in his fur for a moment before she stood. "Stay!" she commanded.

Royal whimpered and sat, watching her closely.

Cally climbed onto the wagon seat without looking back. Haywood climbed up beside her. For a moment she thought he wanted to say something, but he didn't. He turned the wagon in the yard and started down the drive that ran beside the house. Before they got to the road, Royal was trotting along at the horse's side.

Haywood reined the horse to a stop. "Cally," he started.

"Haywood, you can't lock him in the barn. He needs to be able to run around. Let's talk the Gwynns into letting me keep him there."

Haywood shook his head. "It's no use. Besides, it won't be forever, Cally. I'll get a chain. A long chain. One that will let him run all the way from the house to the barn. When he gets used to being here, we can try again to set him free."

To Cally's dismay, Haywood put his arm around her shoulder and pulled her close. His hand began stroking her hair. She had sworn not to cry, but she would if he continued. She looked up to find his face only inches away, his lips near enough to touch. He was going to kiss her. For a few seconds, she would feel safe. She leaned toward him slightly and closed her eyes.

But he didn't kiss her. He sat up abruptly, easing her out of his arms. Muttering to himself, he jumped from the wagon and called Royal. Royal didn't even glance at Cally. Her loyal dog followed the sheriff to the barn, leaving her alone with thoughts that centered more on the sheriff than the dog.

In a moment she heard Royal's muffled bark, and Haywood climbed up beside her again, starting the team moving forward. Cally sat stiffly as far from him as the wagon seat would allow.

When they reached the Gwynns' house, Noella stepped onto her porch and motioned them to drive the wagon around to the back door, where both sisters met them.

"I'm glad to see you've come to your senses," said Noella.

Easter looked uncomfortable with her sister's greeting, but said nothing to soften it. "Bring her things into her room, Sheriff," she instructed.

Haywood carried the trunk, and Cally followed, struggling with the rocking chair. When they walked back to the wagon, the sisters were examining the crates of canned goods. They looked pleased but said nothing about them.

Cally lifted a half-filled crate and Haywood a heavier one, and they made a second trip into the house. When Haywood would have set the crate on the table in the kitchen, Cally brushed past him. "Put all these in my room, too," Cally whispered. Haywood followed her directions, and she thought she saw him smile.

Noella pointed out the entrance to their cellar, and Cally watched her potatoes disappear under the Gwynns' house. She knew they would spoil if she tried to keep them in her room. For a moment she wished she had left them at Haywood's or even the farm.

Finally the wagon was unloaded, and Haywood was ready to leave. It seemed odd to hate to see him go.

The sisters had no trouble dismissing him. "Come along inside, dear," said Easter, following her sister into the house.

Haywood came to stand close beside her. "Good luck, Cally."

She nodded, hoping none of her fear showed on her face.

"If you need anything, you know where to find me."

She bit her lower lip and vowed not to look at him, even as she turned her face toward him. "I'll be over to milk and such toward evening."

He nodded, ready to desert her. Quite suddenly, he bent and kissed her cheek, then turned and climbed onto his wagon. Cally hurried to the house so she wouldn't have to watch him drive away.

The Gwynn sisters were waiting for her in the kitchen. Noella glared at her. "You must bathe and change into appropriate clothes. I daresay you can handle that yourself this time. We'll return in an hour and give you instructions for lunch." The tall woman turned on her heel and left the room, Easter following.

"I don't think I much care to have instructions for lunch," Cally muttered to the closed door. "I'm used to more tasty food than instructions." She stood in the huge kitchen for a long moment and considered running, then with a deep sigh, she turned to put water on the stove to heat for her bath.

The little soddy had been vacant only a few hours when the new tenants arrived. Val Milton, Parker Stedwell and Wade Terris pulled up sharply in the dusty yard and looked around.

"This don't come close to what you described, Milton," Terris groused.

"Oh, I don't know, Wade," Stedwell said, tipping his head and closing one eye. "It almost looks habitable."

Milton sighed. "The old man talked about his neat little farm and his cozy little house. I had no idea his standards were so low."

Terris glared at him. "Are you damn sure you've got the right place?"

"I'm afraid so. The sheriff gave precise instructions."

"You should have told him to ride along," Terris suggested with a grin.

Val chose to ignore him. He was somewhat disappointed in his new farm, but he, of course, would be staying in town. Part of him felt pleased that his companions wouldn't be particularly comfortable.

He dismounted and the others followed suit, taking down their carpetbags and sacks of supplies. Terris was the first to venture into the sod house. In a moment he came out, shaking his head. Val noticed Stedwell watching his companion with amusement. "What do you think, Wade?" the forger asked.

"I think it beats a jail cell, but not by much."

Stedwell followed Terris back inside to see for himself. Val decided to give them a few minutes to accept their hideout and led the horses into the rundown barn.

When he joined the other men a short time later, they both had found chairs and were staring at their surroundings, Terris in obvious disgust and Stedwell in good-humored resignation. Finding no other chair, Val perched on the end of one of the bunks beside a haphazard pile of clothes.

Terris lifted a tin plate from the stack on the table and let it fall from his fingers with a clank. "Do you suppose DuBois' daughter intentionally made a mess for us before she left?''

Val shook his head. "Looks to me like the after-effects of some very fast packing.''

"Well, we're all familiar with that," Stedwell said, leaning back in his chair, completely at ease.

Terris gave a short, humorless laugh. "Probably glad as hell to get out of here.''

Stedwell said. "You haven't told us the plan yet, Val. How long will we be out here?''

"Not long," Val said, trying not to look too closely at his surroundings. "The plan is to rob the bank and frame Haywood. We need to know as much as we can about both before we make our move.''

"Meanwhile, you'll be in a hotel in town," growled Terris.

Val knew better than to smile. "I'll be the one asking questions, since neither of you can. Fancy should get here in the next day or so. You two can check out Haywood's house while she finds a way to keep Haywood busy.''

Val found it hard to ignore Terris's snort. He knew what the bastard was thinking. He couldn't be completely certain that wasn't exactly what Fancy would be thinking too, especially after she saw Sheriff Haywood.

"We'll need a place to stash the money that will implicate Haywood," he went on. "Someplace we can get to fast that won't be too hard for a deputy to find. But it's still got to look like a reasonable place for a thief to choose.''

Terris seemed to be only half-listening. He picked up a dented tin cup. "Say, Parker, when that sister of yours gets to town we ought to get her out here to tidy up the place."

Parker Stedwell grinned and winked at Milton. "He doesn't know Fancy, does he?"

It was almost dark by the time Cally was able to leave the Gwynn house to do her chores. The sisters had followed her around all afternoon, instructing her on cooking, serving and cleaning. It was easy to see they thought she was completely stupid. They had even shown her how to dust; how else would anybody do it?

She held the borrowed lantern in front of her as she walked through the shadowy streets. She didn't look forward to carrying both it and the full milk bucket back to the Gwynns' in the dark. In the future she would have to talk the old ladies into letting her leave earlier, perhaps before she cleaned up the dinner dishes. Surely they wouldn't insist on watching over her shoulder every day.

She had changed back into the men's clothes she had refused to burn. Her hair was still in the tight chignon Easter had shown her how to make and, thinking it would keep her hair out of her way, she had left her hat behind. A few blocks from the Gwynns' she began to regret it. She felt exposed without the hat to hide her face.

A light burned in Haywood's house, and Cally wondered what he was doing. She imagined him noticing her and her lantern going up the drive. Would he be glad that she had finally arrived to do her chores, or had he even noticed or cared whether they were done or not?

Before she was past the house, she heard Royal bark. One soft word from her, and the dog was quiet, but in a second he came bounding toward her. She set the lantern on the ground and crouched to greet him, forgetting about her possible audience in her pleasure at seeing Royal again. She hugged him and ruffled his fur, discovering that he had a chain around his neck.

"Poor Royal," she murmured. "I know it's not easy. But at least the mean old sheriff lets you have a long leash."

"The mean old sheriff didn't intend for him to roam quite that far."

Cally gasped at the sound of Haywood's voice. She knew her cheeks were burning but hoped she was too far from her lantern for him to tell. He stood in nearly total darkness. "Don't sneak up on me," she said, hoping to sound indignant enough to take his mind off her insult.

"Sorry," he said, moving into the circle of light. He didn't look as angry at her as she had expected, but he didn't look especially sorry, either. Actually he looked amused. The cruel man enjoyed frightening her, she decided.

"Get the lantern," he said, starting toward the barnyard. "Come on, Royal, let's try this again."

Cally didn't understand what he meant until she discovered Royal's long chain wasn't connected to anything but a broken stake. She grinned to herself as she followed, secretly proud of her dog for besting Haywood.

"How about a tree this time, boy? You can't break that, can you?" He talked to the dog as if he were *his.* "There we go. You stay here, now." He straightened from the task and walked toward Cally, making her wish she hadn't followed so closely. "Everything's done but the milking," he said.

Cally felt a surge of anger. Did he have to take over everything? She opened her mouth to say so, but he spoke again. "I'm sorry, Cally, but I haven't milked in years."

"I don't want you to milk my cow," she stated, her voice growing louder with each word. "I don't want you to feed my animals. And—and—I don't want you pretending like my dog is yours!"

He seemed completely surprised by her outburst. So was she, but she wouldn't apologize. It had been a terrible day and having to talk to him made it worse.

"It was getting late," he said in that warm honey voice. She knew by now to be wary of it. "I was afraid you wouldn't be able to get away. Actually, I was about to give up on you and try to milk as well. I didn't think you'd mind, Cally. I only wanted to help."

He moved toward her as he spoke. He was close enough to touch, close enough for her to imagine her head on his shoulder or his lips against hers. She shook herself. "I'll milk Belle," she said quickly, nearly running past him to the barn. Royal, following as far as he could, set up a tremendous barking that Haywood quieted with a word.

Cally wanted to swear the entire time she milked. She had to force herself to be calm to get Belle to cooperate. Finally she left the barn, lantern in one hand, bucket of milk in the other. To her dismay, Haywood waited by the back door. He lifted a small basket and stepped out to meet her. Royal came to meet her too, at least as far as the chain would allow. She stopped to say goodbye to Royal, ignoring the sheriff standing nearby.

When she had reminded Royal to stay, she gathered her burdens and started down the drive. Royal sat and whimpered.

Haywood fell into step beside her. "There were only two eggs," he said, indicating the basket.

Eggs. She hadn't even thought about how to carry them back as well. "Keep them," she said, hoping she sounded generous instead of desperate.

"Cally," he started.

"Yes?" She walked a little faster.

"Let me carry the bucket."

"Why?"

"I'm walking you home. Let me carry the bucket." Cally stopped abruptly. "You're what?"

"It's dark. I'm walking you home." He sounded hurt that the notion would surprise her. He was always so sure of himself.

Cally took a deep breath. "Home? You took my home." Her anger at the whole situation seemed to explode. The next moment she shouted, "You took everything. You even took my dog."

Royal barked and Haywood turned toward him, giving Cally a chance to hurry on her way. At first, she expected him to follow, then realized he had to quiet Royal or the neighbors would complain. Maybe Royal was still on her side after all.

Chapter Nine

Andrew fought the urge to go home early. He had nearly given in when a woman entered his office. He came slowly to his feet. Sunny blond hair caught the lamplight. A deep blue dress of the latest fashion hugged a very shapely body, and eyes of the same shade looked casually around the office before turning to him. Her smile was warm but formal.

Andrew smiled back. "May I help you, ma'am?"

"Why, I hope so, Sheriff." She presented him with a gloved and somewhat limp hand. "You are the sheriff, aren't you?"

"Yes, ma'am. Sheriff Andrew Haywood."

"Francine Wells," she said smiling sweetly.

"How might I be of service?" Andrew motioned toward a chair and, once she was seated, returned to his own.

She folded her hands demurely on her lap. "I will be moving to your fair city soon, and, well, sir, a woman alone just can't be too careful, you understand."

Andrew nodded. While he waited for her to go on,

he studied an artful curl at her ear that was supposed to have escaped its place in her perfectly styled hair. A real woman was just what he needed to get his mind off Cally. He hadn't talked to her for two days. He missed her spunky wisecracks. Yesterday, she had slipped in to do her chores and out again before he got home, which was why he had been thinking of going home now. Not a good sign, he decided. He was grateful to this beautiful woman for stopping him from making a foolish mistake.

"I have quite a sum of money I wish to transfer to the local bank," she explained in silky tones. "I must be certain that my money will be safe."

"It's a very stable bank, to my knowledge, ma'am."

"I'm sure it is." She turned her head slightly giving him a view of her pretty profile and long slender neck. "You see, sir, I've heard so much about robberies here in the West. Her gaze turned on him again. "I want to be sure they've taken every precaution."

The rose-petal lips gave him a shy smile. She did everything but bat her lashes. Andrew was flattered. He was also suspicious. He cleared his throat, successfully clearing his head as well. "I'm sure the bank president would be glad to give you a tour."

She frowned a very becoming frown. "I would like to do as you suggest, of course, but I've been through this before. Ladies, especially attractive ones—" She paused for confirmation, which of course she got "—we're so often treated as if we haven't a brain in our heads. Businessmen are especially fond of telling us not to worry, they'll handle everything. But I believe a woman needs to look out for herself. Don't you agree, Mr. Haywood?''

Andrew couldn't help but think of Cally's determination to do just that. And his own conviction that she couldn't. ''Yes, of course,'' he said.

''Lawmen seem to be a little more in tune with...reality, shall we say. That's why I've come to you. You've been inside the bank, I'm sure.''

Andrew nodded. He described the general layout of the bank and answered her questions about the number of tellers and each one's ability to stay calm in an emergency. He felt a little odd discussing the bank with this stranger, but he didn't tell her anything she couldn't find out simply by walking into the place herself.

Finally she asked him about the safe, the size, the style, the make. The woman knew more about safes than he did. He couldn't keep the surprise from his face.

She took a deep breath, stretching the material across her breasts to a dangerous degree. ''I've made it a point to know these things. It is, after all, my money. You do understand, don't you, Andrew? It's all right if I call you Andrew, isn't it?''

''Quite all right...Francine?''

She smiled. The perfectly shaped lips revealed perfectly straight teeth. Her eyes sparkled like blue diamonds. Andrew found himself saying, ''I'll check for you first thing in the morning.''

She rose to leave, and Andrew hurried to escort her to the door. When he reached for the knob, she stopped him with a hand on his arm. ''You won't tell the banker why you're asking, will you?'' She closed the already small space between them, and her voice dropped to a sultry whisper. "I couldn't bear thinking you and he were having a laugh at my expense."

Andrew had a feeling she could bring tears into the blue eyes at a moment's notice. He patted the hand on his arm reassuringly. "Of course not," he said.

The moment he had closed the door behind her he headed back to his desk and began opening drawers and shuffling papers, looking for his sketches of the woman who had gone to visit Stedwell before his escape.

Cally saw the beautiful woman leave Haywood's office and turned quickly into a side street, changing her plans as she went. The Gwynns had finished their dinner earlier than usual, and she had had some harebrained thought of paying the sheriff a quick visit on her way to his house to do her chores. Now she couldn't remember why she had wanted to do such a stupid thing.

She was glad the woman's presence had stopped her. She might have walked into Haywood's office and apologized for the things she had said last time they were together. She might have told him Pa was more to blame for her plight than he was. Haywood had found her a home, a job and a place to keep her animals, and she hadn't even tried to act grateful.

"And I don't want to start now," she muttered as she walked. She touched the tight bun at the nape of her neck and wondered if it looked as ridiculous as it felt. Compared to the blond woman's hair, it certainly did. She looked down at her gray dress and slightly smeared white apron and compared them to what the woman had worn, as well. How horrible if she had stepped into the office, clutching her milk bucket and egg basket, and interrupted Haywood and the woman!

By the time she arrived in Haywood's yard, she had decided not to think about him. It had worked before, if she reminded herself enough.

Royal came to greet her again, breaking the chain where she had tried to repair it that morning. With a sharp command from her, she had been able to walk away from him, but he couldn't seem to resist running to meet her when she approached. It happened every time, morning and night.

After kneeling to give Royal a hug, she took the chain from around the dog's neck and let him walk beside her as she did the chores. The thought came to her that she might have told Haywood about the broken chain, too, if she had actually gone to the office. Another reason to be grateful to the beautiful woman.

"The old ladies like my cooking," she told Royal. "I heard them talking after dinner. Of course, they wouldn't say so to me. They want to throw a dinner party to show off their new cook." She slipped the two dogs each a bone she had smuggled from the Gwynns' kitchen. The sisters would probably have been more than happy to have the bones fed to the dogs as long as the dogs weren't on their property. But Cally didn't want to ask and then be grateful. This way the gift to the dogs was from her.

"They said I need some more instruction first," she confided with a sigh, "so tomorrow will be another miserable day." That might have been another reason she wanted to see Haywood. He was at least straightforward. The Gwynns talked in circles and gave each other knowing nods. They thought she was stupid.

But then Haywood knew she was stupid. Even the Gwynns didn't know she couldn't read.

"But I won't feel sorry for myself," she muttered as she entered the chicken pen. The hens flocked from the new pen into the little house, and she raised the ramp, hooking it in place to shut them in. Haywood had worked on the pen the past two evenings, she supposed, and had turned the hens into it this morning.

Some things weren't too bad, she reminded herself as she milked Belle. The bed was comfy and the kitchen was so big it was almost a pleasure to cook. And there was always lots of food. She didn't think they even knew how much food they had.

"I wonder if my squash are ready," she whispered as she fed Jewel. "Shall we ride out and see come a moonlit night?" Cally was smiling when she left the barn, Royal at her side.

Haywood, standing at the tree, the broken chain in a pile at his feet, wasn't.

"We're in trouble now, Royal," she murmured, setting the bucket of milk in the shade of the house next to the basket of eggs. She walked toward the sheriff, Royal trotting innocently at her side. She was reminded of the evenings she had walked toward his office, building up her courage for another try at breaking Pa out of jail. She felt defenseless now for more reason than just the absence of a concealed weapon.

He pushed away from the tree and came to meet her. He was looking at her dress. She wanted to defend her decision not to change her clothes twice. The sisters would probably throw a fit if they knew she hadn't burned the pants. She didn't want them to catch her in them.

She chose not to say anything. It was probably silly to think Haywood cared what she wore. At the same time, she couldn't help thinking of the beautiful woman's elegant gown and imagine him making comparisons.

"How are you, Cally?" he asked softly.

The tone and the question both took her by surprise. She merely nodded.

"You look good, I mean...like you're doing all right."

Cally cringed. "I look silly." She spread the dress out and leaned over slightly to look down at it, exposing the toes of her oversize work shoes. She looked up in time to see him grin. Shoot. She had meant to keep quiet.

For some reason, the grin faded as he continued to look at her. "Do you have everything you need? Is there anything...?" The question trailed off as she shook her head. He seemed uncomfortable for a moment, then said, "I'll see what I can do about Royal's chain."

He went into the barn for tools, and Cally knew it was her chance to leave. She was still thinking about a hasty escape when Andrew emerged. *I waited because Royal would have followed me.* She decided it sounded too stupid to say aloud. Instead she stood and watched him.

The end of the chain was securely fastened around the tree in a few minutes. Haywood called Royal, who eagerly ran to him. That was when Cally surprised herself by mumbling, "I don't really blame you."

Haywood looked up at her. "Excuse me?"

Now she had done it. She would have to say it aloud. Or at least say something. "It seems a shame to—chain him up, I mean."

He grinned at her. She felt the blood rush to her face. He had heard her fine the first time! She spun on her heel and nearly ran to the house, scooping up the bucket and basket so fast she spilled milk on her shoes. She heard Royal bark but didn't want to turn, even to say goodbye.

Haywood's voice, talking to the dog, relieved her fears of being followed. The relief turned to anger as she stomped down the street. He was laughing at her. Laughing at what she had said, how she said it and probably everything else about her. She didn't want him to think she was silly. Or stupid. She wasn't sure what she wanted where Sheriff Haywood was concerned.

Andrew watched her storm away feeling inordinately pleased. She didn't blame him for all her troubles after all, though she hated to admit it. He knew he shouldn't have grinned the way he had. And now he should be sorry that he had upset her. Somehow the fact that a mere grin from him could make her angry meant that she cared what he thought. He didn't examine this idea very closely.

He had other things on his mind. Like the wisp of bright hair that blew across her face, and the blushing cheeks sprinkled with freckles. The simple gray dress made her look delicate in a way the baggy pants never could. He was in the house sketching her picture before he stopped to think about the implications of any of these thoughts.

By morning he had thought about them, though. His edge as a lawman was in serious danger because of an innocent young woman. Thinking of her as a child hadn't saved him. Finding her work and decent living conditions hadn't ended his worry about her welfare. Meeting a much more elegant woman hadn't shaken his preoccupation.

Sketches of Cally were scattered across his floor. He hadn't acted like this since he was an adolescent. He frowned down at the mess. He hadn't acted like this *when* he was an adolescent.

Picking up a random sketch, he tried to eye it critically. A smile slowly formed on his lips. She looked furious. She was about to quit his yard because he had caught her trying to take back a painful admission. He realized with a start that he was grinning down at the picture in the same way he had grinned at her last night.

He let the sheet flutter to the floor with the rest and shook his head. He couldn't look at her critically, not even his own pictures of her. He simply couldn't think about her reasonably. And he didn't have the first idea what to do about it.

Nothing, he decided. At least, nothing today. Surely this infatuation would wear off if he spent more time with her. He was her guardian, so to speak. He should go to visit her, encourage her to come see him. In a very short time he would get tired of her quick temper, her illogical notions, her freckled nose.

He was grinning again.

He turned away from the pictures, more than a little irritated with himself. He had other things to think about. Like Miss Francine Wells and her unusual request. He had told her he would go to the bank first thing this morning. A small inheritance, currently invested in an eastern bank, would serve as his excuse for asking questions. He would find out what she wanted to know, at least in part, and then start finding out what he wanted to know about her.

He opened his back door, grabbing his coat from its hook at the same time, and tripped over Queen. One arm partway into the coat sleeve kept him from catching himself. His shoulder hit the ground, and he rolled to his back. For the third morning in a row he stared up at the sky and counted to ten.

Queen crept toward him, nuzzled his arm and licked his face. When he didn't speak, she stretched out beside him, head on her paws, and watched him with sad eyes.

"Cally's going to be the death of me. One way or another, she's going to be the death of me."

Queen whimpered.

Stedwell and Terris waited for Milton to ride by and signal that Haywood was in the bank before they crept along the hedge toward the house Milton had told them was Haywood's. The front door was in clear sight of his neighbors, but the backyard was virtually hidden. They paused and studied the situation for a minute. There were two dogs, one chained to a tree, the other sleeping at the back door.

"They don't look too unfriendly," Stedwell commented. "You're the safecracker. You can break into the house."

Terris shook his head. "Look, I'll bet the bigger dog's unpredictable or it wouldn't be chained. The one by the door's probably harmless. You break into the house. I'll make sure that one stays quiet."

Stedwell looked at his companion and frowned. "How?"

"How do you think?"

"Wade, we don't want it to look like anyone's been here. I think the man will suspect something if he comes home and finds his dog dead."

Terris snorted. He pulled a paper parcel from his coat pocket and unwrapped it, revealing a small beefsteak.

Stedwell nodded his approval. "You've already checked out the place."

Terris didn't answer. He started forward and Stedwell followed. As soon as they set foot in the yard, Royal started barking.

"Hush now," said Terris, walking cautiously toward the dog. "See what I got?"

Royal barked louder.

Stedwell, halfway to the door, turned and hissed, "Toss him the meat."

Terris did. It didn't help. Royal strained against the chain, barking and growling, ignoring the steak that landed on the ground not two feet away.

Stedwell, worried that the neighbors might come to investigate the noise, was paying more attention to Royal than Queen until the older dog stood and bared her teeth, issuing a long low warning.

"Oh, for Christ's sake," muttered Stedwell, backing off a step. "You go get the steak."

A yell from Terris spun him around. The chain had given way, and the dog had nearly flown at Terris. The man turned and fled, the dog close on his heels. A tug on his own pant leg just below the knee reminded Stedwell there was a second dog to worry about.

He tried to shake his leg free only to be nearly pulled off his feet. With a surge of panic, he tore himself away, running out of the yard at a right angle from the retreating safecracker and his pursuing dog.

When Andrew left the bank, having thanked the banker for his help, he went directly to the City Hotel and inquired after Miss Wells.

"Room seven, at the front," Mr. Ossman told him.

Andrew smiled. "Would you ask her to come down, please?"

The manager spoke to a tall, thin boy scrubbing the floor, and the youth headed up the stairs. Andrew ignored the man's curious glances while he waited for the boy to return. Mr. Ossman was known as the town's most inaccurate gossip.

"Here on business, Sheriff?" the man finally asked.

"That's right," Andrew answered with a politician's smile. He was relieved to see the boy on his way down the stairs.

"She said she'd be down in five minutes, and you should wait in the dining room." The boy returned to his bucket and brush.

Andrew expressed his thanks to them both. It was

midmorning, and the dining room was nearly empty. Andrew asked for coffee and settled in for a wait. If a woman says five minutes she means fifteen, he reasoned.

Not in Miss Francine's case, however. It meant forty-five. During that time, Andrew's impatience turned to mild concern and back again. A woman always thought if she made herself lovely enough it was worth any wait to a man. Andrew had never found himself agreeing, though he had pretended to more than once.

When Francine stepped through the double doors that connected the dining room to the hotel, the notion suddenly made perfect sense. Andrew stood and watched her walk toward him. Her cream-colored skirts were too wide for the overfurnished room, but she brushed past the tables and chairs without seeming to mind.

"I'm sorry to keep you waiting, Andrew." Her cheeks were flushed and her voice was somewhat breathless. He felt flattered that she had hurried down to meet him, though he presumed the breathlessness could be caused by a too-tight corset. Her waist looked uncommonly narrow.

He pulled a chair out for her and returned to his own. "Would you like some coffee? Breakfast?"

"No, but that's very kind of you, Andrew." She touched the creamy lace at her throat and unnecessarily adjusted the front of the navy bolero jacket that rode precariously on the peaks of her unnaturally high breasts.

Andrew averted his eyes to his coffee cup. She had been busy, all right. Looking up, he said in his best business voice, "I just came from the bank." He caught a glimpse of surprise in her face before she smiled.

"How kind of you. What did you find out?"

He told her the size, type and brand of safe. It was no secret. The safe was new, and the banker was proud to tell everyone about it.

She leaned toward him, looking very earnest. "You didn't tell the banker why you were asking, did you?"

"No. I told him I had some money I was thinking about moving." It was the truth, though he had considered telling the banker about her. If his suspicions were correct, the man deserved to be warned. But right now, all he had were suspicions. It could be coincidental, her questions about safes while a safe-cracker was on the loose.

"You've been very kind, Andrew. How can I repay the favor?" She lowered her head and looked at him through her charcoal-smudged lashes.

Andrew smiled. "It's been my pleasure, Miss Wells. Now, if you'll excuse me, I have work to do." He left without a backward glance so he missed the pretty pout that settled on her painted lips.

As soon as the breakfast dishes had been washed and put away, Noella and Easter took Cally to the dining room and showed her where they kept the good china. Cally stood by and watched as Noella set one place at the table, using a startling number of pieces.

"The edge of the plate should be one inch from the edge of the table. Put the bowl on top," Noella instructed.

"The soup bowl, not the dessert bowl," added Easter.

"The knife here, fork here, spoon here, and of course, the soupspoon here."

"The soupspoon's the big one." Easter smiled at Cally. She tried to smile back. The silly old lady thought this was fun.

Noella went on as if there had been no interruption. "Bread plate, butter knife, sauce dish, saltcellar, dessert dish. Unless the dessert is the kind that's dipped up in the kitchen and brought to the table. Water glass here. Wineglass here." She stepped back and motioned Cally forward to view her handiwork.

Cally thought it looked like a mess. How could anyone actually eat this way? They must knock things over a lot, she decided.

"Now you do one, dear." Cally saw Noella cast Easter a disapproving look for the endearment, but Easter missed it. Cally carried one of each of the different dishes to the table and, by referring often to Noella's model, set a fair place. Noella even said so.

"I won't remember it though," Cally pointed out. She didn't mean to be arguing with the women, but if they thought she would be able to set a whole table after this one lesson, they needed to know the truth.

"That all right, Cally," Noella said stiffly. "One of us will set one place for you each time until it comes naturally to you."

Each time? How often did they plan to have these dinner parties?

Noella was already removing the serving dishes from the bottom of the sideboard. "Now you must learn how to serve the food," she said.

Easter took a place at the table, and Cally watched as Noella explained with one dish after another. She served make-believe soup, meat and vegetables into the two table settings while Easter added her encouragement. She repeated the process until even Noella was satisfied.

After the lesson she was sent downtown to shop. Before she left the house, she wrapped two muffins left from breakfast in a cloth and tucked them into her basket. She didn't look too closely at her motives. She told herself simply that her animals might suffer if she and Andrew were fighting. Andrew. She rather liked the name, though she would always call him Haywood or Sheriff, of course.

The new shoes the sisters had bought her with money withheld from her pay, tapped rather than clumped along the boardwalk. They made her feel light and purposeful. There was something very efficient about shoes that fit. The shoes were the reason she walked toward the sheriff's office with such eagerness, not because of any desire to see the sheriff.

She had already decided the sheriff's office would be her first stop. Again, it wasn't that she was eager to see him or in danger of losing her courage if she put this errand off. She simply needed to deliver the muffins before she started filling the basket with the items on the Gwynns' list.

She hadn't gotten used to the difference between walking along these streets now, in her gray dress and apron, and before in her men's clothes with Royal by her side. People still noticed her, but it was different. They were looking at a woman rather than a curiosity, and she had to admit she liked it.

The sheriff's office seemed different, too, with sunlight streaming through the windows. She had come so often in the evenings to see Pa. For a second she expected Pa to be in the cell. The eerie feeling passed with the sight of the man at the desk. It wasn't Andrew.

"Can I help you, ma'am?" the young man asked as he stood.

"Where's Andr...Haywood?"

The man's friendly face opened in a broad grin. "He's been called out of town on business. I'm the deputy. I don't suppose there's anything I can do for you?"

Cally couldn't help but remember the last time Andrew had left town. He had dragged her into town claiming she wouldn't be safe while he was gone. This time he didn't even let her know. She knew it was stupid to feel hurt.

"It was nothing important." She forced herself to smile at the deputy. "I just had some muffins left over. You can eat them as well as he can, I suppose." She handed the parcel to the deputy.

He sniffed appreciatively. "I'll be sure to tell him you came by, Miss...ah?"

"Miss DuBois," answered Cally, feeling more angry at Haywood by the minute. "But you don't need to mention the muffins unless you want to."

She turned and left the office, wrinkling her nose at the pictures on the wall. She had almost forgotten about them. Her loneliness made her forget a lot of things. She walked toward the grocer's store, deciding she was glad that Haywood hadn't been in his office.

While she was downtown shopping, she decided

something else as well. Tonight she would check on her garden.

Just before dark, Val headed toward the soddy. Last time he had visited his cohorts he had gotten the distinct impression that Terris wasn't exactly waiting patiently. The man was liable to do something rash and ruin everything.

Val was well aware that he needed these two more than they needed him. His job was to make them think otherwise. With that in mind, he had done as he had promised and found them another place to stay. The rest would have to be bluff for the moment. But then, he was a gambler.

As he rode up to the soddy, Stedwell met him at the door, calling cheerfully over his shoulder, "Company, Wade."

"Tell me we're getting outta this dump," Terris growled from the bunk. "I'm damn tired of sitting around here."

"Lying around," Stedwell corrected with a grin.

"As promised, gentlemen," Val said as he stepped inside, "I've found you a place in town." Having both men's full attention, he explained, "There's a room in the back of the saloon. It can be rented for poker games or whatever. Jesse James holed up there about a year ago, or so the man says. There's a peephole so you can see what's happening in the saloon half a flight below, and a trapdoor to the roof if you need a way out. The owner will bring up your food and keep his mouth shut."

"Sounds risky," muttered Terris.

"Sounds like heaven," countered Stedwell.

"Whatever." Val took the empty chair and went on, "It's the best I can do. The more questions I ask, the more dangerous it becomes."

"I can see your point," said Stedwell. "When do we move?"

"Now."

Terris swung his legs off the bunk and started to rise. With a groan, he dropped back to the bunk.

"What's his problem?" Val asked.

"Oh, he sprained his ankle running from Haywood's place," Stedwell explained, not unsympathetically.

Val eyed the man's stocking feet. One might have been slightly larger than the other. He wasn't interested in examining them too closely. "But you did find a place to stash the money?"

Stedwell shook his head. "We didn't even get inside the house."

Val frowned. "Well, don't worry. I'll come up with something."

Terris sat up again, careful not to put his right foot on the floor. "You'll damn sure come up with something. That's the whole idea, ain't it? *You'll* make all the plans. Well, how *are* those plans coming, Milton? I'm beginning to wonder if you're just stringing us along."

Val stood. "The plan's taking shape. But these things take time. You want to walk away from this one without shackles on your feet, don't you? Hell, if we pulled the job tonight, you wouldn't *walk* away at all!"

The words had the desired effect. Stedwell gathered up their few belongings as Val went to saddle the horses. Terris was able to hobble out to his horse and, with Stedwell's help, made it into the saddle.

The sprained ankle clearly didn't improve Terris's disposition, and Val wasn't sure it would make him any easier to control. It did, however, buy Val a little time.

Chapter Ten

Andrew had trouble sleeping. A minor altercation in a small town at one corner of the county had kept him away most of the day. It had forced him to put off his plan to get over Cally by overexposure to her temper.

He had come home late to find Royal chewing on a remnant of a steak bone. Cally had brought it, he supposed. He checked the dog's chain and discovered another of Cally's repairs.

At the door, he found Queen chewing on a piece of cloth with a gusto that matched Royal's. It didn't seem like an equal gift, but he assumed Queen had already devoured her treat. Since he didn't recognize the cloth as anything he owned, it was a mystery hardly worth pursuing.

A bigger surprise was Queen's trying to follow him into the house. She hadn't done that before, though he was sure Cally had always let her in at night. He had even considered allowing it, thinking he wouldn't trip over her if she was inside. In the end he had decided it wasn't something he wanted to get started, and had pushed her back out.

Now as he paced his bedroom in the dark, he decided the mystery of Queen's behavior and the square of cloth would be a better excuse for calling on Cally than his original plan of calling on her as her guardian. He had already determined that the Gwynns' house would be a better setting for their meetings than his yard when she did the chores. She tended to run away from him here.

Yet she had come to his office. Bill had enjoyed passing that information on to him. She had come, leaving muffins, which reportedly were delicious, but no message. Bill seemed to think the muffins represented a woman's usual route to a man's heart. Andrew tended to think of them as a peace offering. Bill had handed him the cloth the muffins had been wrapped in, suggesting he return it personally.

He found himself smiling again. It just reinforced his conviction that he needed to do something about his tender feelings for Cally. He didn't need the big-hearted girl complicating his life. He had two good reasons to call on her, and tomorrow he would do it. She would be her usual illogical self, and he would feel much better.

He walked to the window and gazed down into his moonlit yard. Royal was alert, intent on some sound or other. Andrew had become used to seeing the big dog at his post under the tree. He rather liked having the dog, though he had very little time for him. The poor beast had adjusted well, considering he had been used to spending every waking moment at Cally's side.

As he watched, the dog came to his feet. With one wild lunge, he snapped the chain. Andrew groaned. The dog would be out chasing rabbits all night. He tried to decide if there would be anything gained by going after him, but Royal trotted back into the yard, a small figure at his side. From Andrew's position at the window, the figure looked like a pile of rumpled clothes with a floppy hat on top.

"Cally, what are you doing here in the middle of the night?" he murmured, shaking his head. "Something I won't like, I'm sure." He watched her remove the chain from the dog's neck and wondered if she came to see him every night. It would be like her, he thought.

The two companions walked to the barn and disappeared inside. Andrew leaned on the window frame and sighed. Of course the dog adjusted more quickly than the girl. She had, as she said, lost everything. The dog was her best friend, and they ought to be together. The current situation was far from perfect.

Standing at the window he found himself sorely tempted by the open barn door. Any thoughts he had of comforting Cally, however, were dangerously mixed with the image of her in the white gown. He had to resist.

Yet he couldn't pull himself away from the window. He had to wait for her to reemerge. When she did a short time later, he was taken by surprise. She led Jewel out of the barn and turned to close the door. He stared in shock as she swung onto the mule's back. With Royal at their side, mule and rider trotted down the drive. Andrew wasted a full minute blinking down at his now empty yard.

"She's going home," he muttered, turning away at last. He took only enough time to slip into his pants and boots before he headed down the stairs.

Grabbing his coat as he reached for the doorknob, he was brought up short by the note tacked inside the back door. "Dog," it proclaimed in large black letters. He would have tripped again if his note hadn't reminded him.

"They would go home, wouldn't they, girl?" he asked Queen as he stepped over her, throwing on the coat at the same time. "Cally wouldn't just run away, would she?"

He became more worried about her with each second. He saddled his horse and headed toward Cally's farm, knowing if his guess was wrong, he would have to wait until morning to try to track her.

He hadn't guessed wrong. He was barely out of town when he saw the strange trio silhouetted in the moonlight. For some reason, he couldn't bring himself to confront her. He was too curious about what she intended to do. Surely she didn't plan to run off the new owner.

She disappeared into the shadow of the trees at the creek and Andrew slowed to give her time to cross. Once in the creek himself he discovered she had left the mule in the trees. He left his horse as well and followed quietly.

After a moment he saw Cally and Royal creeping forward. It seemed the house wasn't her destination, after all. While Royal watched the house, Cally crept into the garden.

Andrew returned to the trees to wait. After a few

minutes he saw her hurrying awkwardly back to the mule.

Andrew mounted his horse and drifted farther away. He wasn't sure the gambler was actually staying in the soddy, but, if he was, Andrew didn't want him to overhear when he confronted Cally. He was glad he had taken the precaution. Royal warned her of his presence with a bark that could have been heard for a mile or more.

"It's me," he said, as much for Royal's sake as Cally's.

She brought the mule up to within a few feet of him before she spoke. "You followed me," she accused.

He leaned toward her. "You trespassed," he countered.

She shook her head. "That's my garden."

"Not anymore." He wanted to impress upon her the danger she was in when she did foolish things like this. At the same time, he sensed she wouldn't be convinced by the usual arguments. She wasn't a logical person.

After a full minute Cally broke the silence. "Are you going to arrest me?"

Andrew wanted to laugh. He hadn't thought of that, but it made perfect sense. "I'll release you into the custody of the Gwynns in the morning."

Cally tried to turn Jewel, but the old mule was far slower than Andrew's mare. "You can't arrest me," she protested, as he took the reins from her.

"Why?" he wanted to know.

Cally tried to think of something that would appeal to the coldhearted sheriff. Nothing came to mind.

She glanced at Andrew's face in the moonlight. He looked rather pleased with himself. He was finally getting his revenge for all the times she had tried to free her father. She couldn't hardly blame him for that, she supposed.

"The old ladies will kill me," she muttered. She could imagine how upset they would be to find their breakfast wasn't ready and their cook in jail. "Oh, the scandal!" Miss Noella would say.

As they reached town, Cally began to hope that he wasn't serious, that it was just a bluff to get her to do as he said. But as they rode past Andrew's house and didn't turn off on the Gwynns' street, her hopes sank. Andrew dismounted in front of the jail and tied the mare and the mule to the hitching post.

Cally made no move to dismount. There had to be some way to convince him not to lock her up. When he reached up to help her down, she whispered, "I'll do anything."

She wondered at his reaction to the words. His hands were on her waist, and he eased her slowly to the ground. "Anything, Cally?" he whispered. "That's quite an offer."

She had no idea why the words made her pulse race. Or was it his voice and his touch? He hadn't stepped away from her. She had to crane her neck to look at him. An instant before it happened she knew. He was going to kiss her! She raised herself to the tips of her toes.

Her hat fell to the ground. The mule sidestepped, bumping the mare. The mare danced as far away as her tether would allow. None of this mattered to Cally. The mysterious feelings stirred inside her again as she was encircled in his arms. The warmth of his lips spread through her body until her fingers and toes tingled.

Abruptly he pulled away. Cally slowly settled back down to the soles of her feet, eyes still closed, savoring the strange feelings she had, until recently, thought of as a dangerous illness.

She opened her eyes when she heard Andrew take a ragged breath. "Go home, Cally," he whispered. "To the Gwynns', I mean. Now."

She hesitated a moment, afraid her knees would shake. Then she remembered the threat of jail, and turned, grabbing up her hat before hurrying down the boardwalk. Was that all she had to do to stay out of jail? Kiss the sheriff? She found herself grinning. She wished she had thought of that sooner. She was nearly to the Gwynns' back door when she discovered Royal had followed her.

Cally took Royal back to Andrew's the next morning. She had known when she let him in that the sisters would be furious if they caught her, but she slept so much better with the big dog beside her bed. Too much better. It was almost dawn when she awoke. She dressed in the pants knowing she could work faster in them. She slipped out the back door in a matter of minutes and ran all the way to Andrew's.

She didn't bother trying to fix Royal's chain but hurried to the barn to milk Belle, hoping she could get away without meeting Andrew. Would he be sorry he hadn't locked her up last night? Would he threaten her again? Would she be able to change his mind with a kiss?

She caught herself before she giggled. This kissing business had turned out to be much more interesting than she had first thought. If it could make someone as tough as Sheriff Haywood back down, it had great powers, indeed.

It occurred to her that she had a little trouble seeing the sheriff as a bloodthirsty snake anymore. She wondered if that might be *his* kisses working on *her.* Perhaps kissing was something she ought to be very careful of.

She hurried out of the barn as Andrew came out of the house, stepping over Queen. He walked toward her, but she pretended she didn't see him. She didn't stop until he called her name. "I'm late," she said.

"I want to talk to you." He sounded a little uncertain. A strange sound for him, she thought.

She turned toward him to be sure he could hear but continued her escape by walking backward. "The old ladies will be upset if breakfast isn't ready." Her own voice shook just a little, but only because she was afraid she would trip.

"All right." He was letting her go! "Can I come by to see you later?"

Cally shrugged. She didn't know what to make of the question so she simply nodded. "Keep Royal here, will you?" She turned and nearly fled the yard.

She hadn't been fast enough. Noella waited in the kitchen when she came in. The woman's face went from stern to shock to open reproach in the time it took Cally to set the bucket of milk down and close the door.

"I thought you burned those clothes." Noella's nose wrinkled in extreme distaste.

"I washed them, instead," Cally said. "Milkin's a sight easier in pants."

Noella tapped her foot. "But *I* remember distinctly telling you to burn them."

Easter came sleepily into the kitchen, having heard her sister's voice. "What?" she asked, then staggered back a step when she caught sight of Cally. She shook her head, clicking her tongue.

"Exactly," declared Noella.

Cally was bewildered. They had seen her in the pants before. Not since they had told her to burn them, of course, but really, they weren't that horrible. She *had* washed them. Maybe the old ladies were like Haywood and expected every order to be obeyed.

Noella slumped into a chair. "I am at a loss as to what to do with you, young lady."

"Perhaps she just doesn't know," suggested Easter.

Noella studied her sister then returned her gaze to Cally. Cally wanted to tell them she knew a lot they didn't, like how hard it was to milk a cow when you were wearing a dress and how hard it was to keep the hem clean in the chicken house, but was afraid it would nettle them more.

Noella and Easter were studying her so intently she squirmed. She felt she ought to say something. "I'm sorry I overslept," she offered. It wouldn't be a good idea to explain that she was out last night harvesting her squash, which the sheriff had stolen away from her.

The apology didn't seem to ease the tension even a little bit. The two women continued to study Cally and exchange knowing looks. Cally was ready to scream by the time Noella finally spoke. "I think you're right, Easter. Growing up without a mother, the girl just doesn't know."

Easter took a seat at the table and divided her attention between Cally and Noella. Obviously, she waited for her sister to explain whatever was on both their minds. The tension made Cally want to fidget. "Can I strain the milk now?" she ventured.

"No, Cally. Come sit down." Noella indicated the chair across the table from her and waited until Cally was seated to go on. "Did your mother ever talk to you about...well, where babies come from?"

"Babies?" Cally blinked. She knew a little about babies, at least where cows and dogs were concerned. But she hadn't learned it from Ma. "I was still mostly a baby myself when she died."

"You poor dear," said Easter.

Noella scowled at her sister then turned her attention back to Cally. "It's important that a young lady know these things to protect herself."

"From what?" Cally had noticed that quite often these two women didn't make sense.

"From men." Noella straightened in the chair, and Cally could tell she was ready to launch into her explanation. She braced herself.

"Men are like...bees. They will try to take nectar from as many flowers as they can. It is up to the flower to stop him."

Cally blinked. The woman thought that made sense? She pictured a flower bending its stem to avoid a bee and caught herself before she grinned.

Noella didn't seem to notice. "Men aren't entirely to blame, you understand. It is simply the way they are made." Her voice grew more stern with every word, and Cally was afraid she was becoming truly angry. "They cannot help themselves and, quite frankly, are not expected to try. Society leaves it up to women to be constantly vigilant."

What this had to do with her being late, Cally had no idea. Did they think she had been with a man? Were they going to tell her she couldn't go to Andrew's to do her chores anymore? She wanted to look at Easter for encouragement but was afraid to take her eyes off Noella.

"When you wear pants," the woman continued, striking her fist on the table, "you remind every man who sees you that you have two legs. If he thinks about the fact that you have two legs, it will naturally bring to his mind where they meet. You, young lady, are inviting disaster every time you wear pants where any man can see you. I can be excused if I find it truly shocking!"

With this final pronouncement, Noella rose shakily to her feet. "Strain the milk, change your clothes and start our breakfast. I will see to burning those vile pants, myself." She turned and left the room.

Cally stared after her in disbelief. Could this have anything to do with tingling kisses? But Andrew had kissed her first when she was wearing her nightgown. According to Noella's explanation she should have been safe then. Besides, as she walked around town she saw women in dresses, and they had husbands and babies. She wondered if Noella knew anything at all.

Then she remembered how the fever had come over Andrew in her cabin and had taken possession of her as well. Perhaps there was something to what Noella said.

Easter was still at the table, watching her sympathetically. "I know Noella seems angry, dear, but she's just worried for you. Once a reputation is ruined, it can never be gotten back. And in spite of what they might say, a man never marries a fallen woman. Miss Noella just wants to protect you."

Cally noticed that both Noella and Easter had protected themselves clear into spinsterhood. She made one last effort to save her pants. "She thinks my pants are going to make some man want to make a baby?"

"Oh, dear child, men never want to actually make a baby. Well, I suppose some do, but usually they don't. They just want...the nectar."

"Like the bees?"

Abruptly Easter smiled. "You understand now, don't you?" She patted Cally's hand and rose. "You can go about your work now."

Cally sat at the table for a full minute after Easter left. The old ladies were batty. All the same, she was going to be in trouble with the Gwynns if Andrew came to see her. And she had just told him he could come. She would have to get away after breakfast and go to him first. If she couldn't sneak out, she would have to think of some believable excuse like shopping for an appropriate dress to do the milking in.

Andrew had already sent a few telegrams. The pictures of Francine Wells would follow by mail. One of the sheriffs or someone in the U.S. marshal's office might recognize the woman and know if there was a connection between her and either Stedwell or Terris.

That was why Andrew tried his best to remember the woman's face exactly. He had an artist's eye for detail, and Francine was very attractive. He was sure that his drawings would be nearly as good as a photograph.

When he heard the door open, he took a last few strokes on her pointed chin before he looked up. "Cally. Is everything all right?" He dropped the pencil on the desk and came around to stand near her.

"Yes, mostly," she said.

He watched her stroll around his office as if putting off what she had come to say, or perhaps to move farther away from him. When she glanced at his drawing on the desk, she turned away quickly, flustered. He found it completely charming. Not at all the effect he had hoped for.

Finally she quit wandering and faced him squarely. "I came to tell you not to come visit me at the Gwynns'."

She had stopped where the sun streamed through the window, and he had a feeling he could count the freckles on her nose. He grinned when he said, "I planned to offer them some squash, fresh from the garden."

Her response was a scowl. "Stolen from me, you mean."

"Confiscated," he corrected.

She shook her head. "Anyway, you can't come to the Gwynns' house."

She was truly upset about something. He found himself reaching out to her but quickly dropped his hand. "Why not?" he asked gently.

"Because you're..." She stopped. He raised his

eyebrows to prompt her, but she only cleared her throat.

Andrew took a step toward her, stopping himself before he touched her. "I'm what, Cally? You can talk to me."

She took a deep breath and said in a rush, "Because you're a man, and they don't like men. At least they don't seem to. I know I'll be in trouble if I let you come see me, so I don't want you to come." She took another deep breath as if satisfied with her explanation.

Andrew wasn't. "Why would you be in trouble? Cally, they've never acted like they didn't like me."

Cally cringed. "They don't not like you exactly. They just won't like you coming to see me. Oh, I can't explain it! Just don't come!" With that, she darted out his door.

Andrew found himself chuckling by the time the door had closed behind her. What had she really come to say? He was certain that the sketch of Francine was what had prompted her silly statement. He wasn't going to take it seriously. It was important that he spend as much time as possible with her in order to cure himself of his infatuation. He smiled as he returned to his drawing. He already looked forward to their next encounter.

It was well past midnight, and Cally couldn't sleep. She kept thinking about the picture of the woman on Andrew's desk and how close she had come to calling him a bee. She felt the color rise to her cheeks even now. She hadn't said it, but he had laughed at her anyway. It seemed she never said or did anything right. She bet that beautiful woman knew just the right thing to say to get Andrew to...

To what? What was it she wanted from Andrew? Could she be falling in love with him? Could that be what this fever really was?

She wished she had someone to confide in. It seemed she was more lonesome in town surrounded by people than she had ever been on her farm.

When I'm with Andrew I don't feel lonely.

She tried to brush the thought aside. She didn't want to be less lonely when she was with Andrew. She rolled over, giving her pillow an angry punch. It had all been so much simpler when she hated him!

She had to admit that she didn't hate him anymore. In fact, remembering how she used to hate him made her feel ashamed. He had helped her bury her father, given her animals a home, found a place for her, and all the while he had treated her kindly. And just thinking about his kisses made her tingle down to her toes. She sighed and stretched under the covers.

Her thoughts were interrupted by a familiar bark. *Royal!* Cally threw off the covers and ran quickly to the back door. Outside she clamped her hands around the dog's muzzle for a moment to keep him from barking again. "What are you doing here?" she hissed.

Royal panted cheerfully.

She didn't think she could risk keeping him inside another night. She had gotten into enough trouble this morning. "I have to take you back."

Cally was afraid to go inside even to dress for fear Royal would bark and wake the sisters. "I shouldn't have let you in last night," she whispered as she started through town clad only in her nightgown. "I knew better, too, but I missed you so much." She stopped and hugged the dog, then hurried on.

She was shivering by the time they got to Haywood's backyard. "Oh Royal, what am I going to do with you?" She knelt on the ground to hug the dog again, as much for warmth now as affection.

"I might ask the same thing of you, Cally."

She sprang to her feet as Andrew wrapped a warm coat around her shoulders. "Royal," she protested as he led her toward the house.

"He won't leave the yard as long as you're here," he said. "Come inside before you catch your death of cold."

They stepped over Queen, and Cally let Andrew hurry her inside. He led her through his dark house, keeping her close beside him to avoid furniture she could barely see. Finally he stopped and lit a lamp revealing a cozy room cluttered with tables, chairs, books and all manner of other things. Andrew's things. Cally wanted to wander around and study each and every one of them.

"I'll have a fire going in no time," he said, drawing her attention.

Cally stared. Andrew wore only pants. His chest was sprinkled with fine curly hair. He turned away from her before she could decide if they looked soft or scratchy. He poked at dying embers; he lifted logs and set them on the ashes; he worked quickly, without glancing in her direction. The muscles she had admired once before for their labor potential completely fascinated her now. She felt little shivers in her stomach that had nothing to do with the cold. The fever, she thought, or love? She forced herself to turn away.

Her gaze fell on an untidy pile of papers, papers with sketches like the one she had seen on his desk. Before she could stop herself, she took a step toward the pile, dreading to see if they were more pictures of the beautiful woman but somehow needing to know.

It wasn't the same woman. This woman wasn't beautiful. She was angry, her eyes narrowed under puckered brows. Her mouth was a thin line; her turned-up nose was covered with freckles.

Freckles? Cally touched her own nose. Was this a picture of her? He drew pretty pictures of the beautiful woman, but this angry creature was what he thought of her?

"Cally?"

She spun around guiltily. He glanced from her to the pile of sketches and back and seemed to hesitate before coming closer. "Cally, come sit by the fire," he said softly.

She obeyed. She found herself shivering in a chair he had set before the fire, his coat still around her shoulders. She was surprised that it could hurt so much to know how he saw her. She gritted her teeth and vowed not to look at him.

It didn't work. He knelt in front of her. "Cally," he whispered. "Tell me what's wrong."

She couldn't. She jerked her head away when he tried to lift her chin.

"Is it the pictures? Does it bother you that I sketch you?"

She shook her head. She wanted to say she didn't care at all but her jaw was too tightly clenched.

"Cally?" There was desperation in his voice that made her want to either cry or kick him, she couldn't decide which.

She tried to pull away from him. "It's ugly," she said finally. She had meant to insult his drawing but decided it was her own appearance she had insulted instead.

"Here, look, they're not all that bad." In a moment the pile of sketches was on her lap, and he knelt beside her again. He seemed eager to show her the pictures. She wasn't sure she wanted to see them.

"I drew this one after...well, I had made you pretty mad, I guess." He grinned at her as he dropped the sketch on the floor. "This one's better. See? I drew you in the dress, your basket on your arm. It's pretty good."

The sheer size of the stack of pictures had startled Cally into relaxing. She turned toward him as he picked up the next sketch. He went through the stack, pausing only briefly on each one. After a few, Cally found herself paying more attention to his face than the pictures. The firelight cast a warm glow on his features, already bright with interest.

"This is one of the first I drew," he said. "I drew you on Jewel. I need to work on the mule's legs." The picture drifted down with the others. Cally hadn't even seen it.

"Look. I drew this one this morning. I call it the midnight raid." He chuckled at the drawing of a mule and rider silhouetted against a huge moon before dropping it on the floor.

Though Cally knew she probably shouldn't bring it up, she had to say it. "The other woman is beautiful."

Chapter Eleven

"What other woman?" Andrew seemed to be more interested in his drawings than in what Cally had to say. He held up the next sketch. "This one's pretty good."

A big-eyed girl, her face surrounded by a cloud of hair, looked back at Cally. She had a pretty innocence that was compelling. It was definitely more flattering than the first sketch.

But Cally was distracted only momentarily. "The woman you were drawing in your office. She was beautiful."

"She's a suspect." The pretty sketch followed the others. "Here I tried to draw Royal running to meet you. I'm not any better with dogs than I am with mules, I'm afraid."

"A suspect?"

The sketch he was about to lift from her lap fluttered back in place. Quite suddenly, she had his full attention. "Cally?" he whispered. "Are you jealous?"

"Of course not."

He grinned, that mischievous grin that made her heart skip a beat. She narrowed her eyes into a scowl, and he laughed. "Look at these, Cally. All these are of you. And there's half a dozen more at the office. I can't seem to do anything else." He stood suddenly, pacing across the room. "I can't believe it! All this time, I thought I felt responsible. I thought I was infatuated. Even after I realized I liked you I didn't understand." He stopped and gazed at her. She stared back in dismay. "Don't you see?" He came back to kneel in front of her. "Of course you don't. I barely see myself. I think I'm in love with you."

Cally's heart beat faster. No one had ever said that to her before. And she had been wondering if she was in love with him. Was that why she wanted to be with him all the time, annoying though he could be? Was that why she wanted him to kiss her every time they were close? If he knew he loved her, maybe he could help her figure out her own feelings.

She swallowed. "Why do you love me?"

He laughed again, ruefully this time. "There's never an answer to that question." He gathered up the pictures, from her lap and from the floor, reaching over to toss them on a nearby table.

"Then you don't really want to love me?" She stiffened again.

"I guess not, exactly," Andrew said thoughtfully. "But that doesn't seem to make any difference, I'm afraid." He turned to her again. "Oh, Cally, don't take it like that. I may not have wanted to fall in love with you, but I'm not sorry it's happened." He ran a gentle finger down her jaw, making it relax.

The fever was back in his eyes, mixed with something sweeter, more compelling. Love, she decided and wondered if her own eyes reflected the same. She leaned toward him.

The coat slid from her shoulders as he gathered her into his arms. He lifted her off the chair and into his lap on the floor. "I love you because you're so lovable," he whispered, smoothing her hair away from her cheek. "I can't seem to help myself."

She was snuggled up against his bare chest, much as she had been in more than one dream. In the dreams there had always been a crisp white shirt, however, instead of his bare skin. It was incredibly warm and safe in his arms. And exciting at the same time. Against her ear, his heart was beating like the hooves of a runaway horse, and she realized hers was as well.

Her hands were drawn to the soft hairs on his chest, testing the texture, finding it extremely pleasant. She lifted her face to see his expression and found her lips caressed, slowly, tantalizingly, by his.

She shouldn't let him kiss her, she supposed. She should be vigilant as Noella said. The tingling had increased to an intensity that made her tremble. She put an arm around his neck to pull him closer. Surely if he loved her it was all right.

She didn't know he had lifted her until she felt the rug-covered floor at her back. In a moment, he braced himself above her. "You're so beautiful," he whispered before bending slowly to kiss her cheek then trail kisses down her jaw and neck. "I want to love you, Cally." More kisses followed. "Do you want me to love you?"

Earlier he had told her he didn't want to love her,

but it was a fine point she decided not to argue. She didn't think she had the strength anyway. The best she could do was murmur a slurred "Yes, Andrew."

Only moments before, Cally had been shivering from the cold, now she felt incredibly warm, like the warmth of a lazy summer afternoon. *It's the fever,* she thought absently, *that wonderful fever.*

She closed her eyes and lay still, enjoying the sensations. She had become used to drifting off to sleep tingling with the memories of Andrew's kisses. She didn't think she could fall asleep now, though. This felt more like tremors! She did, however, feel strangely weak and didn't think she could get up and go home, either.

She realized that Andrew was no longer touching her and ran her own hands down her body, thinking to still the tremors. She sighed deeply. She wished he hadn't moved away. She missed his touch.

She felt Andrew's return at her side and turned toward him. His arms went around her, and she could feel the full length of his body. His naked body! The rough hairs of his leg rubbed against her thighs. With a shock she realized he had removed his pants, but his hand began gently kneading her breast and it slipped her mind. Altogether new sensations spiraled through her body, and she could think of nothing else.

"I love you, Cally." His whisper fanned her temple and let her know where to seek his mouth with her own. He accommodated her quickly, pulling her still closer against him.

His lips abandoned her, and she moaned softly.

"Love me, Cally." His honeyed voice made her tremble, and she realized he trembled too. His kisses became urgent, hungry. The bewildering sensations intensified.

Cally didn't want the feelings to end, but their power frightened her. She clung to Andrew, pulling him more tightly against her. Her gown had worked its way up to her waist, and his leg nudged between hers until he made contact with her most intimate spot.

The jolt from the contact made her jump, and she would have hit her head on the floor if he hadn't been cradling it with one hand while he plundered her lips. There were too many mysterious feelings to keep track of them all. At the same time she knew they somehow weren't enough. She had to get closer to ease the yearning that built apace with the pleasure.

She didn't know that her response to his first kiss had seemed like an invitation, that the way she clung to him now drove Andrew beyond the point of reason. As he hadn't realized that he loved her until he had said it, he hadn't realized how hungry he was for her until he had found her in his arms. He had just enough restraint left to enter her slowly, to stroke her back to passion again before he moved, to carefully, slowly, carry her over the brink with him.

The earth exploded. Cally thought she had died and floated up to heaven, but gradually she found herself drifting back to earth. She was on the floor beside Andrew, her head on his shoulder, his arms wrapped around her and one leg thrown over hers.

He kissed her temple. "Did I hurt you, sweetheart?"

Cally didn't feel hurt. Curiously tired, perhaps, and maybe a little sore. She shook her head.

So this was what it felt like to be loved. She had never imagined it would be so glorious. Now she was Andrew's mate! She wouldn't have to go back to the Gwynns' ever again! She snuggled against him.

Andrew held her close to his side. It felt so right for her to be there. In fact nothing had ever seemed so right before. But *seemed* was a key word here. Cally had never been part of his plans, and he didn't change his plans easily.

"I'm not sure this was a good idea," he said gently. "No. That's a lie. I know it wasn't a good idea. We rushed into this without thinking." He hugged her a little closer. "Though I don't know how I could have resisted you.

"I don't mean that I blame you," he added hastily. "I take full responsibility for what happened. I'm older, and I knew you were innocent. I should have found the willpower—somewhere."

He waited for a response and decided she was digesting what he had said. He ran back through it in his mind and realized it sounded like he regretted their intimacy. "I do love you, Cally. I don't want you to doubt it. And I didn't mean to take advantage of you, or anything like that. It's just that I'm not sure love is always enough."

He expected some kind of outburst. When did Cally ever listen quietly and reflectively? "Cally?" He stroked her cheek before tilting her chin upward. She was sound asleep. "Wake up, sweetheart." He planted a kiss on her lips.

She stirred and then smiled at him. "I don't want to wake up."

He almost groaned. "You have to, Cally," he said softly. "You have to go home."

"I am home."

"No, sweetheart. You're at my house. You have to go back to the Gwynns'."

"No, I don't," she murmured, trying to reach his mouth with her lips.

It was all Andrew could do not to cooperate. He shook himself. "Yes, you do, Cally. Come on." He sat up, bringing her with him. "You have to get back before they miss you."

Cally rubbed her eyes. Through the window she could see a faint hint of dawn. "It doesn't matter if they miss me. I'll stay with you."

Andrew ran his fingers through her hair, attempting, she supposed, to untangle it. "Try to understand, sweetheart. You can't stay here. It'll ruin your reputation. And mine. I'm a sheriff. I have to run for re-election. I can't have a woman living with me. I think there may even be a clause against it in my lease."

Cally came awake real fast. A shiver of alarm replaced the warm tingles. "Why would they care if we were married?"

Andrew didn't answer, and the sisters' conversation came back to her. She tried one more time to make things right. "Don't you want to marry me?"

"Well, Cally, I need some time to think about it. I've never believed law officers should be married. They lose their edge. Most people agree with me, I'm afraid."

"Most people" evidently meant the voters. And she knew that tone he used. It was his patient-and-reasonable tone. The tone she could learn to hate.

"You don't have to be a sheriff," she suggested, thinking to be as reasonable. He *had* said he loved her. Shouldn't she be the most important thing in the world to him?

"But I *am* the sheriff. I *like* being sheriff. I want to continue being sheriff."

Cally watched him with narrowed eyes. "Even after—" she glanced at the rug and looked away "—what happened, you won't marry me?"

He hesitated. "I'm not saying I won't marry you. I need some time to think about it. And so do you. Whatever we decide, right now, you need to get back to the sisters before they miss you."

He was so calm it made her furious. "The old ladies were right! You just wanted the nectar! And now I'm a fallen woman."

"Cally! Wait a minute!" Before Andrew could catch her, she was on her feet, running for the door. "Let me walk you home! Cally!"

Andrew grabbed his pants, trying to step into them as he followed. She went out the door without bothering to close it behind her. "Cally."

By the time he was outside, she was headed full speed down his lane, Royal on her heels. She probably wouldn't stop until she got to the Gwynns'. He had to let her go.

"Royal. Come back, boy." The dog at least obeyed.

He knelt beside Royal and rubbed his ears to encourage the dog to stay in the yard. He was absolutely certain that his yelling had awakened all his neighbors. Any of them could have seen the white-gowned girl fleeing from his house. They were, no doubt, watching him through their windows and guessing why hc was clad only in pants, unbuttoncd pants at that.

"This is not good, Royal," he murmured.

Royal seemed unconcerned. When Andrew stood to go back into the house, Royal trotted off in the direction Cally had taken. The dog knew where she lived now and no chain was going to hold him.

Andrew called Royal back and the dog obeyed. With a sigh, he let him into the house. Queen followed, spreading herself across the threshold as soon as the door was closed.

"Oh, wonderful," Andrew muttered.

Royal followed him into the living room and stood at his side when Andrew sagged into a chair. Andrew rested his hand on the dog's head as he gazed into the dying fire. He had just seduced an innocent girl. A girl he had promised to look out for. He had been honest when he said he loved her, but equally honest when he said he didn't want to marry her. She was more likely to believe the latter than the former. Maybe it didn't pay to be honest with women.

More likely, honesty wasn't the problem. Fairness was. She had every right to be furious with him.

Andrew sighed. Surely there was some solution he could be comfortable with. He stared at the embers for a long moment before he whispered, "Nectar?"

Val Milton padded across the hall in his stocking feet. At Fancy's door he stopped, looked up and down the hall once more then reached for the doorknob. The knob didn't move. The little minx had locked the door!

From an inside coat pocket he withdrew his collection of picks. He didn't have Terris's skill at safecracking; still, he could manage a simple lock or two. The soft click told him he had been successful. He slipped inside, closing the door as quietly as possible.

Pale moonlight streamed through the window. Of course Fancy hadn't pulled the shade; she didn't like the dark. Val smiled as he walked toward the bed. He studied the curvaceous body outlined beneath the sheet as he undressed.

The bedsprings squeaked when he slipped in beside her. He lay still for a moment, listening to her even breathing. Her back was to him and he reached out, caressing the warm skin on her shoulder. When his hand moved down to her firm hips, she sighed. He trailed his hand up her side and slipped it around her to fondle a soft breast.

Her body responded to his touch before the sleep left her brain. She moaned, scooting her backside against him. "Val?" she murmured.

Who in the hell was she expecting? The sheriff, maybe? He tried to brush his jealousy aside, reminding himself that she had locked her door. She hadn't been expecting anyone. "You wake up so sweetly, my love," he murmured.

She sighed, pressing his hand more firmly against her breast. "You're full of such nice surprises."

Later, when they were both sated, Val stared at the ceiling while Fancy cuddled up against him. He thought she had fallen asleep until she asked, "Do you have a plan yet?"

He shifted slightly as he considered how much to tell her. "Not completely. I have a few problems to iron out. Do you think you can lure Haywood away when the time comes?''

She took her time answering. When she did, it wasn't what Val wanted to hear. "I think he's in love.''

Val had to force himself to relax. "What makes you think so?" he asked, trying to sound unconcerned.

"He ignores me," she said with a pout.

Val let out a sigh of relief. It wasn't Fancy the sheriff was in love with.

Fancy continued, "I can sit right in front of him, and you'd think he didn't see me at all.''

Val wanted to laugh but thought better of it. Fancy wasn't likely to take it well. "He just pretends not to notice you, sweetheart," he soothed. "If we can find out who this lover is, we might be able to use her. Your brother could forge a note to lead him into a trap. Something like that. See what you can find out.''

He felt her head nod. She yawned and cuddled closer.

"Fancy?" He waited for her response before he went on. "Don't try too hard to get the sheriff to notice you.''

She had the audacity to giggle.

"Could I have some time off this morning?" Cally asked Noella after breakfast. "I haven't done my morning chores yet.''

"Did you oversleep, Cally?" she asked coldly.

"Yes, ma'am," Cally lied. She hadn't wanted to go back to Andrew's until she knew he was gone.

"You may go then, but don't make a habit of it. A maid has no business sleeping late."

Easter cast her a quick smile while Noella wasn't looking. "Were you up late reading, dear?"

"I can't read," Cally answered absently. She would have to come up with different excuses each day if she hoped to avoid seeing Haywood ever again.

Noella's stern voice interrupted her thoughts. "Well, that doesn't matter. I don't see why a maid needs to be able to read, do you, Easter? No," she answered for her sister. "It isn't necessary at all. Well, clean up the dishes, and you may go. But don't dawdle."

Cally watched Noella leave the room. She thought about asking Easter how she would know for sure if she and Andrew had made a baby but decided Easter probably didn't know. Besides she couldn't possibly tell her what she had done. And now he wouldn't even marry her to make it right!

She realized that Easter had been watching her brood. She grabbed a pile of dirty dishes and hurried to the kitchen. She didn't know Easter had followed her until the woman spoke. "I could teach you how to read if you'd like. We could work during Noella's afternoon nap."

Cally was startled. "But don't you nap, too?"

"Oh my, no! I read!"

That same morning Andrew put off leaving for his office as long as he could. He wanted to talk to Cally. He had done her chores so she would have time to listen to him. He had even milked the cow.

By the time he decided he had to leave, he was

sure she wasn't coming at all. He put the milk in a jar and put it in his icebox, then wanting her to find it, he drew a picture of his back door with Queen in her usual place. The open icebox and the jar were visible through an imaginary hole in the wall. He tacked the drawing to the barn door. He wanted to leave another note asking her to come to the office to see him, but was uncertain how to get that point across in a drawing.

Royal was his next problem. If Cally did come, he would follow her. There was little use chaining him up again. With a sigh, he called the dog to his side, and was about to head for the office when his deputy hailed him.

"Swineferd's at it again," Bill said, catching his breath. "His boy came in."

"Poor kid," Andrew said, already turning toward the corral. "Where is he now?"

"I left him at the office," Bill said as he followed, "but I doubt if he'll wait very long. Somehow he thinks he ought to be able to protect his mother. I told him coming in was the best thing to do."

"Keep him there as long as you can."

"Don't you want me to come with you?" Bill asked. If he noticed the odd picture tacked to the barn door he didn't comment.

Andrew threw the saddle on his mare's back. "No. Stay with the boy. I'll take my new partner." He indicated Royal with a tilt of his head.

Bill nodded rather quizzically but headed back toward the office without further comment.

In a few minutes, Andrew and Royal were on their way.

* * *

Cally wondered briefly if she was the only person in the world who didn't have an icebox. It seemed strange to go into Andrew's house and get the jar of milk. Cally was sure that was what he intended her to do or he wouldn't have drawn the picture. Just the same, she went in and out as quickly as possible.

Cally saved the picture he had tacked to the barn door. She wasn't sure why, but it didn't seem right to leave it out in the weather. She tucked it away in her old trunk.

She spent the morning trying to tell herself she shouldn't be worried about Royal. Andrew's horse was gone as well. Royal never wandered away. The dog had to be with Andrew. But where was Andrew?

The sisters hadn't given her any jobs to do during the afternoon, and, by the time she cleared the table from lunch, Cally was considering a visit to the sheriff's office just to reassure herself. Not that she wanted to see Andrew again! She just wanted to check up on her dog.

When Easter came into the kitchen after lunch, Cally had to fight back a groan. The old lady must have thought of something. She steeled herself before she turned toward her. "Yes?" she asked.

"Books!" Easter's eyes sparkled as she laid a stack on the table. "None are really meant to be primers, but I think we can make do." She sat down at the table and began dividing the books into different piles. "You ought to buy a slate and chalk next time you're at the store. They still use slate and chalk, I believe. Some things won't ever change."

Cally watched with a mixture of excitement and

fear. What if it was too late to learn to read? What if she wasn't smart enough? She approached the table slowly as Easter seemed to settle on a particular book.

"Ah, poems," the old woman said. "Let's see. Where shall we start?"

Cally took the seat beside Easter, all other concerns momentarily brushed aside.

Andrew led the still-swearing drunk to the cell and locked him in before he removed the handcuffs.

"You got no call for this, Sheriff. She's my wife," Swineferd slurred for the twentieth time. "I can do as I please."

Andrew didn't comment. He tossed the keys on the desk in front of Bill and muttered, "I'm going to dinner."

Andrew was so angry at Swineferd he had been tempted to beat the daylights out of him, to give him a taste of what he liked to give his wife. The woman had managed to hide from the lout, and their son had gone for help. This time.

The son hadn't liked leaving his mother in danger, and Bill had only managed to keep him in town long enough to give Andrew a head start. Next time, the boy would likely shoot his old man. What kind of way was that to start a life?

Andrew knew he would be forced to let Swineferd out of jail in the morning. Without his wife's signed complaint he couldn't charge him, and he could almost bet that she wouldn't sign one. Andrew would wait for her to come to take her husband home, and try to convince her. In the past, she had always tried to assure the sheriff that she would be fine.

With Royal at his side, Andrew decided to walk around town, burn up some of his frustration before going to dinner. In front of the Antlers, he nearly collided with Val Milton.

Royal growled but quieted after a word from Andrew.

"Well, hello, Sheriff." The gambler greeted him cheerfully, keeping an eye on the big dog. "Can I buy you a drink?"

"No, thanks," he said, almost absently. "I was on my way to dinner."

"Dinner then." Milton clapped him on the shoulder and suggested a restaurant across the street. "Kind of late for dinner, isn't it, Sheriff? Hard morning?" He stepped out of the way when Royal decided to cross the street between the two men.

"A little long, I guess. And yourself?"

Milton shrugged and didn't speak again until they were seated in the restaurant, with Royal lying under the table. Andrew could tell the dog made the gambler nervous, but the mood he was in, he didn't care.

"That little farm I won isn't exactly what I expected," the gambler said finally.

Andrew chuckled, nodding his understanding. "It is a bit run-down."

Milton's eyes widened at the understatement. After ordering steaks, Milton added, "I've decided to sell it as soon as possible. I'm not cut out for farming, and Salina's a little too tame for me to—shall we say, pursue my chosen profession?"

Andrew nodded absently, thinking more about the drunken Swineferd than what Milton was saying.

Milton continued, "I may have even found a buyer.

The fella who owns the place next to it made me an offer. Ned something or other.''

"Ned Christianson," Andrew provided. Suddenly he came alert. "Ned's buying Cal...the DuBois farm?"

Milton nodded, interest in his eyes. "He didn't offer me much, though.''

Andrew remembered Cally's dislike for Ned because he had always wanted her farm. If her trip to the garden was any indication, the poor girl still thought of the place as hers. Losing it to Ned would be another hard blow, and she had had too many already.

"What did he offer?" he found himself asking. He hadn't thought about doing this. It was just a whim. He never did anything on a whim. He was, in fact, the most deliberate person he knew.

Until today. He waited expectantly for Milton's answer.

"Fifteen dollars an acre. Can you believe that? And there are only ten acres left. The rest of the original claim already belongs to this Ned. He said what's left is mostly creek, and I have to agree that DuBois' idea of improvements doesn't raise the value much.''

"The going price for farmland is closer to twenty," Andrew said.

Milton laughed. "You think you can find me a better offer?''

"I'll make you a better offer. I'll pay twenty.''

Milton was pleased, perhaps a little too pleased, but Andrew barely noticed. He had bought Cally's farm from the gambler.

* * *

Val waited at the bar for a chance to slip into the back room of the Antlers. A trip to the bank after dinner had finalized the sale. The notion of selling the farm to the sheriff himself delighted his sense of irony. Stedwell, at least, would agree.

Terris was another matter. He was difficult to control to begin with, and was becoming more so. Val's plan was taking shape and the time was near, but he wanted everything to work perfectly.

Finally he saw his chance and slipped through the door. Terris stood near the peephole, his right knee resting on a chair. Stedwell, in the middle of a game of solitaire, offered Val a seat.

"Took you long enough to get in here," Terris said.

"I didn't want to be seen coming in." Val sat down with his back to Terris and listened to him hobbling around. He spoke mainly to Stedwell. "I sold the farm to none other than Haywood himself."

Stedwell grinned. "We should go into business together with these gambling debts."

Val eyed him until the grin faded. "Yeah, I forgot. I'm supposed to drop out of Fancy's life. What does she think about this, by the way?"

"She doesn't know. And she isn't going to."

Stedwell raised a hand in surrender. After a moment he asked, "What's the next step?"

Val watched Terris join them at the table before he spoke. "We still need a place to stash the stolen money."

"How about Haywood's office?" suggested Stedwell.

Val nodded. "Or the alley behind it. It's in the middle of town, though. Haywood's house is better."

Terris growled, "You can check it out any time you want to."

Val decided not to comment. "There are a couple other things that need to be ironed out as well. And you, Terris, will need to be able to move faster than you can now."

"Don't worry about me," Terris growled. "Say, if you sold the farm, how about splitting Haywood's money? Before you forget."

Val hesitated a moment. "If Haywood's the thorough lawman you two claim, he might check back with the banker. He's liable to become suspicious of Fancy if she doesn't deposit any money. I thought I'd give it to her."

Terris caught him by his shirtfront and hauled him up against the wall. "Think again. According to this half-baked plan of yours, the bank's money frames Haywood and goes straight back to the damn bank. We get nothing! Nothing!" He punctuated the last with a shake that knocked Milton's head against the plank wall.

"But revenge," Stedwell put in, a tad too cheerfully for Val's peace of mind.

"You're right," Val said quickly. He raised his hands to the safecracker in supplication as Terris slowly let him go. He adjusted his shirt and cravat, thinking fast. "Of course, you're right." For a moment he had forgotten. *He* didn't plan to leave a dollar of the money behind. He prayed he hadn't already given too much away. He reached for his wallet, handing each of his companions twenty-five dollars.

"You sold the farm damn cheap," accused Terris.

"It's a little farm." Terris reached for him again, and Val took a step back. He had let Terris surprise him once. He didn't plan to let it happen again. "This place isn't free. Neither is the hotel. When we're ready to move, I'll divide whatever's left."

Terris reluctantly gave in, and Val prepared to leave. He gave Stedwell one last glance as he slipped out the door. The forger had watched the proceedings just a little too placidly. Surely he wasn't considering a plan of his own.

Chapter Twelve

Andrew couldn't believe he had bought Cally's farm. It had felt right at the time. He had done it for the woman he loved. Even after thinking about it for a while it still felt right. It just didn't feel sane.

He walked slowly toward the Gwynns' house, Royal at his side. He had some notion of telling her what he had done. The more he thought however, the more slowly he walked.

What was he going to do, give it to her for her birthday? A farm was a somewhat extravagant gift. And if he didn't plan to turn the place back over to the girl, how was she any better off than if Ned had bought it?

His logical nature made him feel he should make sense of his own behavior. He reminded himself that, from time to time, he had thought it would be nice to own his own home. Of course, the home he had just bought was barely habitable. Then again, he reminded himself, he owned the land so he could build a new house.

He also owned Cally's garden. Whatever else he

might decide, he did want to let her know she was free to raid her garden any time she pleased. He and Royal were halfway to the Gwynns' house before he started to see the situation from Cally's point of view.

He was the sheriff who had arrested her father, let him die in his cell, then taken her farm from her for the gambler. He looked down at Royal and added stealing her pets to his list of offenses. He was also the man who had seduced her and refused to marry her. She wasn't going to see his ownership of her farm as an improvement.

He could argue that he hadn't exactly refused to marry her. He had just asked for time. But he knew that he wanted the time to convince her that marriage was a poor idea.

He shook his head, turning around to go back. He realized he had carried on an entire argument with Cally without her being present. Not a good sign.

On the back-street route home, he came face-to-face with the subject of his thoughts. "Cally, you've done the chores already? Can I help you carry things home?"

Cally narrowed her eyes and kept walking. Andrew and Royal fell into step on either side of her. "We need to talk, Cally," Andrew said gently.

"No, we don't."

"Listen to me, please." Lord, he didn't know where to start. "I meant it when I said I love you. You need to believe that."

Cally stopped and turned toward him. "I can't believe it. I won't believe it. Not when you won't marry me. But it doesn't matter, because I don't want to marry you, anyway. I don't want to ever see you again.'' Her chin high, she marched toward the Gwynns'.

Royal started to follow her, but Andrew called him back. With a sigh, Andrew watched her go before turning his own steps toward home. He wanted to talk to her, but he didn't know what to say. He needed to sort some things out for himself first. He would call on her tomorrow.

By the time he stepped over Queen and entered his house, followed by both dogs, he decided that love did strange things to a man's mind. Perhaps it would be better to think about anything but Cally for a while. He would pretend he was the same rational man he had been before he met her. He would plan the house he wanted to build on her farm.

His farm, he corrected himself. He tried it aloud. ''My farm.'' Heaven help him, it just didn't sound right.

Cally could see a light burning in one of the downstairs rooms of Andrew's house. The room where they had made love. She stood in the shadows for a moment, watching. She had to fight the temptation to sneak up to the window and see what he was doing this late at night.

Shaking off the foolish notion, she reminded herself why she was here. She had wanted to take Royal with her to stand guard, but neither of the dogs was anywhere in sight. Perhaps Andrew had locked them both in the barn.

She tried to work up her old hatred for the man who would treat her dogs so cruelly, but she knew he wasn't cruel to her animals. Any thought of Andrew at all brought a hollow feeling inside. "He's cruel to me," she muttered under her breath, hoping to dismiss him from her mind.

She hurried to the barn, opening the door only a crack before slipping inside. No dogs greeted her. In a matter of minutes, she led Jewel out and closed the door behind her. "I guess it's just us tonight," she whispered before she swung onto the mule's back.

She wore one of the gray dresses, and it hiked up to her knees. "Stupid dress," she muttered, angry again with herself for getting caught in the pants. She had used some of Pa's clothes to protect her jars during the move into town, and she had searched through them. There wasn't anything there that would be wearable without considerable sewing. She had hopes of remodeling some of them sometime, but she really hated to sew.

She hoped Easter could talk Noella into letting her have some bloomers. The pictures in the catalog looked funny to her, but Easter seemed to think the short flounce of a skirt made them less scandalous than men's pants.

The ride to the farm was lonely without Royal, and she missed having him to stand guard while she gathered things from the garden. Still, the place felt empty to her. She supposed the gambler was staying in town. For a moment, she wondered if he would let her live here since he didn't want to. She shook her head. If he didn't want to live here he would be looking for someone to buy it.

She had sold a few cans of tomatoes from Mr. Lafferty's feed store, and Andrew had left the confiscated squash there to be sold too. However, the money was not coming in as fast as she had hoped. If she was ever to buy her farm back she would have to rob a bank!

When her bag was filled with squash and one small pumpkin, she straddled Jewel and headed for town. She stopped at the creek and listened but no one waited for her. She must have slipped past Andrew after all. She tried to tell herself she wasn't disappointed.

When Jewel was safely in the barn with the door closed behind her, Cally crept into the shadows. It occurred to her that Andrew might have decided to wait until her return to catch her. She wondered if she would have to kiss him again to keep from going to jail. She felt a tremor in her stomach just thinking about it. Yet if she let him kiss her again, that hollow place would just get bigger.

Studying the house and yard, she tried to guess where he might be waiting. Probably along the lane, her usual way to leave. Maybe she should cut across the neighbors' yard.

The same light still glowed in the windows. The sack clutched in her hands, she moved toward the house, trying to stay in the shadows.

She crouched under a window, gathering enough nerve to look inside. She would be in more trouble if he caught her peeking in his window than she would for raiding her garden. How could she ever explain why she was spying on him? She had made it to the farm and back without his knowing; she shouldn't be pushing her luck.

She was checking on her dogs. She didn't care why Andrew was up late. Of course, if she saw him she would know he wasn't waiting for her elsewhere. That was why she hoped to see him. The only reason. Her heart was pounding only from the fear of being caught.

She set the sack on the ground and craned her neck to see inside. Sheriff Haywood was sprawled in a chair, fast asleep. His sketches were everywhere. One even lay on Royal's back while he slept curled up beside the chair.

Cally squinted, trying to make out the pictures and decided they were of some house or other. At least he hadn't stayed up late drawing pictures of that beautiful woman. Of course she wouldn't have cared if he had! They were both just flowers to the bee!

He had taken off his boots and gun belt and loosened his shirt at the throat. His normally perfect hair was mussed; his face peaceful in sleep. He looked rather pleasing, she decided. She tipped her head to one side, trying to stop the smile that curled her lips. Actually the whole scene was charming, the handsome man asleep by the dying fire, the dog sitting beside his chair.

The dog *sitting* beside the chair! Cally dropped to the ground, her heart racing again. Royal had seen her! He would wake Andrew any second! She grabbed the sack of squash and ran.

A pain in the side of Andrew's neck brought him awake just before dawn. He groaned and massaged it, causing several sketches to flutter to the floor. As he flexed stiff muscles, he remembered what he had been doing the night before. Wanting to become engrossed in something that would keep his mind off Cally, he had stayed up late planning a new house. "A little too late," he muttered, ruffling Royal's fur as the dog came to his feet and stretched.

Andrew reached for one of the sketches that cluttered the floor. The picture startled him. He grabbed another, then another. He glanced at all the pictures in turn, stacking them on his lap. He tried closing his eyes for a moment and looking at them again. It didn't help.

With a groan, he collapsed back into the chair. In every drawing, no matter what style he had drawn the house, he had included a tiny sketch of Cally, or Royal, or Queen, or all three. A face at a window. A figure in the yard. He hadn't been able to imagine his house without them—without her.

There was no way around it. He was going to share his life with Cally. Somehow she had wormed her way into his heart. Her courage, her tenacity, her loyalty, even her tomboy ways made him love her. And the fact that he didn't want a wife didn't change it.

It occurred to him then that she had never said she loved him. Dear little Cally. It wouldn't be fair to her to marry him if she didn't love him. He thought for a moment that he had hit on a perfect excuse, but it evaporated just as quickly. Of course she loved him. He would see to that.

But a week later Andrew had made no progress in his plan to win Cally. She had become very good at avoiding him. He seemed to be called out of town for minor altercations on a daily basis. The only thing he had managed to do was order lumber for his new house. The foundation had been started but the carpenters would have to stop once the frame was up. He couldn't decide on the room arrangement. He wanted to discuss it with Cally, but he was afraid of her reaction.

As he walked toward his favorite restaurant for lunch a sign in the window of the dry goods store caught his attention. "Dressmaker by appointment," it said.

The idea of seeing Cally in a dress like one of Francine's seemed too good a notion to dismiss. Besides, her birthday was only a few days away. Her guardian, of all people, should get her a present. He was smiling when he entered the store.

"Good afternoon, Sheriff." The proprietress greeted him from her place behind the counter. "Can I help you?"

"I hope so, Mrs. Walters," he said. He glanced around the store and was glad to see they were alone. "I'd like to make an appointment with the dressmaker."

Mrs. Walters placed a pair of half glasses on her nose and reached for a notebook under the counter. "When can the lady come in?"

"Well, I don't know that she can."

She looked at him over the glasses. "We have to have her measurements, Sheriff."

He hadn't thought of that. "She's this tall," he said, measuring against his chest, "and about this big around. That won't do, will it?" Mrs. Walters shook her head. "I wanted it to be a surprise."

The proprietress closed the book and removed her glasses, nodding sympathetically. "Perhaps something else. Is the lady a relative?"

He shook his head.

She smiled. "A sweetheart, then."

"No," he said quickly. "Just…uh…an acquaintance." At her raised eyebrows he added, "With a birthday."

"I see," she said. The expression on her face told him she didn't see at all. "Perhaps something a bit more practical then."

Andrew cringed. Something useful like a new milking stool? He didn't think so. This was turning out to be more difficult than he could have imagined. Mrs. Walters waited for a response. He took a deep breath. "I want to give her something pretty and feminine," he said. *Something intimate.* No, that thought was too dangerous.

"She's eighteen," he added, hoping Mrs. Walters could somehow name the perfect gift for an "acquaintance's" eighteenth birthday and let him escape.

Mrs. Walters moved out from behind her counter. "Something pretty and feminine," she repeated thoughtfully. She walked around the store. "We have reticules, and hats. Some lovely gloves. A hand mirror and brush set?"

She obviously had an erroneous picture of the young lady in question. Andrew saw no way of correcting her. Maybe it was his idea of the gift that was in error. Pretty and feminine? Should he reconsider the milking stool?

"We have some nice brooches."

Andrew stepped to her side. Of course! Something pretty to pin to the plain gray dresses she hated. Mrs. Walters set a felt-lined tray on top of the counter. She suggested a cameo of an elegant woman, but Andrew shook his head. His eyes were drawn to the simplest pin on the tray.

Mrs. Walters smiled at his choice. "Can I wrap that for you?"

Andrew was about to agree when the door opened and three housewives came in. They greeted him formally then stood and openly watched him. "If you could just put it in a box," he said, reaching for his wallet.

In a few minutes he stepped outside, the box tucked in his shirt pocket. At the restaurant he placed his order and, while he waited, retrieved the little box. The pin was perfect for Cally, he thought. It was unpretentious, simple but beautiful. It spoke to him of things not quite tame, things far hardier than they appeared. He touched a finger to the tiny bouquet of gold wildflowers and whispered, "Cally."

Cally finished polishing a silver knife and reached for another. She had been told to polish all the silver, presumably for the dinner party. But, as far as Cally knew, the party was still just talk. If it never amounted to more than that, she would be happy. Meanwhile, however, she wasted her time on things like polishing silver.

When she heard the knock on the door, she put the polish-coated rag aside and started to wipe her hands on her apron. Catching herself, she grabbed one of the clean rags. Miss Noella had been harping at her lately about how dirty her apron got. She had wanted to offer to wear an apron over her apron to protect it but didn't think the old lady would appreciate the comment.

The knock was repeated, and she heard Noella's shrill voice from the parlor. "Cally! Get the door."

"I was halfway to the door before you screeched," she muttered. She caught herself muttering a lot lately.

She quickly called to mind the proper way to greet a guest. *Good morning. May I help you?* It wasn't as if Noella hadn't drilled it into her, it was just something she hadn't had to use but once or twice. The old ladies didn't get many callers.

Cally turned the knob on the big door and dragged it open. "Good morn—" The words died on her lips.

"Good morn, yourself, Cally," Andrew said. "Can I come in?"

"No." The word came out a croak. She quickly stepped through the door, pushing Andrew precariously close to the edge of the porch as she closed the door behind her. She couldn't imagine why he was here. She hadn't seen him for three days, not since she had spied on him. "I told you not to come here."

The man just grinned. "I want to ask you on a picnic tomorrow afternoon." He didn't even keep his voice down.

She tried to set an example by whispering, "You know I can't do that."

"But Cally, tomorrow's Sunday. Surely you get Sunday afternoon off?"

Cally just stared at him. The Gwynns hadn't suggested she take any time off. Perhaps she was supposed to ask. It just hadn't occurred to her. She had never taken a day off on the farm.

She shook herself. What was she thinking? She didn't want to take time off to be with *him!* "No!"

she said with emphasis, reaching for the doorknob behind her.

"But Cally, tomorrow's your..."

"Cally! Who's out there?" The door swung open just as her fingers closed over the knob, and Cally nearly stumbled into Noella.

Andrew actually smiled! "Good morning, Miss Gwynn."

Cally was dragged back across the threshold before she could even turn around. She was thrust behind Noella, who then ignored her and turned to Andrew.

"Good morning, Sheriff," Noella said. "What brings you to our door?"

Cally tried to lean around the old lady and shake her head at Andrew but Noella blocked the way. She heard Andrew say, "I came to call on Miss Dubois," and rolled her eyes to heaven.

Easter, probably attracted by the small commotion, an event in this household, came into the hall. "Do we have a visitor?" she asked.

Noella barked "No," over her shoulder. "Is it business, sir?" Cally thought she nearly barked that too.

"Well, no. I just—"

"I'm sorry, Sheriff. Cally has work to do and no time to entertain callers."

"But when can—?" Andrew's question was interrupted by the closing of the door.

Noella turned her haughty nose toward Cally. "You are not to receive male callers."

"I didn't receive him," Cally protested.

"You were talking to him, and he looked quite happy to me."

"I was trying to tell him to go away," Cally protested. Really, these women were impossible to please.

Noella rose to her full height. "Don't you suppose saying no and closing the door would have been more effective than stepping out with him?"

Cally considered telling the old woman she could have spit in his face, that in fact she had a time or two, but she knew the look of horror that was so rewarding would be followed by some especially unpleasant housecleaning. Instead, she tried to act sorry. "He is the sheriff," she reminded Noella.

"She's right," said Easter, wringing her hands. "He is."

Noella seemed to think it over. "I suppose it is understandable for you to be intimidated by Mr. Haywood because of his office. You can be forgiven for thinking you needed to talk to him. Now you have seen my example and will follow it in the future. You may return to the polishing."

Cally knew she was supposed to be grateful for getting off so easily. She was expected to lower her eyes and thank the old woman for her kindness. A curtsy wouldn't hurt. Cally looked her in the eye for a good five seconds before turning toward the dining room. She heard Noella's sharp intake of breath and expected to be called back.

But she wasn't. Cally had to smile to herself. The poor old lady found her particularly hard to train. She had overheard her telling Easter this morning that she suspected Cally of being slow-witted. Easter, in protesting that she seemed bright enough to her, had almost let the reading lessons slip.

Noella hadn't been listening, anyway. She had half a mind, she told Easter, to complain to Haywood about sending them such a foolish child. Well, she had had her chance a minute ago. Had she complained?

She wished she could have seen Haywood's face when Noella closed the door. He wasn't used to being treated like that. She wondered if he was angry, surprised or determined to try again.

Cally sighed as she picked up the rag and reached for another knife. She almost hoped he would try again. A picnic on Sunday would be delightful. Even with Haywood, she forced herself to add.

That evening when Cally went to Haywood's to do the chores, she found a picture tacked to Belle's stall. It showed a quilt spread on the ground under a tree. A man and woman sat on the quilt. A building easily recognizable as Haywood's barn was in the background. She carefully folded the picture, tucked it in the bib of her apron and tried not to think about it as she did her chores.

It rustled when she bumped it. It poked her when she bent to lift the milk bucket. It warmed her skin with the memory of his touch.

Back in her bedroom at the Gwynns' she lit a lamp and sat with the drawing in her lap as she took the pins out of her hair. The man in the drawing was in his shirtsleeves. Cally knew he was handsome, though his face was turned toward the woman. She wore a white apron over a pencil-shaded dress. They each held a glass while bread and fruit were scattered between them on the blanket. The drawing was an invitation she didn't want to refuse.

But she must, she knew. Even though she missed him terribly, she couldn't let herself fall into his arms again. The fever came back to her every time she thought about that night, which was every time she thought about *him*. Which, she realized, was nearly all the time. And with the fever was this empty feeling, because he didn't want to be with her always.

Cally stood and dropped the sketch into her trunk. She mustn't think about that night, or Andrew, or kisses. But she had little else to think about. She felt more and more restless every day. And more lonesome.

She gave herself an hour to try to sleep, then gave up. She quietly dressed and slipped out of the house.

As she slid Andrew's barn door open, she tried to think of an excuse for raiding her garden tonight. She didn't need any more squash yet, though the Gwynns certainly enjoyed it. It sold fairly well at Lafferty's, and she would have harvested it all if there had been a way to bring that much back to town.

Perhaps she simply needed to get away from the old ladies' house and see her farm again. It couldn't possibly be that she wanted to see Andrew. Of course not. She never wanted to see him again.

She jumped on Jewel's back and tried to adjust her dress so she wasn't quite so uncomfortable. She rode out of the yard without more than a glance at the house. No lights were shining through the windows anyway.

As soon as she was out of town, she voiced all her problems to Jewel. "It's not fair, none of it. I don't want to be a maid. I miss working in my garden. I miss the soddy, too. The bed may be nicer at the Gwynns' but it isn't *my* bed! I miss having Royal by my side. And you and Belle and Queen, too, of course. I even miss chasing off Andr...Sheriff Haywood.''

To top it all off, she couldn't stop worrying that she might be carrying Andrew's baby. She had tried to call upon all her limited knowledge of the subject. Her restlessness itself was reassuring, when she considered Belle. In order for the cow to keep producing milk, she had to be bred about once a year. Cally always knew it was time to take her to Ned, who would put her with his bull, when the normally placid cow became restless and flighty. Cally thought she knew the feeling. When she brought Belle home again the cow would have settled back down, and Cally would know she was bred.

Cally didn't feel settled down! She felt more restless than ever. A good sign, she hoped.

However, when she thought about breeding Belle it worried her, too. Belle had *always* been bred. She always had nice little calves that Cally had to turn over to Ned as payment when they were just a few weeks old.

By the time she reached her farm she was having a regular pity party, as Pa would have said. She left Jewel at the creek and approached on foot. She was almost to her garden when she stopped to study her house. It felt empty, the same as it had before. Yet something was different.

Odd shadows in front of it caught her attention, and she stepped closer to investigate. She couldn't help the sudden intake of breath. An enormous supply of lumber had been stacked here and there around the yard. Someone was building a house!

The gambler had sold the farm, or he had decided to stay. Either way there was no chance now of her getting it back. It would never be her farm again! She turned and ran to Jewel, scrambled onto her back and started her toward town.

What was she going to do? Would she have to spend her whole life as a maid? It was easy to guess what the sisters would do if she had a baby. They would throw her out. Where would she go? Somehow she had convinced herself that she would get her farm back; if she had a baby, she would raise it there. But now that chance was gone forever.

By the time she rode Jewel into Andrew's yard, she felt desperate. How and when would she know if she was pregnant? How long could she keep it a secret? Her knees shook when she dismounted. For some odd reason she wanted to run inside to Andrew. He was the cause of all her troubles, she reminded herself. Why should she want to lean against his chest and feel his bare skin against her cheek? How could it help to have his arms around her?

As she led Jewel to her stall she realized she knew the answer to those questions. None of the rest, not the farm, not the baby, would matter if Andrew would marry her, if she could be his forever. She was so caught up in her misery as she left the barn that when she found Andrew waiting for her outside, she went straight into his arms.

Royal had awakened Andrew when Cally first came into the yard. He had considered following, but there was no one at the farm to bother her. Let her make her midnight raid, he had decided. Then he had lain awake worrying about her. He had been so relieved to see her come back that he had gone to meet her without a second thought.

He hadn't expected her to walk into his arms. At first he was elated, then he was concerned. This wasn't like her. "Cally, sweetheart, what's wrong?" She shook her head and let him guide her to the house.

Inside his kitchen he lit a lamp. "Are you hurt? Cally, please talk to me."

All she did was shake her head. And cling to him.

Lord, what could have happened? He held her away at arm's length and studied her face. She was fighting tears or terror, he wasn't sure which. "Cally, did someone hurt you?"

She shook her head.

"Then tell me what's wrong."

She seemed about to speak then shrugged. "It's nothing," she said, collapsing back against his chest.

Andrew cradled her in his arms and stroked her hair, knocking pins loose until it all fell freely over her shoulders. He tried to think what could have caused her such worry. "Cally," he whispered. "Was it something I did?"

She shook her head. Then she nodded, pounding a small fist ineffectually on his chest. In a moment she was clinging to him again.

Quite suddenly it occurred to him. She was pregnant!

Chapter Thirteen

Of course knowing she was pregnant would make Cally too upset to speak. And he had refused to marry her! Andrew felt like a worm.

"Sweetheart, it'll be all right," he crooned. "I'll take care of you." He smiled to himself. It felt good to say it. He said it again. "I'll take care of you."

She pulled away and delivered one more punch to his chest. "I don't want you to take care of me." It came out just above a whisper. She took a deep breath. "I can take care of myself," she said more firmly.

"But if there's a baby..." he started.

"I don't know if there's a baby. I don't know how to know. Belle never showed for months, but I'm still restless. Maybe it's different, but I can't talk to anybody." Her voice had grown softer until it was a whisper.

Andrew thought he understood most of it. The key points at least. She didn't know how to know? Obviously her father had neglected her education. Hadn't she had any women friends? Andrew cuddled her

against his chest. He wanted to convince her that
whatever happened he loved her. But he could understand her need to know.

"Your...uh...monthlies, Cally. When was the last
one?" He took her shoulders gently and turned her
toward him when she would have turned away. He
had put it as delicately as he could, but she blushed
bright red. He would have thought it looked rather
cute if the subject weren't so serious.

She glared at him, evidently angry that he had em-
barrassed her. Lord, she was difficult to understand.
Finally she spoke, trying to sound tough. "It just finished, but I don't see how that matters."

Andrew hadn't realized he was holding his breath
until he let it out all at once. At least their shaky
relationship didn't have that to deal with at this point.
She eyed him suspiciously. He explained, "That's
how you know, Cally. When you're...with child, your
monthlies stop."

Her eyes had narrowed. Her worry had turned to
anger. What now? Then it occurred to him; she knew
he was relieved. Well, she should be, too. But it
wasn't quite the same.

He watched her straighten, toss her hair over her
shoulders and turn away. He reached out to catch her.
"Cally?"

She didn't turn back and he didn't follow. She
didn't believe he loved her, and he didn't know how
to convince her. He let her go.

"'I'll take care of you,' he says. '*If* there's a baby,'
he says. He doesn't care about me. Easter was right.
They don't want to make a baby, but they like

to…to…practice.'' Cally realized she was muttering out loud and tried to calm herself. It wouldn't do to be caught coming into the Gwynns' house talking to herself.

At least there wouldn't be a baby. She should be relieved. The knowledge did take away most of her fear. But she had been thinking about all of Belle's cute little calves she had turned over to Ned to raise. And she had even started picturing a tiny version of Andrew she could love forever.

Besides, she still wanted her farm, and she wanted to get away from the old ladies. Before their great dinner party, if possible. She would think of something.

She lay awake the rest of the night. She realized that if she left, she would miss Easter's reading lessons. What she was trying to teach her had just started to make sense. But that was all she would miss. And she thought she had a plan.

The next afternoon, Cally told Easter that she would have to skip the reading lesson. She had planned to demand time off since it was Sunday, but at the last minute she said she had some extra chores to do. She knew Easter wouldn't ask any questions. Neither old lady wanted to know any more than she had to about the livestock. They were glad to drink the milk and eat the eggs, squash and canned tomatoes, but they wanted to pretend they provided it. Cally would have sold it all at Lafferty's to avoid serving any to the old ladies if she hadn't wanted to eat some herself.

With the whole afternoon to do as she pleased,

Cally headed first to Andrew's for Jewel, then to her farm. From the cover of the trees, she sat for a few minutes, watching three men work on the new house. In the dark, she hadn't seen that the house was actually started.

She felt a little apprehensive about carrying out her plan now. She sat up a little straighter on the mule's back. Whoever meant to live here might need a housekeeper, she reminded herself. She would still be a maid, but at least she would have her garden back.

Deciding that riding in with her skirts hiked up to her knees wouldn't make a good impression, she dismounted and led Jewel forward. She walked slowly, shading her eyes with one hand and gathering her courage.

"Shame to spend Sunday afternoon working," she heard one of the men holler over the sound of three busy hammers.

"Once the roof's on we can slow up a bit." The older man paused a moment. "We're getting paid enough to compensate, anyhow."

Because of the noise, Cally was practically at the house and they still hadn't noticed her. "Good afternoon," she called.

All three men stopped and stared. The oldest found his voice first. "Howdy, ma'am. Can we do something for you?"

"Why yes, you can," she said, trying to sound proper like the old ladies. She was only a step or two from the structure and had to fight the urge to study it. "Who is building this house?" Afraid they might not want to answer she added, "I was just curious, you understand."

It was the oldest that spoke again. "We're building this house for the sheriff."

Cally felt her heart pound and her knees shake with anger. "Sheriff Haywood?" she asked, wanting to be absolutely sure.

"That's the one." The man actually smiled.

"Why that low-down, lying thief!"

She turned and stormed into the soddy. It was dark inside. The place was a mess. But the shotgun hung above the door, right where Andrew had left it.

When she walked back into the daylight, the three men were approaching her cautiously. The eldest spoke. "Ma'am? Are you all ri—?" All three stopped abruptly when they saw the shotgun. "Whoa now! Are you daft?"

"I'm not daft," she said. "I'm furious. Get off my land!"

"But Sheriff Haywood—" he began.

"Stole my farm." She brought the shotgun to her shoulder and all three men stepped back.

"Now, miss," the eldest tried again.

"I wouldn't mess with her, Pa. I say it's Haywood's problem."

Pa seemed to think it over as his sons backed away. Finally, rather self-consciously, he tipped his hat. "Ma'am," he offered before turning with the others to saddle his horse.

Cally watched them go with considerable satisfaction. Of course it wouldn't be long before Haywood heard and came to kick her off again. But it would be different this time.

Andrew carefully laid everything out on his kitchen table. Today was Cally's birthday, and he was determined that they would celebrate it with a picnic. He had bought bread, cheese, apples and a bottle of wine. He had considered buying a pie from one of the restaurants but knew it wouldn't be as good as Cally's own.

He had the lunch together. The problem now was Cally. The reception he had gotten from the Gwynns still worried him. Cally had been serious when she had told him not to call on her. The idea that the Gwynns might have caused her trouble because of him made him angry at the ladies.

He consoled himself with the conviction that she wouldn't be at their house much longer. Today, somehow, he would get her alone and win her over. Was that being too optimistic? No, he would give her the gift, and when she said she loved him, he would ask her to marry him. He smiled to himself. It was nothing short of amazing how that simple thought could bring him sudden pleasure.

"I want to ask Cally to marry me," he said to Royal. It sounded good aloud, too.

Just exactly how he would get her to sit down and listen was another matter. Last night's little confrontation hadn't gone well. He didn't think he should knock on the Gwynns' door again. Perhaps he should wait for Cally to come to do her chores. Unfortunately she had become quite good at slipping in and out without his knowing. He would have to watch for her.

"I don't like it, Royal," he said.

The dog cocked his head to one side and pricked his ears.

"By the time she comes to do her chores, her birthday will be nearly over. Besides, with my luck, I'll get called away and miss her entirely.''

For a moment, Andrew imagined sneaking in the Gwynns' back door and kidnapping Cally. He grinned at the image as he packed the food carefully into a basket.

"You know," he said, eyeing the dog, "it used to bother me that I talked to you." Royal settled onto the floor, his eyes never leaving Andrew. "Cally's managed to change a lot of things around here."

Andrew picked up the little box that had been lying on the table with the picnic lunch. He opened it for another look at the brooch, then placed it inside the basket. Everything was ready for his wildflower.

There was a knock at the door, and Andrew glanced at Royal. He was sure the dog's reaction would have been different if the visitor had been Cally. It was too much to hope for anyway. He walked through the house to the front door.

Dean Olson stood on his steps, and his two sons waited by their horses on the street. All three looked more than a little worried.

"Is there a problem, boys?" Andrew asked.

Dean took off his hat and scratched the back of his head before answering. "Well, sir. I hate to sound like a coward, but it seemed better to leave it to you to handle." He paused a moment. "I just let a little gal run us off your farm."

Andrew closed his eyes. "Cally," he breathed.

"She was only about yea high, red hair...."

"I know what she looks like." Andrew took a deep breath. Realizing the carpenters were still eyeing him with concern, he added, "I'll take care of it. Thanks."

As he closed the door, he heard one of the boys say, "It looks like we get Sunday off, after all."

Andrew's long strides carried him though his house toward the back door. In the kitchen he turned back and grabbed up the basket. "Now that's optimistic," he muttered as he and Royal went through the back door, letting Queen out to lie against the doorsill.

What, he wondered, had gotten into Cally's head this time? He had his horse saddled before it dawned on him. She had seen the house! He had hurt her again.

Cally waited at the door of the soddy when Haywood rode into the yard. She raised the shotgun to her shoulder. Royal had been trotting alongside the horse, and Cally was pleased to see him leave Haywood to run to her. She spoke to the dog without taking her eyes off the sheriff. Royal sat down beside her, his tail thumping against the packed dirt.

Andrew dismounted a little awkwardly, and Cally noticed a basket hung from the saddle horn. She didn't take more than a moment to wonder about it because the sheriff was walking toward her. She kept the shotgun trained on him.

"Seems like old times," Andrew said.

He grinned, and Cally clenched her teeth. "It's not quite the same, though, is it?"

He continued to walk toward her, speaking softly. "Cally, put the gun down."

She felt her resolve start to waver. "You planned to steal the farm all along, didn't you? You used me to get it." She hoped to remind herself as much as accuse him.

Andrew was close enough now to touch the barrel of the shotgun. With one finger he eased it aside. "I didn't use you." His voice dropped to a husky whisper. "Your father lost the farm. I bought it. I didn't need you for that."

Cally lowered the stock from her shoulder; it seemed to have become unbearably heavy. Of course he knew she wouldn't shoot him. Yet she had wanted to let him know how hurt she was. Instead she got all melty inside and forgot why she was here.

She watched a smile start to curve his lips and knew he had read her thoughts. "I love you, Cally," he whispered.

Cally brought herself back to the present. "I don't believe you," she said. "And I've decided not to believe there was a gambling debt, either."

"Why?" asked Andrew, suddenly alert.

Cally shrugged, only mildly curious about his reaction. "I've decided you would lie to me. I can't read so I had to believe you." She leaned the gun against the soddy and put a few paces between them.

Andrew took so long to answer that Cally started to lose her resolve. Finally he asked, "Cally, is that what you really think?"

Cally's lips quivered, and she turned away. "Since you're the sheriff and stronger than me, I guess I'll have to be content to work for you."

Andrew actually chuckled! She spun to stare at him as he asked, "You want to be my deputy, too?"

"Of course not!" she declared, stomping her foot.

In seconds Andrew stood in front of her, tipping her chin up. "Talk to me," he whispered.

She looked into his eyes a full minute before she

spoke. Then it all came out at once. "I miss my garden. I don't like being a maid. Easter is teaching me how to read, but I have to milk Belle in a dress. Noella's a sour pickle, and I can't have Royal anymore. I know it's stupid, but I thought I'd get the farm back, somehow. Now it's yours, and you're building a house, and I'll never get it back." She took a deep breath. "Can I be your housekeeper?"

"My housekeeper?"

Cally stepped away, hoping she sounded convincing. "I could clean your house and cook your meals and do all the things I do for the old ladies except I'd have my garden and I'd be with...uh...Royal and the others."

She glanced at Andrew in time to see him grin. "Don't you mean you'd be with me?"

Her chin came up again. "I could suffer through that, I suppose." Unfortunately her voice quavered when she said it.

Andrew chuckled. He stepped toward her, placing his hands gently on her shoulders, the tingling warmth preventing her from moving away. "What else would you be willing to do as my housekeeper?"

His voice was so honey-smooth she couldn't meet his eyes. "I could live with you in sin...if I had to." She punctuated this offer of a terrible sacrifice by leaning into him and closing her eyes.

"If you had to?" he asked before kissing her gently. "But you wouldn't want to." Another kiss brought her up on her toes.

"Of course not," she murmured. Her arms had encircled his waist, and she waited for his next kiss.

He let her wait a full four seconds. During that

time, she imagined living with him, seeing him every day, waking with him in the morning. She shouldn't let him know how much she loved him, she thought as his lips finally claimed hers again. She let his tongue explore her mouth and pressed herself more firmly against him. If he knew she loved him, he would control her life even more than he did already. Besides, he would want to take advantage. The thought made her tremble clear to her toes.

Andrew felt his powers of reason being sucked away by Cally's warm, responsive lips. Something had been nagging at his brain, but he couldn't seem to concentrate on it. Instead all he could think of was how to get Cally to say she loved him.

He had to be sensible before he ended up seducing her again. And hiring her as his housekeeper was not what he had in mind. He broke off the kiss, putting her firmly but gently away from him…at least a couple inches away. In his desperation he fell back on an old argument he had nearly forgotten himself.

"Cally," he said, "a lawman can't be worrying about his woman. It makes him cautious, and that can get him killed." It seemed to him at that moment that being cautious could also save his life. He found himself wanting to shake his head to clear it.

"But you told me a long time ago you worried about me. That was why you wouldn't leave me on the farm alone. This would be better because I wouldn't be alone."

Andrew gazed into the green eyes. She was so beautiful when she smiled. He opened his mouth to speak and closed it again. Twice.

"It wouldn't matter to the folks in town," she went

on, "because I'd just be your housekeeper. Lots of folks have housekeepers, especially people with big houses." She waved her hand toward the skeletal frame visible above the little soddy.

Andrew was at a loss for a second. He knew it was inevitable that this little hellion be part of his household, but not as his housekeeper. She was supposed to love him! Now, if he asked her to marry him, she would think he was worrying about appearances. As if being reelected sheriff was more important than her reputation! He had teased her earlier about living in sin, but even she must know he couldn't live with her and leave her alone.

He imagined himself saying, "You have to stay with the Gwynns until you fall in love with me." Surely there were reasonable arguments against her suggestion that wouldn't damage his own cause, but he couldn't think of them with her sweet body so close. He paced a distance away from Cally and turned his back on her.

The air seemed cooler when there was some space between him and Cally. He breathed deeply, hoping it would clear his mind. And suddenly he knew what had been bothering him. When Cally professed disbelief in the gambling note, his first thought had been that it might be a forgery.

His next thought was that her eyes seemed impossibly green and he didn't like it when she moved away from him. Even now he had to fight an urge to turn to see if she watched him. He forced himself to concentrate.

A forgery. He should have thought of it before. Terris, the safecracker. Stedwell, the forger. Was Val

Milton connected to Francine and her questions about the bank? He had been so pleased to have an excuse to move Cally into town that he hadn't even considered it.

"I'm a good cook," Cally said, bringing him back to the present question.

He turned and studied her for a moment. She looked small and frightened. Above all else, he loved her and needed to protect her.

She might have sensed that he was weakening. "I don't want to go back to the old ladies," she pleaded, stepping closer.

He realized as well that he wanted her to be happy. "You can live in your old house," he said. "But don't run my carpenters off again."

"And when the new house is finished?" she asked.

"When the house is finished...I'll think of something."

Before he had finished speaking, she threw her arms around his neck. "Thank you," she murmured.

Andrew closed his eyes for a moment, savoring the feel of her in his arms. Gently he drew her away. "This is a strange way to spend your birthday, Cally."

Her eyes narrowed. "What makes you think it's my birthday?"

"Your father wrote the date in the Bible. You're eighteen today."

She shrugged her shoulders, making a show of not caring.

"I brought you a present." The delight he had hoped to see on her face looked more like suspicion. She didn't trust him yet. Well, he couldn't really blame her, but he intended to change that, perhaps this afternoon.

He went to his horse and untied the basket. Turning back toward Cally he considered a moment. The soddy was not at all inviting. He thought about spreading the lunch on the floor of what would be his new house but dismissed it. He would not have her thinking of herself as his housekeeper when they shared their first meal there.

The only shade closer than the little creek was the apple tree on the hill. It was near her parents' graves, but he had a feeling that wasn't something that would bother Cally. They could spread the lunch on the far side of the tree, anyway.

"I tried to invite you on a picnic once before," he said, offering her his arm. "Would you join me now?"

Cally eyed him for a moment. She wasn't sure how to take his behavior. He continued to say he loved her, but he didn't mention marriage. That shouldn't surprise her; he had already told her lawmen should be single. While he hadn't exactly agreed to let her be his housekeeper, he had agreed to let her live in her soddy until his house was built. After that was still uncertain. He said he would think of something. Well, if he didn't, she would. She wasn't leaving him again. She tried to amend the thought to "leaving her farm," but it was too late.

Deciding she was thinking too much, she took the arm he offered and let him lead her to the apple tree. She stood by as he spread a tablecloth on the ground. When he set his hat aside she was tempted to run her fingers through the dark hair. She let the breeze do it instead.

It would be easy to let him love her again. She knew it would happen sometime if he let her stay. She imagined lying on the tablecloth, while the breeze played over their bare skin. She felt a smile curve the corners of her mouth. This love fever between them was very strong.

Andrew chose that moment to look up at her. She hoped she had gotten rid of the smile in time. He eyed her rather quizzically so she doubted it. "Cally? Do you want to sit down?"

"Oh. Sure." She sat down quickly then tried to adjust the skirt that had moved a tad more slowly. When she felt decent again, she smoothed the gray fabric on her lap for several seconds before looking at him again.

He was intent on laying out the food, and Cally allowed herself to study him. He was better dressed than usual, and she wondered if these were his Sunday clothes. She wanted to touch the cloth of his coat to see if it felt different, but stopped herself in time. She *had* touched it already, but then she hadn't been thinking about the coat.

She took a deep breath, trying to control her quivering stomach. It would be stupid to give in to any of the things she felt. She had to remember to be cautious, even if he had told her she could live in her old house. There was still a lot at stake.

It hurt to know he wouldn't marry her. She had tried to tell herself it didn't matter. She had never cared what people thought, at least not as much as he did. Still, it seemed like being honest should count for more than it did. Andrew said people wouldn't vote for him if he was married, but evidently it was all right for him to live with her if she was his house-keeper, and she had known by the look in his eyes that she would be more than that. But she was learning from the old ladies that a lot of things about town people didn't really make sense.

"Happy birthday, Cally."

His voice startled her. She focused on his expectant face before she realized he held a small box toward her. She smiled and his expression changed, but she couldn't quite read it.

His fingers brushed hers as she took the box. She tried hard to ignore the tingle the touch produced. "Pa's Bible really says today's my birthday?"

He simply nodded.

She had only vague recollections of presents, birthdays and Christmas. She wanted to savor this rare moment a little before she opened the box. "And it says I'm eighteen?"

He seemed startled by the question. She supposed most people would have known something like that. He was watching her intently, and she felt a warm shiver spread though her body and hoped her cheeks hadn't turned pink. She concentrated on opening the little box. "How old are you?" she asked, hoping to distract him.

"Twenty-seven."

She barely heard. Inside the box was a tiny gold bouquet of flowers. She looked up at Andrew, unable to keep the delight from showing on her face. "It's beautiful."

"Here." Andrew moved closer. "Let me pin it on your dress."

He was so close her lips could have touched his cheek without hardly trying. Cally inhaled the scent of soap that clung to him until she felt her dress tighten across her breasts. As he pinned the flowers near the top button his fingers seemed to tremble. They brushed her neck, and she closed her eyes to savor his touch.

"I think they look like wildflowers." Cally only half listened. "They remind me of you."

Cally's eyes flew open. "What?"

He seemed surprised at the change in her. She realized that he had been about to kiss her but drew back instead.

"Wildflowers make me think of you," he repeated. "They're small and fragile looking but are really quite tough."

Cally's eyes narrowed. "I'm like a flower?" She had meant to sound as if she were trying to understand, but there was a little resentment in her voice.

"I didn't mean it as an insult, Cally."

Now she had hurt his feelings. She hadn't meant to. She liked the gift and loved that he had picked it out. But a flower? With nectar to be sampled? She forced a smile. "It's very pretty. Thank you," she said, hoping to ease the disappointment she read on his face.

Andrew handed her a slice of bread and a large chunk of cheese, without speaking. She felt her stomach turn into one big knot as she tried to eat. Were the sisters right? Would she ever know for sure if Andrew loved her?

"Cally?" Andrew handed her a pretty stemmed glass. "Do you want some wine?"

Willing her stomach to relax, Cally took the glass. It was almost as pretty as the glasses she had practiced filling at the Gwynns'. This was quite a fancy picnic.

She smiled at Andrew as she brought the glass to her lips. The fumes made her cautious. The tiniest sip made her tongue tingle. She thought it tasted sweet. She took a larger swallow and gasped. It lit a warm trail all the way down to her stomach. She coughed twice.

"Are you all right?" He leaned close, steadying the glass.

"Yes," she said, taking a deep breath and deciding that she was. "That's good." She studied the red liquid a moment before taking another sip. It went down easier.

"Drink it slowly," Andrew said.

Cally took another sip and set the glass beside her, careful to find a level place so it wouldn't spill. Andrew moved closer to her, trying to get more comfortable, she supposed. He took a knife from the basket and began slicing an apple.

Cally nibbled on the bread.

"Apple?" He held a wedge between his fingers but when she reached for it he brought it to her mouth instead. She had to grab his hand to steady it as she took a bite. He watched her mouth as she chewed. She swallowed as quickly as she could—then realized she was still holding on to his hand. She swallowed again.

"You have beautiful lips," he whispered, leaning closer.

She trembled and found herself leaning toward him too. His lips tasted like wine; he gave her plenty of time to notice. But it was a sweet gentle kiss, not the passion-filled one she longed for. She tried to lean closer, but his lips moved away.

"I love you, Cally," he whispered against her cheek.

Chapter Fourteen

Cally loved to hear Andrew say it. She didn't think she should believe him, but when he said it, it was hard not to say it back. She bit her lip, tasting a trace of the wine.

He moved away a few inches and gazed at her. She tried to smile. She wanted him to kiss her again. He must have wanted something else because after a moment he sat upright, retrieving the knife and the apple.

Cally tried to eat again. This was a very strange meal. It was a good thing she wasn't very hungry. She liked having him kiss her while they ate. When the apple was gone, he tossed the core away and kissed her. When the bread was gone, he kissed her. When he refilled his wineglass and added a few drops to hers, he kissed her. Each time, he told her he loved her. Each time she resisted repeating the words. It was a resolution that was hard to keep. She had to remind herself how much he liked to run her life and that he wouldn't marry her even if she said it.

At one weak moment, when he kissed her cheek and then her neck, she had almost forgotten. It was on the tip of her tongue, but she had bit it back, literally. He had drawn away when she yelped. He probably thought she was crazy.

Now, as she watched him pack the bottle and glasses in the basket, she considered her situation more carefully. He already owned her farm. If he knew he owned her heart as well, he would realize that he could ask her to do anything. She should let him think there was still a chance she would say no. And she might. She watched the breeze ruffle his dark hair. Maybe.

She decided she needed to think about something else. "Can you bring my things out from the old ladies' house?" she asked.

Andrew stood and helped her to her feet. She held her breath, afraid he had changed his mind. She really wanted to live out here again, away from the old ladies. Out here where he could visit her, where he was building a house, where he planned to live. She shook her head and tried to think about her garden.

They had started down the hill before he spoke. "You better ride your mule back to the Gwynns'."

Cally almost gasped. Briefly she wondered if kissing him might work better than fighting, but she reacted before she could give it serious thought. Stomping one foot and putting both fists on her hips, she said, "I don't want to go back there! If you won't let me stay here, I'll find someplace else."

Andrew had the nerve to roll his eyes in exasperation. "I only want you to go back to pack your things. I think you should be the one to tell the ladies that you're leaving. I'll be along later with the wagon."

"Oh," she said. She left him to walk quickly to Jewel. At least she was going to get to stay. There were no doubts in her mind anymore of what she meant to Andrew. She was his flower! Well, there were worse things. He seemed to really enjoy kissing his flower. She sighed as she untied Jewel.

She had agreed to live with him in sin. She wouldn't let it bother her. She would have her garden and her dogs—and sin. She stifled a giggle. Her thoughts took off on their own far too often. She sprang onto the mule's back, pulling her skirts down as much as possible. "I won't have to milk Belle in a dress ever again!" she said aloud. She knew that wasn't why she was so happy.

Andrew watched her go. His plan to charm her into loving him hadn't made any progress. Instead he had agreed to let her move back into her old house. And as if that weren't crazy enough, she thought she was going to be his housekeeper!

He turned away to tie the basket to the saddle horn. He mounted as she rode Jewel up to join him. When he turned to look at her, she gave him such a warm smile, he knew he had made the right decision.

For about three minutes, he knew. After that, he was uncertain again. As he rode alongside her, he tried to make sense of his decision. She was no safer alone in the country now than she had ever been. The fact that he owned the land and would provide her with anything she needed like firewood and food made little difference. He could ask the carpenters to look out for her during the day, but she would again be alone out here at night.

He looked at the girl beside him smiling so trustingly and resolved to come out every night to guard
the place. The next moment he realized that was stupid. When, exactly, did he plan to sleep? Besides, if
he was caught sneaking out to her farm, whether his
motives were to guard her or bed her, it would look
bad to the electorate. Before the silent pair parted at
Andrew's home, he had decided that women definitely made their men crazy. Smart lawmen should
avoid them completely.

Val Milton watched Haywood ride into town with
considerable interest. At his home the sheriff parted
not unpleasantly from a little slip of a girl on a mule.
Shortly thereafter he left again in a wagon, heading
this time into the heart of town. Val ambled down the
street a ways, watching, until Haywood turned off
into another residential area, avoiding the active main
street. Val stopped; there was too big a chance of
Haywood realizing he was followed. He was on the
edge of the business district as it was, and he didn't
want anyone wondering where he was going.

Val found a shady spot to sit and wait, hoping he
looked like a man of leisure enjoying a warm fall
afternoon. All the while he kept an eye on the corner
where Haywood had turned, assuming he would be
coming back eventually.

Eventually wasn't even thirty minutes. The wagon
came around the corner and turned in again at Haywood's place. The girl was on the wagon seat beside
the sheriff, and her mule was tied on behind. All he
could make out of the contents of the wagon were a
few crates and a rocking chair.

Val chuckled to himself. The illustrious sheriff was moving his honey in with him in broad daylight. He had to admit he admired his style.

It was difficult to find a good vantage point across from Haywood's house without becoming conspicuous. He didn't like to wait in any one place very long. Since he expected the sheriff to take the rest of the afternoon seeing that his lady was settled, he prepared to move on. He was half a block away when a mule's bray brought him around. The wagon pulled out of the yard again, heading out into the country.

Val walked back the way he had come, staring at the departing wagon, forgetting to look inconspicuous. The procession included, besides the mule, a milk cow and both of the dogs that had terrorized Stedwell and Terris. He was even sure he heard the squawk of chickens.

So the sheriff wasn't moving her into his house. Where in the world was he taking her? Was she just a local girl he was helping somehow? No, he was sure he had seen a look exchanged that meant more than neighborliness. Were his dogs to stay with the girl, he wondered? Val walked swiftly to the livery to rent a horse.

Cally was so excited to be home that she wanted to run around and investigate everything with Royal. She wanted to weed her garden and clean her house. She didn't know where to start.

And Andrew was being wonderful except for making her talk to the old ladies herself. And even that hadn't turned out to be as bad as she expected. Easter had actually acted as if she might miss her. Noella predicted Cally's doom if she left. She had just launched into her lecture when Andrew had arrived with the wagon. Her savior, she thought.

Now he carried her boxes of produce to her cellar where she could put them on her freshly dusted shelves. "Soon everything will be back where it belongs," she said as he set the last crate of jars on the dirt floor beside her.

"Including you," he whispered, brushing a strand of hair off her damp cheek.

His tone made her think of kisses, and she turned to him expectantly. He lifted her chin with his finger and she closed her eyes. His kiss was as sweet as ever. If only...she thought and stopped herself. She shouldn't spoil what she was given by wishing for more.

Andrew might have sensed her hesitation because he eyed her curiously after he ended the kiss. She got busy with her jars.

"I want to have a look at the barn roof," he said. "You can finish up here?"

Cally nodded. She unloaded the last crate and, taking it and the candle with her, left the cellar. The barn door stood open, and Cally looked toward it more than once as she stacked the crate with the others and took the candle back to the soddy. The next thing she knew she was heading toward the barn.

"Andrew?" she called as she came through the dark doorway.

"Up here."

Cally climbed the ladder. The sun streaming through the many holes in the roof made it as light as outside. The roof had leaked long enough that some of the floorboards had rotted through as well. Cally never used the loft for anything. It had been years since Pa had put up enough prairie hay to need the space, anyway.

She watched Andrew move around, studying the roof. She looked up herself and cringed. "Are you trying to decide if it's worth fixing?" She wished she hadn't asked; it wasn't her business.

When he turned toward her he smiled. "Except for the roof, it seems pretty sound." A moment after he said it, the floor creaked beneath his foot and he stepped back, looking down at the indentation of his foot in the splintered boards. He walked forward, watching his step a little more closely. "All moved in?" he asked.

Cally nodded. "The house is a mess, but it won't take long to straighten." She almost told him that it seemed awfully small now. She didn't want him to think she regretted talking him into this.

"Would you like some help?"

Cally tried to picture him sweeping her dirt floor in his Sunday clothes. She returned his smile. "Thank you, but I can manage."

"You think I don't know how to clean." He came toward her and she thought of Royal stalking a rabbit. "I'll have you know, young lady, that I do all my own cleaning, or did until I hired two deputy trainees."

"What?" He towered over her. She loved it when he did that. In a minute his arms would go around her, and he would kiss her again.

"Never mind," he murmured, scooping her up against him. His lips weren't as gentle as before. The urgency reminded her of their night of passion, and Cally knew she should resist. She just had no idea how. She wrapped her arms around his neck and stood on her toes instead.

"What are you thinking, Cally?" he murmured a moment later.

Cally giggled as he nibbled the lobe of her ear. "I don't know."

"Sure you do." His voice dripped like honey into her ear. "Tell me."

"I think this is crazy." She closed her eyes and clung to him for balance.

"What's crazy?" he coaxed.

"Kissing you," she said. "I only just quit worrying about a baby."

With a sigh, Andrew gradually unwound her arms from his waist. "You're right, of course."

There was something different in his voice, something almost like anger. He didn't seem angry though. He looked down at her for a long moment, and Cally wondered if she had hurt his feelings. Evidently she hadn't said what he had wanted her to. She was afraid to speak again.

Abruptly he said. "I better get back to town."

She followed him down the ladder and out of the barn. She wanted him to kiss her goodbye but decided that wasn't real smart. She watched him spring into his wagon. He turned and waved just before he drove out of her yard. His yard, she reminded herself. She shook her head, smiling. "My yard."

Val Milton had stopped at the creek. There just wasn't any cover between it and the farmstead. From that distance he hadn't been able to make out much more than the fact that Haywood and the girl had unloaded the wagon. When the girl had set the rocking chair down beside the front door and had sat in it for a moment, he got the impression that both chair and girl had been there before.

The pair's lengthy stay in the barn had made him chuckle.

When Haywood returned to the wagon, Val had headed up the creek to be sure he was well away from the ford. After giving the sheriff plenty of time to get ahead of him, he returned to the hotel for a bath and a tumble with Fancy. He enjoyed a huge dinner in the hotel dining room, then walked the short distance to the Antlers. After two unprofitable hands of poker, he stepped to the end of the bar for a drink. When he saw his chance, he slipped through the door and up the stairs.

The greeting he received was exactly what he had come to expect: a smile from Stedwell, a growl from Terris. The men had been playing cards; Stedwell was obviously winning.

"Any news?" the forger asked.

"A little. It appears the watchdogs have left the Haywood yard. We can hide the money there after all."

Terris moved to the peephole and looked down on the saloon. Val noticed there was hardly any limp left in his movements. "How would you know this?" he asked.

"Watched him most of the afternoon. I think he moved old DuBois' daughter back to her home place."

Stedwell grinned at the idea of the sheriff buying the farm back for the girl.

Terris shrugged. "This is taking too long. I might as well still be in prison, for all the good escaping's done. Let's get on with it."

Now, whose fault is that? Val wanted to ask but resisted. "Soon," he said instead. "Go back to Haywood's tomorrow. Find the perfect spot to hide the money. Someplace that'll look like he stashed it in a hurry but won't be too hard for the deputy to find."

"Where will you be while we're taking this risk?" asked Terris.

"Keeping watch. Remember my face won't automatically land me in jail."

Terris snorted. "Won't the sheriff start to wonder why you're still hanging around town? Selling that farm ruined your excuse for being here."

Val nodded. It had occurred to him. "You find a hiding place at Haywood's in the morning, and we'll do it tomorrow night."

"Damn, this place makes me nervous." Stedwell eyed the empty yard through the hedge.

"The dogs are gone," Terris growled.

"I hope so," Stedwell muttered as he followed the safecracker.

At the door, Terris tested the knob, surprised when it turned easily in his hand. "Trusting fella, ain't he?"

"I like that in a victim," Stedwell quipped.

Terris concentrated on looking for a hiding place near the back door, but Stedwell walked on into the house. "Take a look at this," he called after a few minutes.

"What the hell are you doing in here?" Terris grumbled as he joined him. "I don't want to stay here any longer than we got to."

Stedwell grinned, unperturbed by his partner's tone. "Look at all these pictures. There must be fifty of them, and they're all the same girl." He lifted one and handed it to Terris. "Cally, this one says. The sheriff's got it bad."

"So what?"

"So let's use it. Fancy can't keep his attention. Let's use the girl to lure him out of town. Help me find a love letter."

Terris looked disgusted.

"Come on," Stedwell urged, "I need a sample of her writing."

But twenty minutes later, when they had failed to turn up anything, Terris declared his intention to leave. Stedwell reluctantly agreed. Surely if the girl had ever written to her lover, the note would have been here someplace. He would have to be creative, and hope the sheriff hadn't seen enough of her writing to know the difference.

Andrew thanked the telegraph operator. He walked back toward his office trying not to feel discouraged. It was early yet to expect an answer from anyone to whom he had sent Francine's picture. He just couldn't shake the feeling that she and Milton were tied to the escapees. He had nothing he could call proof.

At the office, another applicant for deputy would be waiting. He fervently hoped this one would be qualified. He and Bill were spread too thin.

* * *

"Let me go over this one more time," Val said.

Terris groaned but Stedwell only looked up from his work at the table and grinned. "Where did you get this paper, anyway?"

"Fancy," Val answered absently.

Stedwell raised it to his nose and sniffed. "Hmmm."

Val cleared his throat. "Just after dark, we'll find a boy to deliver that note to Haywood. When Haywood heads out to the farm to help his lover, Stedwell will be waiting for him. Disarm him, knock him out, wing him, whatever, just get him back to his house."

"Gotcha," Stedwell said, ending the note with a flourish.

"Fancy will have distracted the deputy—"

"Scared to have her around Haywood, ain't ya, Milton?" Terris interrupted.

"Her job," Val went on, ignoring the safecracker, "will be to keep the deputy busy until it's time to get him to the sheriff's backyard to catch Haywood.

"Meanwhile, I'll stand guard while you, Terris, break into the bank's safe and lift the money. I'll cover your back until you can stash the money at Haywood's and hightail it. Understood?"

"I never liked this plan, Milton. Haywood lives, and we leave broke."

"That twenty-five dollars from Haywood will get you away from here, and you'll leave free," Milton argued.

"Small change, and I should get a *third* of what you got for that place."

"Terris." Milton used his most threatening tone.

"You can't stay here or at the hotel for free. I told you that. And need I remind you there are *four* of us working together here? If you want to forget Sted-well's sister, remember how you got out of jail!"

Milton continued to glare at Terris, hoping his last words would put Stedwell on his side. He regretted ever getting mixed up with this one. He didn't trust him.

When he thought the man was close to backing down, he added, "And don't try taking any of the money out of the bag. If it isn't all accounted for, they'll start looking for accomplices. If their questions lead to any of us, we'll bring you down as well, Ter-ris."

"It looks like I'm taking the biggest risk."

Stedwell spoke up, "You wanted revenge for the years we spent in prison as much as I did."

Milton cleared his throat. "As I was saying. As soon as both of you are away, I'll shout for help and claim to have stopped the thief." He glared at Terris. "You'll be gone. I'll be here. That sounds pretty damned risky to me."

"You know, Parker," Terris said to his former cell mate, never taking his eyes off Val Milton. "I just figured out what this gambler expects to get out of this. He's hoping for a reward from the bank. One he won't have to share."

The air almost crackled with tension. Val had no idea how to defuse it. He had risked so much to come this far, and all his plans depended on the safecrack-er's cooperation.

It was Stedwell who broke the silence. "You'll still get your revenge, Wade," he said quietly. "Val's helped us, and he hasn't needed to. If all he wanted was a reward, he could have turned us in long ago.''

Terris grumbled but seemed to relax. Val tried not to show his relief. ''This is the last time we'll get to talk,'' he said after a moment. ''I'll meet Terris at the bank. Are there any questions?''

''Well, I have one last comment.''

Val and Stedwell eyed Terris warily.

''If anything goes wrong, I mean anything, I'll kill Haywood.''

''Nothing will go wrong,'' Val assured him hastily. ''Let's see that note.''

Ten minutes later, with the note tucked carefully into his coat pocket, Val left the Antlers. He was glad to get away from his co-conspirators. He would be more than glad when this was over and those two bastards were back behind bars.

Last night he had hidden a carpetbag full of newspaper in the alley behind the bank. He wanted to make certain it was still there, but it was too dangerous. He couldn't be seen nosing around the bank's back door mere hours before it was robbed. That kind of thing was too easy for witnesses to remember.

The matching carpetbag was still in his room, which reminded him of his need to pack. He was leaving tonight, alone perhaps, because he was still uncertain about Fancy. Her loyalty to her brother made him afraid to mention his double cross. When he called for the deputy to stop the thief, he planned to have the carpetbag full of the bank's money in his hand and both Stedwell and Terris still on the scene. That just might not sit well with the forger's sister.

He would miss her, he was certain of that. He wondered if she was in her room this time of day. He wondered if they could have one last tumble without his giving himself away. Fancy was very perceptive. He found himself walking a little faster. She was also very lusty. For a moment he even wondered if she might be worth more than the money. But only for a moment.

The sun had set but Andrew was still in his office. He knew he should go home. He turned over another Wanted poster and tried another series of sketches. He felt certain that Stedwell, and probably Terris as well, were nearby. He had been drawing their faces from his old Wanted posters, adding several different styles of hair and beards. None of his drawings looked like anyone he had seen in town.

Andrew finally set the sketches aside. It was a big town with plenty of places for a person to hide. And as yet he had no proof. All he had was a young woman who might have been Stedwell's last visitor asking questions about the bank, and a gambler who might have given him a forged IOU. Pretty thin. Way too thin to make any guesses as to their next move.

He stood up and was about to extinguish the lamp when the door opened. He greeted the young boy who entered. "Hi, Taylor. What are you doing out this late in the day?"

Taylor shuffled his feet as if he had been caught in mischief. "I weren't doin' nothin' bad, just runnin' around. Anyhow, I'm supposed to give you this note." He handed a piece of expensive writing paper to Andrew.

"Where did you get this?"

"I'm supposed to tell you a girl gave it to me."

Andrew raised his eyebrows at the boy. "And who did give it to you?"

"A lady."

Andrew held back a laugh. He tossed the boy a coin and unfolded the paper as the boy turned to leave. A glance at the bottom stopped him cold. "Taylor, wait!"

As the boy turned around, Andrew tried to think fast. Someone was trying to lure him out of town using Cally as bait. She might already be in danger. But perhaps they planned to ambush him on the way to her rescue or merely get him away from town. "Taylor, do you know where the DuBois farm is?"

"Yes sir." The boy nodded enthusiastically. "Mikey's pa sent me and Mikey out there once to buy a pie since Mikey ain't got no ma to make 'um."

"Could you go out there now?"

"It's almost dark."

"Damn. Of course, you're right. I'll get Bill. You go on home."

"Is someone gonna hurt Miss DuBois?"

"I don't think so, Taylor. Just go on home now, all right?"

Taylor was obviously hurt that he wasn't included in some adventure. Andrew regretted even suggesting it. Of course he couldn't send a child into possible danger, even if it hadn't been getting dark. It had been a momentary lapse, and it bothered him. He thanked the boy again and escorted him out the door.

Andrew extinguished the light and grabbed his coat. Was the note designed to lure him into a trap or simply away from town? The bank seemed the most logical possibility. He would send Bill out to check on Cally, and he would keep a close eye on the bank.

At Bill's door he waited impatiently for his deputy to answer his knock. Finally his wife came to the door. "Mrs. Edmonds, I need to see Bill."

"I'm sorry," she said, stepping out on the porch. "He's not here."

"Where can I find him?"

"I'm not sure. A woman came and got him just a few minutes ago. She seemed very concerned about something and said she couldn't find you."

Andrew ignored the hint of accusation in her voice. "Did you know this woman? Can you describe her?"

"Well, she was blond, very well dressed. Say, you don't think Bill and she are..." She nearly glared at Andrew.

"I doubt it, Mrs. Edmonds. If he comes home, would you tell him I'm looking for him?" Andrew turned to go.

"What do you mean, *if* he comes home?"

"When," Andrew said, backing down the walk. "When he comes home." Andrew turned and made a hasty retreat. "Women," he muttered under his breath. He would try the hotel to see if Francine was there. She was almost certainly the one who had come for Bill.

Mr. Ossman sent the tall, thin boy up to check Francine's room and watched Andrew curiously.

"Trouble, Sheriff?" he asked after a few minutes.

"Nothing of concern," Andrew said, hoping to stop any gossip before it started. He knew his own agitation was becoming more and more difficult to hide the longer he waited for the boy. He had to fight the urge to head straight out to Cally. What if he was wrong about the bank and stayed in town to guard it while someone hurt Cally?

Finally the boy appeared at the top of the stairs. "She ain't there, Sheriff," he said. "I knocked and knocked. You want I should get a key?"

"No, that won't be necessary. Thank you for your trouble."

Andrew took a quick look in the dining room before he left the hotel, even though that had been the first place he had looked when he came in. Where would Francine take Bill to keep him out of the way? Where would Bill allow himself to be led? Concern for his deputy's welfare was added to his worry about Cally.

On the boardwalk, he took a deep breath of the cool evening air. He had to think calmly. His hunch was still that they planned to hit the bank. His hunches were usually good. With that in mind, he slipped into the shadows of an alley. He needed to catch the thieves in the act, not scare them away.

Taylor didn't go straight home. He went straight to Mikey's house. A pebble tossed against a certain windowpane brought his friend out as always.

"What's up?" whispered Mikey as he sat down

beside Taylor in the shadow of the outhouse and pulled on his shoes.

"You 'member that Miss DuBois what baked the pies?" At his friend's nod he continued, "She's in trouble, and we can save her."

Chapter Fifteen

Mikey stared at Taylor for a long moment. Finally he whispered, "How?"

"Come on. I'll tell you as we go. We gotta stay away from the road." They started through town, disregarding property lines, and Taylor told his friend his story. "I was coming to see if you wanted to help me catch a bat to put in my sister's room when this real pretty lady stopped me on the street. She gave me a nickel to take a note to Sheriff Haywood. I figured this was great 'cause the sheriff would be good for at least a penny, too.

"Anyhow, I give him the note like she says, but when he sees it, he calls me back. For a minute there, I thought he was gonna send me out to Miss DuBois' farm, but I slipped up and mentioned it was getting dark." Taylor shook his head, still unable to believe he had made such a mistake. How much would the sheriff have given him to run an errand like that? Besides, it would have been real deputy work!

"What did the note say?" Mikey asked.

Taylor giggled, and Mikey had to nudge him twice

before he would tell him. Finally Taylor cleared his throat and recited it in his best high-pitched girl's voice. "My dearest Andrew, come to the farm as soon as possible. I need your help. Please hurry, my darling."

Both boys were almost immobilized by fits of laughter. "Please hurry, my darling," they each repeated.

Taylor finished, "It was signed, Cally."

Mikey quit laughing. "Miss DuBois didn't write that."

"How do you know?"

"'Cause of what Pa told me. He said she oughta been in school even ahead of your sister, but her old man never let her go. I don't reckon she knows anythin', specially not readin' an writin'."

The boys trudged on in silence. It was dark enough now to make walking difficult, but when they stepped into the shade of the trees that lined the little creek, it was darker still.

"Shouldn't we follow the creek to the road?" Mikey whispered. "That'd be the easiest place to cross."

"We have to stay away from the road," Taylor reminded him.

"Why?"

"Shhh. Just 'cause. Besides, I know a way." They made slow progress along the eroded bank until Taylor stopped. "See those three rocks? We can use them to cross the creek."

Mikey squinted. "I can't hardly see 'em. I'll fall in."

"It ain't deep enough to drown in anyhow," said Taylor, starting across.

"How'll I explain my wet clothes?" Taylor didn't respond, and with a shrug Mikey started reluctantly after his friend. Taylor waited at the largest rock in the middle to give Mikey a hand. Once across, the boys scrambled up the bank.

At the edge of the trees they paused again. Taylor pointed. "See that tree there against the sky? That's on a hill by her house. There's a grave out there so we can't go near it bein' it's dark, but it means we're close to her place."

Mikey nodded and followed his friend. "What are we gonna tell her?" he asked.

Taylor paused for a moment. He looked at his friend's face, white in the pale moonlight. "We'll tell her the sheriff sent us out here after he got the note she didn't write."

Royal heard the little boys' chatter from some distance away and alerted Cally. By the time they knocked on her door, Cally was up and dressed in her Pa's pants and shirt and had a lamp lit on her little table. A dog standing on either side of her, she yanked the door open and demanded, "What are you doing here?"

She had clearly startled them, but she had meant to. Not all little boys were nice, and if these two were here to bother her, she would make sure they thought twice before doing it again.

They stood, openmouthed, looking at each other for a moment. Finally the taller of the two spoke. "Sheriff Haywood sent us."

Cally grabbed both boys by their collars and dragged them into the house, closing the door behind them. "Tell me exactly what he said."

The one that had spoken before stuttered a moment. "He…he got this note, see."

"Only it wasn't from you," piped up the other.

"He sent me, I mean us, to check on you," finished the first. They looked at each other and nodded.

"He sent two little boys out here to check on me?" Cally had been deeply insulted. How helpless did Andrew think she was?

"Well, not exactly," the shorter one confessed slowly.

"But he would have," the other broke in, nudging his companion in the ribs, "only it was dark."

"But we didn't care."

Cally looked at the boys. They were watching her expectantly, not at all like bullies who had come to torment her. "Do I know you?" she asked finally.

"I'm Taylor," came a quick reply. "This here's Mikey. His pa sent us out for a pie once."

"It was awful good. You got any now?" This question earned Mikey another sharp nudge in the ribs.

"There's something funny going on here," Cally said, opening her door. "You can tell me every detail while we go into town." They looked slightly dismayed by this pronouncement, but they followed obediently.

Cally put the boys up on Jewel, and, with Royal at her side, led the mule toward town. The boys talked as they rode. It became apparent rather quickly that they hadn't been sent by Andrew by any stretch of the imagination but weren't going to admit it. Cally let it pass.

They had gotten no farther than the creek when Royal alerted them of someone's presence. Cally motioned the boys to get down while Royal stood in front of her bristling and growling.

"Call off the dog," a man shouted. A stranger stepped out from behind a tree, gun in hand. "Call him off, or I'll shoot him."

"Hush, Royal," Cally said. With her hand behind her back, she tried to motion the boys away, hoping they would run for cover.

"Now, I've seen that dog before," the man said. He sounded threatening but maybe a little scared too. Cally didn't take her eyes off him, wishing he would step into the moonlight so she could see his face. She couldn't hear the boys and hoped that meant they were gone.

"Don't you dare hurt my dog," she said, trying to keep his attention on her.

The man shook his head. "I won't unless I have to. See, I was waiting for a friend of yours, but it seems he didn't care for my note. Still, I can't have you blundering into him in town, so you can just come with me." He used the gun to motion her forward.

Cally took one step in the direction he indicated then dived out of the way, yelling, "Get him, Royal!"

The dog leaped forward, sinking his teeth into the man's arm. The man's yell mingled with the sound of a gunshot. Cally screamed, afraid for her dog, but Royal was still holding on, growling.

Suddenly both boys ran from the trees, kicking at

the man's legs, yelling like savages. Cally jumped to her feet and, reaching around the dog and boys, grabbed the man's gun.

"Run now, run!" she yelled at the boys. "I've got his gun." The boys scrambled away from the man but didn't go far.

The man yelled, "Call off the damn dog!"

"Royal!" she snapped. The dog reluctantly let go.

"Damn dog! I'm going to bleed to death." He took a handkerchief from his pocket and tried to tie it around his arm. "Come help me with this."

"You got another gun?" Cally asked, glad now for the darkness that kept her from seeing his blood. She had to get away quickly before just the knowledge that he *was* bleeding made her faint.

"Now, little girl, if I had another gun, do you think that dog would still be alive?"

Royal growled deep in his throat.

"We gonna tie him up?" asked Taylor.

Cally stumbled toward Jewel, who had stood placidly during all the excitement. She held her face in her hands a second, fighting off dizziness. "I don't have any rope," she murmured.

"These'll work," the boy said.

Cally turned to see him holding something toward her, but it was too dark to see what it was.

"You got yours too, don't ya, Mikey?"

"We always carry 'em," the smaller boy said, "on account 'a us being deputies in training."

Cally took the object from the boy. A slingshot. Mikey had produced one from his pocket as well, and Taylor helped him take the leather strap off the wooden handle.

Royal growled and brought Cally's attention back to the man in time to see him edging away. "Hold it!" She pointed his pistol at him again, and he stopped. "You're right," she said, trading the whole slingshot for the strap the boys offered.

"Don't try nothin'," she warned, setting the pistol on the ground next to Royal so the man wouldn't be tempted to try to get it. She tied his hands behind his back, and with the second strap, tied his legs together just above his boots.

"That'll hold him," said Mikey. "You want us should stay here and point that gun at him?"

"You can't let them do that, lady," the man said, clearly dismayed at the turn of events.

Cally retrieved the gun. "You boys better go straight home. Can you walk? I'll need Jewel to get to town fast so I can warn the sheriff. I think this man was waiting for him."

"You could ride his horse." Taylor pointed at a horse nearly hidden in the trees.

Cally considered only a moment. The horse would be faster, but she wasn't used to horses. "You boys can ride it if you want." She couldn't wait around to see what they did. "Royal, stay!" she commanded and swung onto Jewel's back. She could hear the man yelling at her and her dog's menacing growl as she splashed across the creek and rode for town.

Haywood saw the flicker of a match through the bank window and left the shadows of the doorway across the street. He made his way quickly to the alley that ran behind the bank. As he flattened himself against the back of the saloon and listened for footsteps behind him, he tried to gauge what his best position would be. He wished, not for the first time, that he had been able to find Bill. He wished even more that he knew for sure that Cally was all right.

He tried to brush any thoughts of her from his mind. He had to be alert. Gun in hand he crept closer to the back door of the bank and blended into the shadows across the way.

He didn't have to wait long. Two men stepped cautiously from the bank, and he made his move. "Stop right where you are," he demanded.

The man in front turned and fired. Andrew felt a sting high in his chest then an alarming weakness spread through his body. He fired a shot toward the retreating figure, but his arm wouldn't respond to his attempt to aim. Terris. He was sure of it. And the other? He was just as sure he had seen him slip back into the bank. He thought it was Milton, though he would have expected Stedwell.

Andrew took a cautious step toward the bank, and the alley came up hard to meet him. He tried to rise and succeeded only in turning himself onto his back. He groaned more in frustration than pain.

And quite inexplicably Cally was there. "What are you doing here?" he found himself asking, though surely there was something much more urgent he should say.

"I saw you go down the alley as I came into town," Cally choked out. "Then I heard the shot. Oh, Andrew, you're hurt so bad."

Cally had to stop the flow of blood. She knew Andrew was trying to say something, but that awful buzzing had started in her ears. She was terribly afraid she would faint. She had all the familiar symptoms—the buzzing, the cold sweat, the darkness at the edge of her vision.

No! She just couldn't faint, she told herself. She had to save Andrew. She groaned aloud as she pressed a handkerchief against the wound. At least against his shoulder where she thought the wound was. She didn't dare take a closer look.

When Milton saw Haywood go down, he stepped through the bank's back door into the alley. The girl was preoccupied with the sheriff. Val had seconds to escape. He took one step, and his chance was gone. He could hear voices, lots of them, approaching the alley. He was about to be caught standing over the wounded sheriff holding a carpetbag full of the bank's money! He saw one chance to save himself. He drew his gun and rushed forward, dropping the bag beside the sheriff just as the first of the townspeople rounded the corner.

"I got him!" he yelled. "I saw him coming out of the bank, right there!" It wasn't hard to sound panicky. "I tried, I really tried to get him to stop, but he wouldn't. I had to shoot him."

The deputy and the banker were both making their way to the front of the crowd, followed closely by the doctor. The banker virtually stepped over the sheriff in an effort to get to the carpetbag. He yanked it open and staggered at the sight of the money.

Andrew heard Milton's accusation but it was so incredible it took him a second to make sense of it.

Suddenly Cally moved away from him. Did she believe he had robbed the bank?

Bill's face appeared instead of hers, only to be replaced just as quickly by that of Dr. Briggs. He had to tell them. Terris and Milton had come out of the bank. Terris had shot him and escaped. Milton was lying. He tried to tell them but his mouth was too dry when he opened it to speak. He tried again but a whispered, "Terris," was all that made it past his lips before he passed out.

When Cally saw the doctor coming, she ran to grab him, to bring him to help Andrew. As soon as she was positive that he would help her man, she stumbled to the ground and tucked her head between her knees. Almost immediately, she felt the black haze receding to be replaced by a sick feeling in her stomach.

She didn't want to faint in the middle of this crowd. She wouldn't know what happened to Andrew. She lifted her head to try to see what went on and the buzzing started again. She was ready to tuck her head down again when the doctor directed two men to lift Andrew. They were taking him away! Her vision cleared quickly, and she scrambled to her feet to follow, feeling only slightly light-headed.

Fancy found herself pushed some distance away from the center of the action. The deputy had abandoned her at the sound of the shot, and she had not been able to keep up. From what she could pick out of the confused conversation, it was Sheriff Haywood who had been shot. Evidently Parker had been unable to detain him. Well, it wouldn't be the first time her brother had screwed up. Had the sheriff shot him? Was he lying dead somewhere? And Val? Where was he?

She found a crate to stand on and looked over the crowd. She caught a glimpse of Val following the banker through the back door of the bank.

Instinct made her step down and walk away. When she was far from the crowd she quickened her steps toward the hotel. Only then did she try to piece it all together. If Val followed the banker into the bank, the money was still there. He would have no reason to go inside if Terris had gotten away with it as planned. Was Val going to make another try for the money? She didn't know, but she knew they would have to get out of town quickly. For whatever reason, the original plan had fallen apart.

She nodded her usual greeting to the hotel clerk and walked gracefully up the stairs, though she wanted to run. In her room she began throwing her things into her bags.

Val crouched beside the unconscious banker and practically held his breath. His only hope was that everyone would be concerned enough about their fallen sheriff-turned-bank-robber that they wouldn't check inside the bank. Val felt sweat trickle down the back of his neck. In spite of the confusion someone might have seen him slip inside the bank. It would only take one curious witness to ruin everything.

The sounds in the alley told him the crowd was moving away. He didn't dare go to the door to look.

He had to stay out of sight until he was absolutely sure.

At the sheriff's office, the doctor sent everyone outside except the deputy. Cally had to push through the crowd that drifted away and pound on the locked door. She was ready to break the door in when the deputy finally unlocked it.

He opened it only a crack. "Go on home. The robbery was foiled, there's nothing to be alarmed about. Right now the doctor needs quiet to work on the sheriff."

Cally stuck her foot in the door just as the deputy would have closed it. She summoned all her courage and stated, "I need to be with Andrew."

The deputy was taken aback. He glanced over his shoulder once then opened the door, closing and locking it quickly behind her. Cally stood just inside, afraid to look toward the doctor and Andrew. She didn't realize the deputy had been watching her closely until he caught her as she started to sway.

"You better sit down," she said. "Say, aren't you the girl that brought the muffins?"

Cally nodded. Yes, she had to sit down. She hadn't come here just to faint. She came to help Andrew.

The deputy led her to a chair. "My name's Bill," he said as if he were talking to a child. "You must be Cally."

She nodded again. She felt a little better now that she was seated and looked across the room for the first time. Andrew lay on a bed in one of the cells and the doctor bent over him. There was blood, and she looked away. The image stayed in her mind, and she felt dizzy again.

Suddenly she realized what she had seen besides the blood, and her eyes flew back to Andrew. There were bars separating them! "Andrew didn't rob the bank," she blurted.

Bill pulled up a chair near her. "Did you see what happened? Were you with Andrew when he...I mean, someone robbed the bank?"

Cally swallowed hard. She wanted to clear Andrew but he was already lying on the ground when she reached the alley. After that there was buzzing in her ears and shouting in the distance, and she had nearly fainted. Just thinking about it made her feel sick. She bent over, lowering her head almost on her knees.

"Put a wet cloth on the back of her neck," the doctor suggested. The words helped revive her. She couldn't have the doctor worrying about her when Andrew could be dying! "I'm all right," she said, making an effort to sit up.

The deputy handed her a damp cloth which she used to wipe her clammy face. He asked, "What were you doing in the alley?"

"I came to find Andrew because...Royal!" She stood up suddenly, causing Bill to reach out to steady her. "Royal's still guarding that awful man that sent Andrew the note that wasn't from me."

She started for the door and the deputy followed. "Do you want to explain what you're talking about?"

"But we have to hurry." Cally ran down the dark street, the deputy close on her heels.

* * *

At the hotel, Fancy carried both her bags to her
door and peeked out. Val's room was across the hall,
overlooking the alley. In a pinch, she could go out
the window, but first, she would pack Val's bags. Seeing that there was no one about, she slipped out her
door, closing it quietly behind her. She set her bags
at her feet at Val's door and looked up and down the
hall again before trying the knob.

It was locked. Whispering a curse, Fancy removed
a pin from her hair and quickly picked the lock. She
eased the door open, set her bags inside and slipped
in after them, closing the door gently behind her.

She lit the gaslight on the wall by the door and
turned around. And stared. Val's bags stood at the
foot of his bed, obviously bulging with his belongings. The door to the wardrobe stood ajar; it was
empty.

At first she was relieved. She wouldn't have to
waste time packing his bags. When he arrived with
the money, they would be ready to go.

They would be ready to go? He had been ready all
along! He had said nothing about leaving tonight. He
couldn't have known ahead of time what would happen. Why the sudden hurry?

Unless, she thought. *Unless he planned to have the
money.*

She walked toward the bags, thinking. He had
planned a double cross all along. Val, who had never
broken the law, at least not much, had masterminded
a plan that fooled two experienced criminals. The fact
that one of them was her brother bothered her for a

moment. But she couldn't get over the notion that her Val had planned it all.

Of course, he had also planned to leave without her.

She walked to the window and pulled aside the thin curtain. The window was open a couple of inches. Crates were stacked below making an easy climb to the alley. Or up to the room.

Fancy moved her bags and Val's nearer the window and turned down the light. She pushed the window all the way open and waited for her lover to appear below.

She didn't have to wait long.

Val crept toward the pile of crates, the carpetbag full of the bank's money clutched in his hand. He had minutes to get his bags and make it to the train station in time to catch the ten o'clock. Unwilling to leave the money even for a moment, he carried it with him up his makeshift stairs.

When he reached for the windowsill he found the window open and Fancy waiting for him. Uncertain what conclusions she might have come to, he whispered what he hoped was the right thing. "Fancy! I was just coming to get you!"

She returned his kiss but didn't move aside to let him through the window. "Why are your bags packed, dear?"

"I see yours are packed, too. Pass them to me, and I'll drop them to the ground."

"Yours were packed when I got here, Val. Were you planning on going somewhere?"

Val felt the press of time. He could explain. He

really could if she gave him a moment to think. But they didn't have a moment. He heard the train whistle in the distance or imagined he did.

"I had a bad feeling, Fancy." He braced the money between his feet on his precarious perch and reached past her for one of the bags. He let it drop to the alley below. "I just had a feeling so I packed." He grabbed a second bag. "I wanted to tell you but you were already out looking for the deputy."

This time he did hear the whistle, distant but definitely the train. He grabbed another bag, one of Fancy's. She must have caught his urgency because she helped him with the last. He reluctantly dropped the money after the bags and started down the crates, helping Fancy as she struggled down above him.

When his feet were on firm ground again, he lifted Fancy down beside him and they turned to grab up the bags. Terris waited for them.

"I shot Haywood," Terris said.

"Good for you," Val said, his own sense of urgency making him incautious. "From what I heard, I don't believe he'll die. Why aren't you away from here?" He couldn't read Terris's face in the shadow, and in the best of times the man made him wary.

"Things went wrong," Terris accused.

"Well, don't look at me. Stedwell's the one who didn't do his job." He heard Fancy's gasp behind him and wished he'd been more careful. He had to get out of here.

"I came to split the money," Terris said, setting the carpetbag on a crate and preparing to open it.

Val reached out and caught his wrist. The train whistle sounded on the edge of town. "There's no time. You were the one who cracked the safe. My plan failed. You keep the money. We're leaving. You should be going too.''

He knew his voice was rising in his panic, but he couldn't help himself. He heard Fancy's weak protest behind him and shoved two of their bags toward her, gathering up the others. "Have a good life," he said over his shoulder as he urged Fancy down the alley.

At the train station, he left Fancy with the bags, all but one. "I'll get our tickets," he said, hurrying toward the office. The train chuffed expectantly, but they had time enough now. They were all but away.

At the office he glanced over his shoulder toward Fancy before saying softly, "One, please." He retrieved his own ticket from his pocket and held the two together when he returned to Fancy.

In a few minutes they were seated across from each other on the train. Val sighed with relief, then looked at Fancy. Her beautiful face was composed, giving him no idea what she was thinking. Finally he ventured, "I wasn't going to leave without you."

She smiled. "Of course not, dear. I wouldn't have let you."

That answer wasn't reassuring. He waited until the train was moving before he tried again. "I'm sorry about your brother."

"Thank you, Val. Did he really ruin your plan?"

His plan. How much should he tell her? "I don't know what happened, but we couldn't stay around to see."

"I understand."

Val wondered if she did. He tapped his fingers on the carpetbag in his lap. Perhaps the easiest way to regain her trust was to show her. He opened the bag, peeking inside before holding it toward Fancy. He yanked it back again, opening it wider. Newspaper! The bag was full of newspaper!

He started to stand, having some thought of going back. Terris must have switched the bags while he and Fancy were climbing from the window. And he had generously told the man to keep the money! Damn!

"What is it, dear?"

Something in her voice made him think she knew. He had no idea how to answer.

"Val, darling," she said. "I was very impressed by your scheme to frame that sheriff." She ran her fingers down the pleats on her dress and looked up at him through her dark lashes. "I was even more impressed when I realized that you had another plan that was just for you...and me."

Val swallowed and snapped the bag shut. "Fancy," he started but didn't know what to say.

"But if you had kept all that money, you'd be rich. I don't think you would have needed me anymore."

She smiled at him sweetly and adjusted herself in the seat as if intending to take a nap.

Val sighed.

Chapter Sixteen

"**W**here is this awful man you mentioned?"

"He's at the creek this side of my farm." Cally thought it was sort of stupid for the deputy to waste his breath asking questions when he needed it to run. He was puffing already and they had only run one block.

"Damn," he gasped. "That's a mile and a half! I'll have to get my horse."

Cally rounded a corner and found Jewel just where she had left her. "I'll meet you there," she said, swinging onto the mule's back.

"Wait a minute," the deputy called.

But Cally didn't; she was too worried about Royal. And the boys, too, if they had stayed. Bill caught up with her so quickly she wondered whose horse he had borrowed. He didn't offer an explanation.

They heard the man talking before they saw him. "Nice doggy. Now I'm just going to... All right, I won't. I'll stay right here. Nice doggy. Ow! Will you boys stop that!"

"There he is, Deputy," Cally said, dismounting next to Royal.

"Oh, thank God! You came back." The man's voice cracked. "Call off your crazy dog. And tell those boys to stop throwing rocks in my face."

"I told you two to go home," Cally said.

The boys rose from their squatting position deeper in the trees. "We stayed to throw rocks at him every time he tried to get free," Taylor said.

Mikey added, "We was starting to have a hard time finding rocks."

"Who is he?" asked Bill, swinging off the horse.

"I don't know," answered Cally. "Who are you?"

"Nobody. I'm nobody. I was just out for an evening ride and when I stopped for a drink from the stream, this crazy girl set her dog on me. Then she and these little thugs tied me up. I've been here for hours!"

"He pointed this gun at me and these two little boys!" Cally declared, pulling the offending weapon from her pants pocket and pointing it at the man. The man ducked, and Bill took the pistol away from her.

Taylor stepped forward. "This is a bad man, and he sent a note to Sheriff Haywood that wasn't from her, and said she'd have to go with him. Her dog bit his arm, and we kicked his legs. Then she took that gun away and tied him up with our slingshots. Us and the dog made him stay here."

Cally nodded. The boy's explanation was fairly complete. Surely Deputy Bill would arrest him now and let Andrew out of jail.

"Look," the man said, his voice sounding far too friendly. "The boys and this girl are obviously nuts. If you'll untie me..."

Royal growled deep in his throat and edged the man back against the tree.

Cally glared at the face in the dark. There was a little moonlight, but the man was in the shadows. She couldn't even see the deputy well enough to know if he believed them. "Royal and I'll just wait here until you tell the truth, mister. Then the deputy will arrest you."

"You want we should go find some more rocks?" asked Mikey.

The man's voice took on a note of desperation. "You can't listen to her, Deputy. I've lost a lot of blood where that dog bit me. I could die here while you humor this lunatic!"

"Then you better hurry up and talk," Cally said, hearing that familiar buzz at the mention of blood. She used all her strength to fight against it.

"All right. I'll tell what happened. Just call off the dog!"

"Perhaps you should," started the deputy. "If he's hurt."

"After," Cally stated.

The man gave in. He gave in completely. Cally listened in fascination as he started with his sister breaking him and a cell mate out of prison and ended with a description of how things were supposed to have happened tonight. When he finished, Cally spoke quietly to Royal, and he turned and trotted to her side. As soon as the dog was clear, Cally stepped forward and kicked Stedwell as hard as she could. He went down on his knees.

The deputy grabbed Cally's arm and pulled her away. "What are you doing? Get away from him."

"He stole my farm." She turned on her heel. "Come on, boys," she said, indicating the mule. With them aboard and Royal at her side, she led Jewel back to town.

Out of habit, Cally tied the mule in front of Mr. Lafferty's and told the boys goodbye. They seemed reluctant to leave and she wasn't sure she had seen the last of them.

She and Royal walked to the sheriff's office, where she sat in a chair and stared at the unconscious Andrew. Royal lay on the floor watching them both.

The doctor had dug the bullet out and was bandaging the wound. She knew he gave her curious glances from time to time, but she couldn't take her eyes off Andrew's pale face. She was afraid to ask how badly he was hurt.

When the doctor packed up his bag and left the cell, Royal trotted in and sat beside Andrew's bed. Cally stood and approached the doctor. "You can't leave him there," she said.

"He'll be all right, miss."

He patted her shoulder, moving around her toward the door. Before Cally could think of a way to stop him, Bill and Stedwell entered. Cally and her slow old mule had beaten them and their horses by a good ten minutes.

"Got another customer for you," Bill told the doctor, giving Royal a wary glance. "I wrapped it up the best I could out there in the dark, but you better have a look." Bill took his prisoner to the cell next to Andrew's. Royal turned to the prisoner and growled softly.

The doctor, following Bill into the cell, glared at the dog.

Cally moved closer to the cell where Andrew lay.

"Can't Andr...Sheriff Haywood go home now?" she asked the deputy. Andrew stirred in his sleep.

"He just needs to rest," replied the doctor.

Cally glanced at the bars that separated her from Andrew. The door standing open didn't make her feel any better. She couldn't help thinking of her father. "But he's not under arrest, is he?"

"No, ma'am," the deputy answered. He stood guard over his prisoner as the doctor bathed a small hole in his arm.

"But..." Cally hated to admit that it gave her the creeps to see Andrew in the cell. She wanted to take care of him, but she couldn't bring herself to step inside. "I don't think he should be in jail." All three men looked at her, then returned to their business, dismissing her.

Cally scowled at them, then turned her attention back to Andrew. He was stirring quite a bit, now. She wasn't sure if that was a good sign or not. Dr. Briggs didn't seem concerned.

When the doctor was finishing with Stedwell and about to leave the cell, Cally stepped up to block his way. "He'd rest better at home, wouldn't he, Doctor?"

"The deputy's here to watch him, Miss DuBois. He shouldn't be alone." He pushed her aside slightly so he could walk around her, then patted her arm as if everything was settled.

Everything was not settled! Andrew should be in his own bed. Somebody who loved him should be looking after him. As she tried to form a sensible argument, the deputy strode toward the door.

"I'm going to see if I can round up the gambler

or—'' he thrust his thumb over his shoulder ''—this fella's sister.''

''See!'' declared Cally. ''Now he's alone. That prisoner will torment him. I can look after him if you'd help me take him home.''

The doctor gave her a sympathetic smile. ''Dear, I know you mean well, but I can't let you do that. People would talk. I'll stay here with him until the deputy returns.'' Cally started to protest, but he raised his hand. ''You're welcome to wait with me if you wish.''

Andrew stirred and groaned. As Cally's attention shifted, a thought occurred to her. She would have to talk fast; she didn't want Andrew to hear. In the end she convinced the doctor and followed him outside.

Several townspeople were waiting for word on Andrew and the robbery, and two men were enlisted to help Andrew from the cell. The doctor was quickly swallowed by an inquisitive crowd.

Andrew was conscious enough to protest the mode of transportation she had chosen, and Cally was pleased with herself enough to ignore him. The two men walked on either side of Jewel to steady him, though Andrew insisted he was fine. By the time they reached his back door he did seem quite recovered. He was helped up the stairs by one man while the other turned Jewel into the corral.

Cally told Royal to stay in the yard, thanked both men profusely, and bade them good-night. She leaned against the door and breathed a sigh of relief that they were gone, then hurried up the stairs. A light cast a golden square on the floor of the hallway, leading her to the open door of Andrew's bedroom.

Andrew was sitting on the side of the bed. ''You're

supposed to rest!'' she cried, running to push ineffectually at his chest to get him to lie back down. It was
like pushing a brick wall. She stood back and scowled
at him, her hands on her hips.

Realizing that wasn't working either, she tried to
smile sweetly. His eyes narrowed suspiciously and
made her wonder if he had heard her conversation
with the doctor. No, he would be more upset than this
if he had. In fact, she suspected he would be furious.
"You're supposed to rest," she repeated. "And I'm
supposed to look after you."

"Why would you want to do that?"

"Because I—" She stopped herself in time.

He grinned at her.

She scowled back. "No reason."

He grinned all the wider.

"All right," she relented. "I'll say it. Because I
love you." His grin was becoming annoying. "But I
still don't believe you love me."

"You don't, do you?"

"No," she said with a pout, but he had already
come to his feet. He should be lying down and letting
her fuss over him, she thought. Instead he towered
over her, teasing her cheek with his fingertip.

"Do you want me to prove it?"

His voice was tantalizing, but Cally wouldn't be
seduced so easily this time. She looked him in the eye
and tried to scowl. It wasn't easy. His chest was
warm, and he was very close. She gritted her teeth.
"You already refused to *prove* it," she said. "A wife
would ruin your edge." She hoped she sounded ap-
propriately sarcastic.

She decided she had failed when he laughed.

"Sweetheart, a wife couldn't possibly ruin my edge any more than you already have."

He kissed her, but when she would have pulled him into a firm embrace he moved away. "Stedwell's in jail," he said casually. "What about the others?"

She decided he must be hurting more than he let on and urged him back toward the bed. "We got the whole story from Stedwell. Deputy Bill has gone to look for the others. You don't have to worry about a thing."

He nodded. "I'm hungry. Run down to the kitchen and fix me something."

Cally grinned at her victory and turned to hurry down the stairs. Andrew's kitchen was smaller than the Gwynns', but still it was full of interesting cupboards and drawers. She lit the gaslight and explored while she tried to decide what to fix.

Royal's sharp, insistent bark made her turn toward the door. She pushed a curtain aside to look through the window but the yard was dark. Opening the door, she stepped out and away from the light.

Royal barked again and growled. She thought she saw a shadow move near the barn, Royal or an intruder, she wasn't sure which. As she watched, the shadow spit a flash of light, and the sharp crack of a pistol made her jump. The next instant she heard a yelp.

"Royal!" she screamed. She ran into the yard. "Royal, where are you!"

Andrew had been halfway down the stairs when he heard the shot. He ran through his kitchen in time to see Cally rush into danger after her dog. His gun was drawn before he stepped through the door.

The light from the house was behind him and he

knew he made an easy target. But so did Cally. "Get down," he shouted as he moved away from the door.

Light from the open doorway glinted off a gun barrel, and Andrew fired. The grunt of pain told him he had hit his mark.

Cautiously, Andrew approached the fallen man. He could hear Cally's concerned murmurs nearby, but, though it tore at his heart, he needed to know that they were in no further danger from this one before he went to her.

The flare of a match revealed the man's gun inches from his still fingers. Andrew stuck it in his waistband before he knelt beside the man. Terris. He wasn't especially surprised. He felt for a pulse, found none and closed the man's eyes.

His bullet had gone straight through Terris's heart. That had been his intention, of course, but his target had been merely a guess in relation to the gun barrel, the only thing he had seen.

He rose to his feet, shaking out the burned-down match. He could hear voices in the street, Bill's among others. "Back here," he called. "Cally," he said more softly. "Where are you?"

"We heard some shots. Everyone all right?" Bill held a lantern high to illuminate more of the yard.

"Terris is dead," Andrew said. "Bring the light over here."

Bill held the light, while Andrew tried to calm Cally and examine the dog's wounds at the same time. Others had gone to see Terris's body.

"I was just coming to talk to you," Bill said, obviously wishing he was with the other group. "The banker woke up by his safe with a bump on his head. The money's gone. Stedwell's sister and her gambler friend left the hotel without checking out. I figured Terris was long gone, too.''

"Cally, sweetheart. He's not hurt bad. The bullet just grazed him.''

"But it's bleeding something awful,'' she whispered into his shoulder.

"Shhh, I know. You don't have to look. But you have to let me go so I can help him.''

A shout from across the yard caught Bill's attention, and Andrew lost his light. He stood and turned, Cally in his arms.

"Where'd you find that?''

"Right over in those bushes.''

"By, God! It's the money!''

The banker ran toward them, the open carpetbag clutched in both hands.

"*He* had the money?'' This was from Bill.

Andrew shrugged. "He could have gotten away if he hadn't wanted his revenge.'' The banker stood before them now, rumpled and pale but delighted. "Go with him to the bank, Bill, and see that he gets it locked in the vault.''

"Yes, sir.''

"Thank you, Sheriff,'' said the banker, starting to turn away. "Oh, and congratulations.''

Andrew frowned at the banker's odd comment, but the man was a bit preoccupied. Royal whimpered behind him, and Cally slipped from his arms to comfort the dog.

"Oh yeah,'' said Bill, clapping Andrew on the back. "Congratulations. Jeff and Martin! You two carry that body to the undertaker's.'' He started away, leaving them in darkness for a moment until his lantern was replaced by that of the mayor.

"Here," the older man said, swinging the light toward the house. "Let me give you light enough to get inside."

"Thanks." Andrew turned to crouch beside Cally. "Let me lift him," he urged softly. "He'll be all right." With Cally's help he got the dog into his arms. The mayor led the way to the light of the back door. The dog was heavy, and Andrew could feel the pull on his own wounded shoulder. Royal, fortunately, didn't struggle. In the kitchen, Cally helped Andrew place the dog gently on the table.

"You folks need anything?" the mayor called from just outside the door.

"We can handle things now, thanks," Andrew said, eyeing Cally to be sure she wasn't about to faint.

"I'll be going then," he called. "Good night, and congratulations!"

"I wish they'd quit congratulating me for killing someone," Andrew muttered as he pumped a pan of water at the sink.

Cally stroked the dog's neck, trying not to look at his bloodied hip. "I don't think that's why," she ventured, then wished she hadn't said anything. He would find out soon enough.

Andrew grabbed some rags from a shelf above the sink and carried them and the pan to the table. Cally was glad he was intent enough on Royal not to look at her. "I don't know what else it would be," he said. "Sure, I messed up the gang's plans, but I didn't really stop the robbery. I wasn't the one who found the money hidden in the bushes."

Cally shrugged, hoping he would let it drop. "Will he really be all right?" she asked, not taking her eyes off Royal.

"Good as new in no time," Andrew said. "It's just a scratch."

Cally breathed a sigh of relief for two reasons.

"Seems odd, though," Andrew said.

"It was too dark for him to get a good shot, I suppose."

"No, I mean everyone's behavior."

Cally bit her lip and glanced toward him, happy to see that most of the dog's wound was covered with white cloth. Andrew was still pretty busy with the bandages. Cally was glad. Maybe he wouldn't put everything together. Maybe they could wait and talk about it in the morning. In the meantime, she hoped to make him happy enough he wouldn't care. "How are you feeling?" she asked solicitously.

She saw him glance at her but only briefly. "I'll be all right." Andrew's hands were working very quickly and gently. The dog barely twitched when Andrew touched the wound.

"How did you get outside so fast? You were right behind me."

He took a moment to answer. "I was on my way down. I was going to look for Terris."

Cally shook her head. He was not a good patient. "You should lie down as soon as you're done."

This time his glance lasted a little longer. A grin quirked at the corner of his mouth. "Will you come, too?"

Cally lowered her face to hide her blush. *Of course,* she thought, but didn't say it aloud.

In a few minutes, Royal was settled near the fire, and Cally tried to help Andrew up the stairs. He didn't cooperate. He kept hugging her and trying to kiss her. Halfway to the top she gave in and let him claim her lips for a long sensuous kiss. After that, she had to let him help *her* up the stairs.

The lamp was still burning in his bedroom, and Andrew turned it down a fraction before pulling her into his arms for another kiss. He undid the top button on the oversize shirt she wore. "You know," he said thoughtfully, his fingers caressing her collarbone, "if you want to milk the cow in a pair of pants, that's fine with me, but I think I'd like to see you in dresses once in a while. You can have as many as you want once we're married."

Cally jumped, then tried to pretend she hadn't. *Married!* Had his crack that she had already ruined his edge been a proposal? Well, she would like to hear it as a question. Suppose she wanted to turn him down. He was taking a lot for granted! Of course, it was exactly what she wanted and coming now could be her way out of trouble. Perhaps she shouldn't push her luck.

He bent and kissed her again, and she lost her train of thought. His kisses trailed across her cheek and down her neck. She hadn't realized he had undone the rest of the buttons on her shirt until his kisses continued downward against her bare skin. When his tongue touched the sensitive tip of her nipple, her knees buckled.

Andrew scooped her up in his arms and laid her across his soft bed. Cally thought she ought to be concerned for his wounded shoulder, but he kissed her breast again, distracting her. She was engulfed in tingling warmth and closed her eyes to enjoy it.

She felt him rise from the bed and smiled to herself. Last time, when he had returned to her side, he had been naked. She opened one eye for a peek and closed it quickly. Surely she wasn't supposed to see this! He looked magnificent, though. She opened one eye again and found him watching her. She was so mortified, she rolled over in the bed, burying her face in the quilt. His chuckling didn't help.

He tugged on her shoulder, but she resisted. "Cally." The word was a caress to her ears. She rolled over, keeping her eyes tightly shut. He was chuckling again. She could feel her cheeks burning and was about to bury them in the quilt again when she felt his hands on the fasteners of her pants. Delicious shivers spread through her body and she decided not to interfere with his work by rolling away. In fact, she scooted around a little to help him pull the pants off her legs.

Then it occurred to her. He was looking at her, naked or nearly so. Why shouldn't she get to satisfy her curiosity as well? She opened both eyes a crack and wondered if he had been waiting for her to do just that. He was standing beside the bed, watching her face.

He slowly smiled. "We gave ourselves to each other once, Cally. I want to marry you so we can truly belong to each other."

He placed one knee on the bed and started to move slowly toward her. She couldn't keep herself from looking at his proud manhood, though she tried to. She was sure her face was going to burst into flames.

He ran one cool finger down her cheek as he moved to lie beside her. "That means you can do what you please with me," he whispered. "Look at me. Or touch me." He ran one hand down the length of her body, brushing the open shirt out of his way. "I intend to do the same to you."

She looked into his eyes and saw the warmth there, an expression she had seen before and recognized now as love. The idea of spending an entire lifetime getting to know, and touch, this man filled her with anticipation. She reached out tentatively and touched his chest, far away from the bandage. She let her fingers trail downward across his ribs and flat stomach. She hesitated then continued onward.

Andrew caught her hand, bringing it up to his heart and pressing it there. A moment later he released her and flopped onto his back beside her.

"Andrew?" Had she done something wrong or was it the injury? She sprang up to hover over him. He looked as if he was in pain. "I told you you should rest." She thought back. "I think I did. I should have, anyway."

He was laughing at her again. For a moment she was relieved. But only for a moment. When she would have drawn away from him, he caught her shoulders. "Rest isn't what I need." He pulled her down on top of him. "I want you so badly it's hard to wait. Suppose you do your exploring a little later."

She smiled at him, and he rolled her onto her back again. His body covered hers, and he brought his mouth down to claim her lips. A long searing kiss had Cally reeling. It wasn't frightening this time, she knew what to expect—and she knew they loved each other.

He entered her so slowly, she thought she would go crazy. She wrapped her legs around him and pulled him toward her. His groan worried her for a moment, but the feel of his skin, his taste, his scent, all had her spinning into wonderful thoughtlessness. She called out his name as all the feeling collided together and she heard him call her name as well.

Later, as they lay cuddled in each other's arms and the foggy glow was lifting, she remembered the townspeople's comments. She would have to explain before he went to work in the morning. She propped herself up on one elbow and studied Andrew's face. He looked as if he was smiling in his sleep. This could be the perfect time. But first, she feasted her eyes on his nakedness, marveling at the differences in their bodies.

When the urge to touch him became too great to resist, she rested her hand on his warm chest, just over his heart. "Andrew?" she murmured. "Remember the congratulations you were getting?"

She thought his grunt might be a yes. "I bet it was because we're engaged," she said softly. She watched his face carefully. Maybe the smile faded a little. She watched him so long she started to wonder if he would answer. Maybe he was asleep.

"I only asked you this evening, sweetheart," he finally said. "None of them would have any way of knowing."

She decided it might be wise to get out of bed in case he reacted strongly. Andrew opened one eye to look at her. She stood a little straighter, bracing herself. "They know 'cause I told them."

"Sweetheart, you were with your dog. You had no chance to tell them."

He thought he was being patient and reasonable. She thought he was being picky. She raised her chin a little higher, forgetting that she was naked.

Andrew's look was frankly appreciative. "Besides," he added, "I don't think you realized I'd proposed until a few minutes ago."

He was laughing at her, she thought. She tried to look serious instead of angry. "I told Dr. Briggs before we brought you home."

Andrew gave her his full attention, his eyebrows questioning quite eloquently.

Cally put her fists on her hips and her chin went up in a perfect imitation of Noella Gwynn. Perfect except for the outfit. "I wanted to bring you home and look after you," she said. "And it just wouldn't have been proper if we weren't at least engaged!"

To her amazement, he laughed. She glared at him as he rose to his feet. "I think we've both had the same thing in mind," he said. "I'll take the blame for not handling it properly, but I intended to propose during the picnic."

"Why didn't you?" What had she done that made him change his mind? What if he changed his mind again?

"Because..." He moved forward and slid his arms around her waist. "I wanted you to say you loved me. You're a very stubborn young lady."

She smiled at the compliment. "I can say it now, Andrew."

As she raised on her toes to encourage his kiss, they whispered in unison, "I love you."

* * * * *

The Jewels of Texas

Bestselling author

presents

Book IV in
the exciting
Jewels of Texas
series.

The town marshal and the town flirt fall in love,
and join forces to save the little town of
Hanging Tree, Texas, from a killer.

The Jewels of Texas—four sisters as wild and vibrant
as the untamed land they're fighting to protect.

Available in September
wherever Harlequin Historicals are sold.

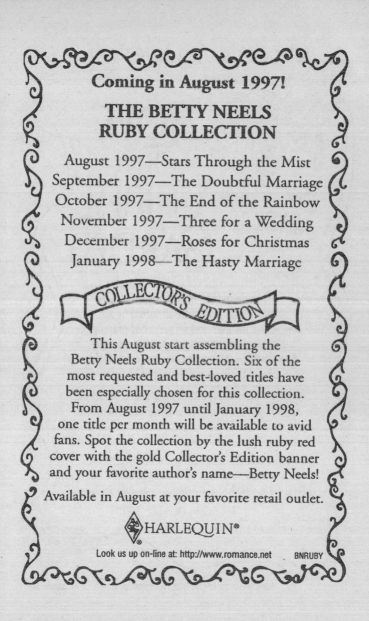

Coming in August 1997!

THE BETTY NEELS RUBY COLLECTION

COLLECTOR'S EDITION

This August start assembling the
Betty Neels Ruby Collection. Six of the
most requested and best-loved titles have
been especially chosen for this collection.
From August 1997 until January 1998,
one title per month will be available to avid
fans. Spot the collection by the lush ruby red
cover with the gold Collector's Edition banner
and your favorite author's name—Betty Neels!

Available in August at your favorite retail outlet.

HARLEQUIN®

China's greatest love story...

Available for the
first time as a
novel in North
America

LOVE IN A CHINESE GARDEN

It's been called China's *Romeo and Juliet*.
Two young lovers are thwarted by an
ambitious mother and an arranged marriage.
With the help of a clever confidante, they
find opportunities to meet...until, inevitably,
their secret is revealed.

Can love prevail against danger and separation?
Against the scheming of a determined woman?

**Find out how to receive a second book
absolutely FREE with the purchase of
LOVE IN A CHINESE GARDEN! (details in book)**

**Available October 1997
at your favorite retail outlet.**

HARLEQUIN WOMEN KNOW ROMANCE WHEN THEY SEE IT.

And they'll see it on **ROMANCE CLASSICS**, the new 24-hour TV channel devoted to romantic movies and original programs like the special **Romantically Speaking—Harlequin™ Goes Prime Time.**

Romantically Speaking—Harlequin™ Goes Prime Time introduces you to many of your favorite romance authors in a program developed exclusively for Harlequin® readers.

Watch for **Romantically Speaking—Harlequin™ Goes Prime Time** beginning in the summer of 1997.

If you're not receiving ROMANCE CLASSICS, call your local cable operator or satellite provider and ask for it today!

Escape to the network of your dreams.

See Ingrid Bergman and Gregory Peck in *Spellbound* on Romance Classics.

FORTUNE COOKIE

Breathtaking romance is predicted in your future with Harlequin's newest collection: Fortune Cookie.

Three of your favorite Harlequin authors, **Janice Kaiser, Margaret St. George** and **M.J. Rodgers** will regale you with the romantic adventures of three heroines who are promised fame, fortune, danger and intrigue when they crack open their fortune cookies on a fateful night at a Chinese restaurant.

Join in the adventure with your own personalized fortune, inserted in every book!

Don't miss this exciting new collection!

Available in September
wherever Harlequin books are sold.

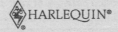